ANOTHER HOME, ANOTHER LOVE

Rosemary Palmer-Farr loves farming and animals — her childhood was spent mostly at Bengairney Farm with her dear friends the Carafords. Now a young woman, she wants to prove her worth in running the gardens of her father's dwindling estate. However, her mother Catherine only wants her to secure a good marriage and believes that tenant farmers like the Carafords are inferior. So when her daughter's childhood friendship deepens into love, Catherine takes action to keep the young couple apart. She throws her daughter into the company of eligible young gentlemen whom Rosemary despises, yearning only for Sam's love . . .

SPECIAL MESSAGE TO READERS

THE ULVERSCROFT FOUNDATION
(registered UK charity number 264873)
was established in 1972 to provide funds for
research, diagnosis and treatment of eye diseases.
Examples of major projects funded by
the Ulverscroft Foundation are:-

- The Children's Eye Unit at Moorfields Eye Hospital, London
- The Ulverscroft Children's Eye Unit at Great Ormond Street Hospital for Sick Children
- Funding research into eye diseases and treatment at the Department of Ophthalmology, University of Leicester
- The Ulverscroft Vision Research Group, Institute of Child Health
- Twin operating theatres at the Western Ophthalmic Hospital, London
- The Chair of Ophthalmology at the Royal Australian College of Ophthalmologists

You can help further the work of the Foundation
by making a donation or leaving a legacy.
Every contribution is gratefully received. If you
would like to help support the Foundation or
require further information, please contact:

THE ULVERSCROFT FOUNDATION
The Green, Bradgate Road, Anstey
Leicester LE7 7FU, England
Tel: (0116) 236 4325

website: www.foundation.ulverscroft.com

Gwen Kirkwood was born and educated in Yorkshire. She moved to Scotland to work, and with her husband, a Scottish dairy farmer, she has spent most of her adult life north of the Border. Gwen has three children and six grandchildren.

GWEN KIRKWOOD

ANOTHER HOME, ANOTHER LOVE

Complete and Unabridged

ULVERSCROFT
Leicester

First published in Great Britain in 2012 by
Robert Hale Limited
London

First Large Print Edition
published 2013
by arrangement with
Robert Hale Limited
London

British Library CIP Data

Kirkwood, Gwen.
 Another home, another love.
 1. Love stories.
 2. Large type books.
 I. Title
 823.9'14–dc23

 ISBN 978–1–4448–1498–9

Published by
F. A. Thorpe (Publishing)
Anstey, Leicestershire

Set by Words & Graphics Ltd.
Anstey, Leicestershire
Printed and bound in Great Britain by
T. J. International Ltd., Padstow, Cornwall

This book is printed on acid-free paper

1

Rosemary scanned the letters in the college mail box. Only a few more weeks and I'll be home for good, she thought. Her heartbeat quickened. Her course in horticulture had given her fresh ideas but there would be storms ahead with her mother. If only they could agree. Her face broke into a smile as she recognized the handwriting on one of the envelopes. It was a letter from Tania, her best friend and the nearest she had to a sister. When she was younger she had spent all her spare time at Bengairney Farm, with Tania and her brothers, Samuel and Alexander Caraford. Her mother had been too preoccupied with her ambitions to bother where she spent her time then but things had changed. Catherine Palmer-Farr had restored Langton Tower, her husband's ancestral home, and transformed it into a successful hotel and conference centre and she was determined that her only child should only associate with people she considered her own class.

'This is 1973, not 1873. Why can't she accept I shall never be the demure young debutante she craves?' Rosemary thought as she opened her letter and settled down to read it.

Dear Rosie,

I hope everything is going well for you. You will be taking your final exams soon but we all know you will do well. At Christmas we talked about a joint celebration for my twenty-first birthday on the 15th May and your eighteenth on the 30th. Both dates are mid-week so Mum has suggested making a family dinner on Saturday the 19th. I do hope you will be able to get home for that? Alex and I will need your support. 'You Know Who' has invited herself. We thought Sam's interest was waning but Lidia is still mooning all over him. Brothers! Grandpa Oliphant and Granny Caraford will be coming.

Mum suggests you and I could have a dance as a joint celebration, when we finish college. We could hire the village hall. I don't want anything grand. I need to earn some money after all these years of studying to be a teacher. Perhaps your parents are planning to invite the 'County Set' to a posh party at Langton Tower for your birthday?

Let me know what you think but please, please try to come to the family dinner *party. Do write soon and good luck with your exams.*

Love, Tania

Rosie grinned as she folded the letter. She doubted if her parents would even remember it was her eighteenth birthday and Tania understood how much she hated socializing with the kind of people her mother would consider 'suitable'. Tania's parents, Megan and Steven Caraford, always treated her like another member of their happy family.

Douglas Palmer-Farr met Rosie off the train at Carlisle on the Friday evening before the dinner party. She was surprised to see he was driving her mother's little Austin car instead of his Jaguar.

'I thought you might like to drive us home to keep in practice,' he said, after greeting her with a hug and a kiss. This was a surprise too; her parents were not demonstrative. Rosie had often wished they were when she was younger and needed comfort or reassurance. She had sought that from Granny Oliphant who had always been ready with a hug and comforting words, even though she was not related to Rosie at all. Her husband, John Oliphant, worked at Langton Tower managing the gardens and grounds. He was waiting until Rosie took over so that he could retire.

Rosie couldn't remember a time without the Oliphants. She loved them as dearly as Samuel, Tania and Alexander.

'Did you think I'd have forgotten how to drive, Daddy?' she teased as she negotiated the evening traffic out of Carlisle.

'No, I know how capable you are. I've persuaded your mother to let you have this little car for your eighteenth birthday. You will be able to drive yourself back to college on Sunday.'

'You're giving me Mum's car?' Rosie squeaked in excitement, turning to look at him, then swerving to get back in line.

'Not if you jump about like that!' Her father pretended to grip the edge of his seat in fear. 'Yes, the car is yours, but you'll have to budget to pay your own petrol,' he warned. 'We've bought an estate car to collect food or wine between hotel deliveries.'

'That's super. I can't believe it. Can I go back in it on Sunday? I wouldn't need to leave until the afternoon.'

'So long as you're not too tired after the party.'

'It will not be very late. It's a family party but Tania wants me to be there too. Her Grandma Caraford will be eighty-three this year.'

'Bengairney has always been your second

4

home. I believe the Carafords regard you as one of their family by now.'

'Yes. I shall be able to drive Papa Oliphant there and back for once, instead of him taking me to Bengairney, as he has done all these years. Oh Daddy I do appreciate it. I didn't think you'd remember it was my birthday.'

'Of course I remembered. I've missed you, Rosemary. I'm glad you decided to follow your heart.'

'Wh-what do you mean, 'follow my heart'?' For a second she thought her father had guessed her most secret dream.

'I mean you have had the courage to choose your own life in spite of your mother's ambitions for you. You'll be home soon instead of spending years at university, and maybe never returning. I shall be glad to have your cheery company again.'

'I'm looking forward to getting on with managing the gardens. I have lots of new ideas. Mr Hudson, one of my lecturers, has compiled a list of gardens and nurseries for me to visit and there are weekend courses too. I intend to go on learning you know — as Papa Oliphant has done all his life.'

'Yes, John is a good man. He's proved himself knowledgeable and adaptable over the years. He's missed your company. He says you're like a ray of sunshine, but I hadn't realized how much I missed you until you went away to college.' Rosie reflected on this conversation many times and was thankful her father had revealed his inner thoughts.

On Saturday morning Tania arrived at Langton Tower to collect Rosie. Her eyes were sparkling.

'We'll go for a cup of coffee in Binns first. I know it's a family party but I've booked a hairdo for both of us with an old friend from primary school. Betty has opened her own salon and — '

'A hairdo?' Rosie's blue eyes widened. 'Gosh, I can't imagine anyone taming my mop. I've never been to a hairdresser. Mother trims the ends when it gets too long. Tania I-I don't think I — '

'You'll be surprised what Betty can do. I told her you had curly blonde hair. 'Oh lucky girl', she said. Please give it a go, Rosie, to please me?' Tania begged. 'Betty will thin and style your hair, that's all. She's going to have a go at putting mine up to make me look more elegant. I'm determined we must look our best tonight so I need your support, Rosie.' She sent a pleading glance to her young friend. 'I'm sick of Sam's girlfriend preening and patting in every mirror. I told Mum she should take them away.'

'She does seem a bit vain,' Rosie agreed,

tugging her own hair.

'A bit? She thinks we're all country bumpkins. Please don't look so worried, Rosie. Betty's salon is new and quite small. She will be glad of our custom. I know you're pretty enough without all this but it's just for this evening. Lidia Blade is even worse now she's moved to this area and got work in a chemist's shop.'

'All right. I'll give it a go. I can always wash it when I get home if I don't like it. I'd planned to wear my new jeans with flared bottoms and stud trimmings. I've got a new top too but Mother says they're not suitable for an evening dinner party, 'Even if it is in a farmhouse,' ahem!' She pulled a face as she mimicked her mother's snooty attitude. 'She has bought me a new dress for my birthday but she says I must wear it tonight. She sent to London for it.'

'Oh gosh,' Tania knew Mrs Palmer-Farr liked to organize everybody. Rosie didn't stand a chance of getting her own way. 'What's it like?'

'I can live with it to keep the peace. At least it's a nice colour — a sort of mid-sky blue. The style is so simple there's not much I can criticize, but it hangs on me. The length is just above my knees.' Tania concentrated on parking the car on the Whitesands.

'There,' she said with satisfaction. She turned to look at Rosie. 'I could lend you a necklace and you might be able to trim your dress with a belt. We could look for one in Binns or Barbours.' She gave a mischievous grin. 'You could hide it in your bag until you get to us.'

'So I could. A belt would pull it up a little. Mum has a lapis lazuli necklace. It's the right colour and it's not as though I'm wanting to borrow her diamonds. I'll ask her. Thanks, Tania. You've cheered me up — except for this hairdresser experience. I'm still not sure . . . '

'You'll be fine, Rosie. Don't worry.'

'What are you wearing, Tania?'

'I've got a new dress too. It's red cotton with straps and a little matching bolero with white piping. Mum thinks it's a bit short but I like it. We'll be able to wear our jeans for our dance, if we ever get it organized when we both finish college. Come on, let's get our coffee and have a look at the hats in Binns. I love trying them on, even though I'm not buying one.' She giggled, then sobered as they found a table overlooking the High Street. 'Do you remember Struan Ritchie?'

'Er sort of.' Rosie frowned in concentration. 'Wasn't he in your year at the Academy?'

'That's right, and we were at Edinburgh

University together. He finished his BSc in agriculture last summer. We've been writing to each other while I've been doing my teacher training. I went to his twenty-first birthday party in January, during the Christmas holidays, so he's coming to mine tonight.'

'Oh ye-es?' Rosie's eyes twinkled.

'We're just good friends,' Tania protested, 'so there's no need to look like that. We've known each other ages. Dad and Sam like him. His sister, Pamela, is eight years older and lives in Australia. Sam is a bit envious because the Ritchies own their farm and we only rent Bengairney.'

'They'll be like Mr Turner at Martinwold then? Your father always says he is the most up-to-date farmer in this district,' Rosie said.

'The Ritchies are building a milking parlour and a new dairy with a bulk tank and a huge shed to house the cubicles for the cows in winter. Dad says Mr Ritchie was wise to wait until he knew Struan would be carrying on the farm. His mother wanted him to have an office job, but he loves the farm.'

'Mmm — ve-ery suitable,' Rosie teased, her eyes full of mischief.

'Rosie! There's nothing serious. But he is one of the nicest people I know. He understands I want a career and I need to earn some money before I think of settling down and he needs to get some practical experience now that he's learned the theory — his words, not mine. Besides we're too young to consider marriage yet. His father was forty but I wouldn't want to wait until I was that age.'

'Meanwhile it's good to have a friend to discuss things with,' Rosie nodded. 'I've missed Alex for that. But don't tell him I said so. I love him like a brother, if I'd had one, but I can't imagine him as someone I might want to marry. Do you understand, Tania?'

'Yes, and so does Mum. She thought you were wise to make a break when you both finished school. We guessed he was getting too serious. Mind you, I'd have loved you to be my sister-in-law, Rosie. I hope Alex makes a better choice than Sam when he does get a girlfriend.'

'Lidia is stylish. She's so tall and slim.' Rosie was unaware she sounded wistful. She was five feet three and she had always wanted to be tall and statuesque.

'She's only half an inch taller than I am but she looks more because she's so skinny,' Tania said. 'We've always been such a happy family. I wish I could like her, but I've tried and I can't.'

'So you do think they're serious?'

'I fear brother Samuel is playing with fire if he's not, and I wouldn't like to see him get burned.' Tania had learned a lot about life during her three years at university. Her parents thought moral standards had begun to fall during the war but she guessed they had no idea how much freedom girls had now they could get oral contraceptives and indulge their passions. She suspected Rosie was still ignorant about such matters, but she thought Lidia Blade would make use of the new woman power.

The two girls enjoyed their coffee and scones and shared a huge cream cake between them, amidst much laughter and licking of fingers. Afterwards they wandered around the store, trying on hats and examining the dress materials.

'We'll both be earning soon then we'll be able to come shopping and choose our own clothes,' Tania said.

'Maybe. I lie awake some nights thinking of all the things that could go wrong with the gardens.'

'Grandpa Oliphant is sure you'll do well. He says you have an instinct for growing things.'

'I shall need to do bookkeeping and records for the tax man, and pay wages and National Insurance. Then there's the electricity for the big greenhouse, and maintenance and buying and selling. The grocer in Darlonachie says he will take our surplus vegetables to sell. I thought I might start keeping hens again like Granny Oliphant used to do. I could sell the eggs to Mother for the hotel. The manure is rich in potash so it will be good for the onions and the fruit bushes.'

'You'll be fine, Rosie, and you've always worked hard,' Tania reassured her as they made their way to a side street and Betty's hairdressing salon. She was pleasant but efficient and Tania was relieved when she put Rosie at her ease, then left her to look through the *Hairdressers' Journal* while she trimmed her own hair. Out of the corner of her eye Betty noticed Rosie kept turning back to the same picture.

'Excuse me a second,' she whispered to Tania and stepped across to Rosie. 'That's the 'Euro Look',' she said, pointing to the picture. 'It would suit you beautifully and I think your hair will lend itself to that sort of style.' Rosie burst out laughing.

'You'd never make mine look that elegant in a million years.' She sobered. 'It looks expensive.'

'I would thin and style it, then do the new blow dry to smooth it out to curve around your face in a loose wave. That will be about . . . '

'This is Mum's treat, Rosie. She's given me the money,' Tania called. 'Remember this is your eighteenth birthday celebration as well as my twenty-first.'

'Oh . . . ' Rosie looked up at Betty. 'Do you really think mine will look like that?'

'I reckon you'll look twice as pretty,' Betty smiled. 'Most of my customers would envy your natural blonde colour as well as your curls. You have a lovely complexion too. I should think Tania's brothers will be head over heels in love with you tonight,' she teased. Rosie blushed.

They chattered on while Betty's young assistant answered the telephone and swept up the trimmings. Rosie was scarcely aware of being transformed from a curly-headed urchin to a glamorous young woman. Betty advised her what shampoo to use and how to style her hair herself while it was still damp.

'You really need to come in for a trim about every six weeks, if you want to keep the style.' She smiled disarmingly. 'I would be glad of your custom. I'm just starting up my own business too, like you.'

'I'm going back to college on Monday. I shall not be back until we finish in June,' Rosie said, 'but I'll come then. We're going to have a joint dance, aren't we, Tania?'

'Yes, we are. You must come too, Betty, and

bring your boyfriend. Is it still Bruce?'

'Yes it is. We're saving up to get married, but we'd love to come to your birthday dance. How about if I give you both a hair do as my gift?'

'Och we don't expect gifts!' Tania and Rosie said in unison, then burst into laughter.

'I'd like to do that,' Betty insisted. 'Regard it as advertising. You're both lovely models, and such a contrast when you get your long chestnut tresses arranged so elegantly on top of your head, Tania.'

'All right, that's a bargain,' Tania agreed.

'I wish you success with your business,' Rosie said.

★ ★ ★

Catherine Palmer-Farr didn't see Rosie until she was dressed to go to Bengairney and for the first time she realized her daughter was an elegant young woman.

'I didn't know you were having your hair done, Rosemary. It's beautiful.'

'Mrs Caraford paid for Tania and me. We went to a salon called Betty's. She was at school with Tania and she has just started on her own.'

'You must get me the address. She has made a good job. You suit your new dress too.'

14

'Thank you. Could I borrow your blue necklace for tonight? Please, Mother?'

'The lapis lazuli? Of course you can. There's a bracelet and earrings too. You can keep the set. It will match your blue eyes and I never wear it. I can't believe how grown up you look.'

Douglas was smoking his pipe in the family parlour. 'Your mother is right, Rosemary,' he said, eyeing her with pride. 'I can't believe I have a beautiful young lady for my daughter. You'll be breaking a few hearts tonight. Which of the Caraford boys will it be, I wonder?'

'Oh Daddy! Alex is like a brother to me, at least how I imagine a brother would be.' Her father nodded but he noticed she had not mentioned Samuel Caraford being like a brother. He liked the Caraford boys but he doubted if such a match would ever get Catherine's approval. She preferred to move in more exalted circles with the Wilshaws who still owned several farms, including Bengairney, or the Braebourne family. They still considered themselves superior, even though their fortunes had dwindled as much as his own. Catherine had high ambitions for Rosemary and he guessed she would soon start introducing her to eligible sons in the county. He hoped Rosemary would be

15

discerning enough to recognize the more pretentious of them.

* * *

'It's good to have a driver,' John Oliphant said as he settled himself into Rosie's car. He turned to look at her. 'You're very stylish tonight. You've always been a pretty lassie with your happy smile and sparkling eyes, but tonight . . . aye, you're a proper young lady.'

'I've been to a hairdresser's, Aunt Megan treated Tania and me.' She smiled at him. 'After all the years you've taken me to Bengairney it's time I drove you instead. You'll enjoy a drink of whisky.'

'Aye, so I will. You're a good driver, Rosie, but I always knew you would be. Have you any regrets about choosing horticulture?'

'No. I shall always love the farm and the animals but I couldn't have had a farm of my own. I'm looking forward to running the gardens but sometimes I'm afraid I'll be a flop.'

'Never. You're young and full of energy and new ideas. I shall still be around to lend a hand.'

'Thank you, Papa Oli.' Rosie drew the car to a halt in Bengairney yard and leaned forward to kiss his leathery cheek. 'I don't know what I'd do without you.'

'Hey, what's this?' Samuel knocked on the car window, then opened his grandfather's door. 'Are there kisses for everyone?'

'Only for one special man,' Rosie said. His grandfather chuckled and climbed out of the car.

'My word, Rosie, you're beautiful. Tania said you'd had your hair done but I had no idea our pretty wee tomboy could look so elegant.'

'Wait a minute while I put my belt on. Mum bought me a new dress but Tania and I bought the belt in town.' Sam nodded. They all knew Catherine Palmer-Farr liked her own way.

'Are you going to stand out there all night, Samuel?' Lidia Blade demanded from the door-way. 'You've not changed out of your smelly clothes yet!'

'No.' Sam sobered and looked down at Rosie apologetically, then at his grandfather. 'The vet's just been,' he said. 'We have a heifer calving, and the calf is not coming straight. It was Mr Fisher himself. He thinks we should give her another couple of hours to see if she opens up. If not he's going to do a caesarean. She's one of the Lily family . . . '

'Aye, it's often the best ones when there's a problem,' his grandfather nodded. He had been in charge of the large dairy herd belonging to Mr Turner of Martinwold before he had retired and gone to work at Langton Tower. He had never lost his interest in dairy cattle. 'I hear the young vet is nearly as good as Patrick?'

'Iain McNaught? Yes, he is,' Samuel agreed. 'Dad thinks so, too. They'll both come to do the operation if Iain is free.' He heard Lidia's exasperated groan. 'I'd better have a quick change. We don't want to leave in the middle of dinner if the vets return.'

'You should leave it to the workers,' Lidia said, coming out onto the step.

'I am one of the workers,' Sam said. John Oliphant looked up.

'Why, here's someone dressed for work, Sam,' he said, trying to dispel the tension. 'She's got her bib and bracers on.' He had no idea Lidia's hotpants were supposed to be the latest fashion statement. She glowered and turned on her heel. He raised his eyebrows at the exaggerated sway of her hips when she turned away. Queer outfit for a dinner party, he thought.

Lidia hovered in the hall as though she were the hostess. 'Are you another cousin then?' she asked Rosie. John Oliphant put an arm around her shoulders.

'We adopted Rosie as another granddaughter before she could toddle, didn't we, lassie?'

'I'm not sure who adopted who,' Rosie laughed, 'but you and Granny Oli were all I wanted.'

'So you're not a relation then,' Lidia persisted. 'It's supposed to be family only tonight.' Rosie's brows rose at her hostile tone and she lifted her chin.

'Mmm, that's what I thought, until I saw you here.' Angry colour stained Lidia's heavily made-up face as Rosie moved on into the sitting room. There was no doubt of her welcome there. Lidia heard the greetings, and the laughter. She scowled. She had noticed Samuel greeting the blonde girl with affection too. She hoped Rosemary Palmer-Farr was not a regular visitor at Bengairney.

As a child Megan had lived at Martinwold where her parents had managed the dairy herd so she understood the welfare of animals came first and emergencies could happen at inconvenient times. Lidia noticed how calmly she served the meal, with help from Sam's cousin, Avril Scott, and the Palmer-Farr girl. As the birthday girl Tania was happy to entertain her guests, especially Struan. He had been at Bengairney with other young farmers for stock judging competitions but this was the first time he had been at a family gathering. He could be rough on the rugby field or in the tug of war, but his upbringing had been strict and he was polite and considerate in company.

The pea and ham soup was attractively presented with a swirl of cream on top, along with a basket of warm crusty rolls and curls of golden butter. Lidia nibbled hers, leaving most of her roll and half of the soup. Tania caught Rosie's glance and rolled her eyes. Rosie tried not to laugh out loud. The roast beef and Yorkshire puddings were accompanied by a red wine gravy and horseradish sauce and served with dishes of vegetables fresh from the garden, as well as roast and creamed potatoes. Everyone seemed to sample everything and clear their plates as though they were starving. Lidia turned to the man on her other side.

'I believe you are Tania's uncle and a surgeon, Mr Gray?'

'You could say I'm an uncle by long association and mutual adoption,' Lindsay said, raising a quizzical eyebrow at Tania. She nodded and grinned at him. 'I have been a friend of the family for many years. I am Avril's stepfather.'

'Your wife is not here tonight. Is she in the medical profession too? On duty perhaps?'

Lint stiffened. He still missed Ruth, even after all this time.

'My wife died seven years ago,' he said and changed the subject. 'The birthday girls are looking very elegant tonight, don't you think?' They both smiled at him with relief.

'I don't know how they manage to eat so much stodgy food,' Lidia commented, helping herself to a third glass of wine. 'You must be more careful what you eat, being a doctor and — '

Avril gave a spurt of laughter. 'You don't know my father,' she chuckled. 'He enjoys his food as much as anyone. Of course he works hard too, like the rest of the men here.'

'A day at Sylvanside in the fresh air gives me an appetite. Fortunately all the women I know are excellent cooks. Are you a good cook, Miss Blade?'

'She can arrange a plate of lettuce leaves and carrot sticks,' Sam said, earning himself a furious glare. Megan and Avril rose to bring in the sweets.

'I made a selection,' Megan said, 'so you can help yourselves.'

'Oh great, Mum, you made a trifle.' Sam beamed. 'It's my favourite.

'Mmm mine too,' Alex echoed. 'Granny Oliphant always made us a trifle. Rosie can make it too.'

'Aye, Rosie is a fine wee cook,' John Oliphant chipped in. 'Your grandmother taught her to cook most things a man might yearn for, didn't she, lassie? I've missed her while she's been away at college.'

Rosie knew how much he missed his wife's cooking, as well as her company.

'Tania will soon be home and she spoils you too.'

'Aye, there's not many old men who have two beautiful young women to look after them,' he chuckled, his eyes twinkling. He looked at Lidia. 'The way to a man's heart is his stomach. You'll need to learn to cook more than lettuces if ye want to snare one o' these young fellows.' Lidia glared at him. Her father had accused her of wanting to snare Sam when she moved to Dumfries to be nearer.

Rosie was seated between Struan Ritchie and Alex. She had felt shy at first but Struan was a pleasant young man, and he seemed interested in her plans to take over the gardens as a business.

'You're very enterprising,' he said. 'Tania told me you're tougher than you look and a hard worker too.' He smiled and Rosie noticed his grey eyes crinkled at the corners and he had nice even white teeth. His fair skin had a well scrubbed look and his hair was almost the same colour as Tania's, a dark glossy chestnut with more than a hint of copper. They could almost have been siblings.

Sam was sitting opposite with his father and Avril's husband, Dean Scott. They all had an interest in farming and the conversation returned to the problem with the heifer as the meal drew to an end.

'Will you go through to the sitting room,' Megan suggested, 'and I'll bring the coffee and mints through there if — '

'I think that's a car,' Steven said, pushing back his chair. 'It will be the vet.' He strode to the window. 'Yes it is. Come on, Sam, we've work to do.'

'Er, would you mind if I came to watch, Mr Caraford?' Struan asked. 'I've never seen a caesarean operation.'

'Of course you can, lad. Alex will find you a pair of wellingtons.'

'I have a pair of clean wellingtons in my car boot. Father is strict about washing them before and after, ever since the foot and mouth in the sixties.'

'That's good advice. You come along then,' Steven said regarding the young man with approval. It was too soon to know whether he was a prospective son-in-law or not but he liked a young fellow who was interested in his work. Alex rose to follow his father.

'I wouldn't mind coming to watch so long as I'll not be in the way,' Dean said.

'Aye, come if you like, Dean,' Steven said. 'She's in a separate pen so there's plenty of space.' Dean had spent a year at Bengairney as a student, before he went to college, so he was familiar with the farmyard, as well as the Caraford family. He glanced at Avril's father.

'Are you coming to see how they operate on animals instead of humans?' he asked. He knew Lint was as interested in farming as any of them, even though he was a surgeon.

'Yes, I'd like to see how it's done,' Lint said, excusing himself to Lidia and giving Megan a rueful glance. 'I'm afraid we're all deserting the ladies.'

'No doubt you'll all be back, and if the vets are with you, you can have your coffee in the kitchen,' Megan said.

'Samuel,' Lidia called, and hurried out to where the men were pulling on overalls and wellingtons in the back porch. 'Samuel, there's no need for you to go. There's plenty of others to help.'

'I told you, she's one of our best heifers. Nothing would keep me away.'

'Not even me?' Lidia said pouting and fluttering her eyelashes at him.

'Not even the Queen of Sheba,' Sam said, hurrying after his father, leaving Lidia with angry patches of colour and a mouth thin with resentment. He would pay for this. Her mother was right, all men needed to be brought to heel like dogs.

Hannah Caraford and John Oliphant chatted in front of the sitting room fire. At their ages they had seen most aspects of farm life and they also had their family in common. Avril and Rosie admired Tania's birthday presents, especially the gold watch which her parents had given her, and the ruby necklace and earrings which had belonged to her grandmother but which Hannah wanted to pass on.

'I have a set similar to this,' Avril said with admiration. 'My father bought it for my mother.' Lidia was not interested in looking at other people's gifts. It was left to Megan to entertain her. She had never had difficulty making pleasant, if trivial, conversation, but Lidia Blade was simmering with resentment and there were awkward pauses.

'Come and tell me how the children are getting on, Avril,' Hannah Caraford said, patting the settee beside her. 'William must be four months old, isn't he?'

'He is, and so far he is a good wee fellow. Anne will be starting school after the summer holidays and . . . ' Lidia gave an impatient sigh. Avril turned to her with a smile. 'Sam is good with children. He teases and entertains Anne whenever he comes over to Riverview. Do you like children, Lidia?'

'So long as they belong to other people.' Lidia said flatly. 'I suppose it's different when you're older. Samuel and I are too young to be burdened with howling kids.'

'I see,' Avril murmured, biting back a smile, but Tania couldn't resist joining the conversation.

'Avril is only six years older than you and Sam.' Megan was relieved to hear the men coming back in at last. She escaped on the pretext of making coffee for them.

They were subdued. The calf was dead, as they had half expected, and the heifer was very sick.

'She might survive, but I doubt if she'll have another calf, Steven,' Patrick Fisher said. 'Don't you agree, Iain?'

'Yes. I don't think there was anything more we could have done. The calf was deformed. It had already damaged her internally. We did our best. I expect techniques will get better as time goes on.'

'Aye, not so long ago we would have had to shoot her to put her out of her pain.' Patrick said. Steven nodded silently. He would have a big vet's bill for this night's work and nothing to show for it, but at least they had minimized the animal's suffering as far as possible.

'So how is the birthday girl?' Patrick asked in an effort to find a more cheerful subject. 'It seems no time since she was a toddler. Sam had just started school the first time I came to Bengairney. I must be getting an old man. It's time I was considering retirement, Iain. I hope you're looking round for another partner to buy me out.' His tone was jovial but he was serious beneath the banter and Steven knew they would be lucky to get another vet as conscientious as Mr Fisher, and one with his experience.

'I'll tell my father to come through and say hello before you go,' Megan said as she refilled the coffee cups. 'He's supposed to be retired himself but he still works every day at the gardens up at Langton Tower.'

'Aye, tell John I'd like to see him. We go back a long time. I was a young vet when I first went to Mr Turner's at Martinwold and your father was a young herdsman who thought none of his animals should die.' He chuckled. 'We were both idealists then. There's been a lot of changes at Martinwold over the years. Murdo Turner is one of the most progressive farmers I know. It's a pity he has no family to carry on. He can't stand the sight of his son-in-law and Natalie was ruined from the day she was born.' He shook his grey head. 'He thinks a great deal of you, though, Sam. I believe you do the relief milking for him once a fortnight, when his dairyman is off? And aren't you doing your student year there as well, young Alex? You couldn't get a better placement by my reckoning.' Megan passed round the tray of shortbread and birthday cake before she went to fetch her father. She knew the men would enjoy time to relax and talk about other things after the night's labours.

'Isn't Samuel coming through here?' Lidia demanded, when Megan put her head round the door to call her father through to the kitchen.

'Not yet, dear.' Megan said. 'You know how it is. The men like a gossip when they all get together and they need time to relax after tonight's work.' Lidia scowled and pursed her lips. She had not come here to make small talk with a room full of women. She stood up and smoothed her hot-pants over her slim hips. John Oliphant marvelled again at the length of her legs. She was an attractive young woman. No wonder young Sam was smitten. He made his way through to the kitchen but Lidia followed him. Her manner was curt when she saw Sam sitting at ease with the rest of the men, munching shortbread and drinking coffee.

'So you're here, eating again, Samuel! I've had a completely wasted evening waiting for you. It's time for me to leave now.'

'Is it? All right, Lid. 'Night then. I might see you at the dance on Saturday.' Sam turned his attention back to Iain McNaught who was recounting a story about his experiences in Canada. Lidia was furious.

'My name is Lidia! You should know that by now.' She was aware of several pairs of male eyes on her and she tossed back her long blonde hair. 'Come and see me to my car.'

'Your car is right at the door, woman. It couldna get much closer,' Steven said irritably, before Sam could speak. It was rare for Steven to be rude to anyone, least of all a guest, but he had had a long frustrating day and he was tired. The girl was a stunner to look at but he couldn't stand her pretensions.

'Go on Iain, what happened?' he prompted the vet. Lidia's eyes widened. She opened her mouth to speak but when she looked across at Sam he shrugged as though he was under his father's thumb and she knew damned well he was not. She stomped out on her high cork platforms and left without a single goodnight, or word of thanks to Megan.

A little while later when the vets had left, Dean moved closer to Sam and said in a low voice, 'I think you're in the black books with your girlfriend, Sam.'

'Och, it'll be all right,' Sam said. 'She'll come round — and if she doesna it's not the end of the world.'

'Oh Sam, be careful,' Dean warned, no longer smiling. 'She looks to me like a woman who intends to get her own way — by hook or by crook.'

'You're talking rubbish, Dean.' Sam laughed and patted him on the shoulder. Although Dean was ten years Sam's senior they were good friends. They had lived and worked together, first at Bengairney when Dean was a student and later when he was dairyman for Mr Turner at Martinwold, while Sam was doing his own student year there.

'It's not rubbish. I wouldn't like to see you trapped by — ' Dean broke off. How could he tell Samuel he thought his beautiful girlfriend had only room for one love, and that was herself. He might be misjudging her but he didn't trust her. 'What if she got pregnant? You would feel it was your duty to marry her, and so would your parents.' He had seen more of life than Sam and he was convinced Lidia Blade was more interested in what she considered Sam's assets than any deep emotion she felt for Sam himself. His young friend deserved better than that. Sam's face coloured. So far he had resisted Lidia's invitations to have sex.

'She's on the Pill,' he muttered. 'She reckons it's given women the same freedom as men.'

'Aye and she might forget to take the Pill one of these days.' If it suited her purpose, he thought. 'All I'm saying is you should be careful unless you can trust her and you love her more than life itself.'

2

Lidia appeared to have forgiven Sam by the time he collected her on Saturday evening. She was looking even more glamorous and was in a flirtatious mood. He enjoyed seeing the envy of most of the men at the dance. It was around midnight when he drove her back to her flat. It hadn't occurred to Lidia he would refuse to come in. She was convinced he would be unable to resist her when he saw her in her new negligee. She couldn't believe it when Sam kissed her goodnight in the car and came round to open the door for her to get out.

'But you must come in,' she wheedled.

'Not tonight. I'm milking at Martinwold in the morning,' he reminded her. 'I have to be up by quarter to five to bring the cows in. The milking has to be finished and the milk cooled in the bulk tank before the tanker arrives, otherwise the creamery will reject it. That would cost me my wages, and more. Come and help me if you're so keen to be with me,' he teased.

'No bloody fear!' Lidia snapped. Sam frowned. She knew he didn't like women swearing but she was furious with him. She tossed her head. 'It's ridiculous you working as a labourer.'

'Mr Turner pays me well. If I didn't do relief milking I couldn't afford the money to buy all the drinks you had tonight.'

'Your father should pay you more then you wouldn't need to work for somebody else.'

'We only take money from our own business when we need it for food and clothes and essentials. We live comfortably enough but we don't squander money. Anyway, working at Martinwold in the milking parlour is good experience.'

'You think taking me out is squandering money?'

'Don't spoil a good evening by quarrelling, Lidia.'

'I asked you a question.'

'You have to understand farmers have most of their money tied up in cattle and machinery. We don't have cash to spend on getting drunk. One day we hope to rent another farm so that Alex and I will have a place each. We need to be thrifty now so that we shall have enough capital.'

'You should be taking over Bengairney now you've finished college. You're the eldest son. It's time you stuck up for your rights then you wouldn't have to scrimp when you take me out. Your father should retire and let you run the farm.'

'Retire? Father?' Sam gave a spurt of laughter. 'Don't let him hear you. He's only fifty-one. Anyway I don't want him to retire. He has plans and ideas of his own to carry out. Besides, he carries most of the responsibility so I have more freedom than if I was in charge.'

'I think your parents are greedy, hanging on to the house and everything.'

'Ach, Lidia,' Sam was tired. 'You don't understand anything about farming. Mum and Dad have worked hard to get us where we are now. They have made sacrifices to give Alex and me a better start than they had. Besides, I might go abroad through the Young Farmers Association when Alex comes home to take my place. It would broaden my experience. I couldn't do that if Mum and Dad weren't there to manage everything.'

'You're going abroad?' Lidia's eyes lit up. 'We could get married and go for our honeymoon. I'd love that.' Sam stared at her in dismay. He had no plans for marriage.

'It's not a holiday. It's meant to be educational. I'd be staying with farming families. Other students might come to Bengairney in exchange. That's the way it works.' He yawned. 'It's time I was home and

34

in bed.' He gave her a swift kiss, jumped into his car and was gone before she could protest.

★ ★ ★

Tania and Rosie finished college and prepared to take on the world. Rosie had sailed through her exams and been offered a job in one of the large commercial nurseries. Mr Hudson told her it was a great opportunity but understood when she explained that John Oliphant was seventy-five and waiting for her to take over at Langton Tower.

Tania had taken a holiday job for the summer, working in a children's home until term started and she could begin teaching. She and Struan spent most Saturday nights together now, going to the dances or to see a film. He had grown quite at ease with her family but Tania was diffident about going to Shawlands. His mother was sixty-one but she talked as though she were ninety. Her ailments changed every time Tania visited.

'They change so often I can't see how her illnesses can be serious,' she confided to Rosie.

'Maybe she's a hypochondriac. What is Struan's father like?'

'He's the opposite. He always makes me welcome. He was seventy-one in July and he still supervised all the work until Struan came home from university. He rides a great big stallion. He used to follow the hunt but Struan says he doesn't go so often now. They both regard Struan and me as children.' She chuckled at the thought. 'Mr Ritchie is strict but he's quite kind. Struan says his mother started with her ailments when his sister went to live abroad. He's sure they're imaginary.'

Rosie had taken her lecturer's advice and joined one of the horticultural societies he recommended. She had every intention of keeping up to date with new ideas and varieties of seed and she had subscribed to two magazines.

'I know I have a lot to learn,' she told John Oliphant, 'but Mr Gillis, another of our tutors, said I had been well taught in practical work. That's thanks to you, Papa Oli.' She gave him one of her wide smiles. They always lifted his spirits. There was an innocence and sincerity about Rosie which made her very loveable in his old eyes. He knew she wanted to prove she could be as good a business woman as her mother, as well as a good gardener and he was determined to do anything he could to help her succeed. It had often grieved him and Chrissie to see how hard Rosie tried to win her mother's approval but Catherine Palmer-Farr never showed any motherly love. She had spent her childhood since she was eight at boarding school and he wondered if that had suppressed her natural emotions.

One thing which pleased him was Rosie's appreciation of Paul Keir's methodical work and his desire to learn. The lad had grown tall in the past year but he was still a slender, fine-boned young man and his fair hair and pale complexion gave him an air of fragility which was deceptive. He was diagnosed with leukaemia when he was eleven and his father had died when he was thirteen, leaving Mrs Keir a wealthy but anxious widow. She had been grateful when John Oliphant and Douglas Palmer-Farr agreed to give Paul a trial in the gardens. She would have had him work for nothing to give him an interest outdoors, but John Oliphant had suggested he should be paid according to his efforts to give him a sense of his own worth. Money did not guarantee health or happiness and John felt Mrs Keir was over protective, although he couldn't blame her considering Paul had not been expected to survive.

'You don't need to prove anything to me,' Rosie assured him one morning. She gave a little grimace. 'If there's one thing I've learned from my mother it's to assess your workers and make the best use of their abilities. I already know you are reliable and conscientious, as well as intelligent. I believe you're as keen to learn as I am. I will pass on some of my gardening magazines and newsletters and you can make a folder for yourself with notes on the things which interest you. It will be a help to have someone to discuss things with when I'm considering changes.'

'Thank you, Miss Palmer-Farr.' Paul's thin face flushed with pleasure. 'Mr Oliphant said I had nothing to worry about because he was sure we should get on, but I was anxious. Mum is too. I enjoy it here and fresh air is what the doctor recommended.'

'Then don't worry any more. Rodney is a different matter.' She frowned, wondering how much she should discuss her other worker. 'He is strong as a horse and so willing and eager to please that it's hard to be angry with him, but sometimes he doesn't listen, or he doesn't take things in. We must never allow him near any of the fertilizers or disinfectants. I have locked them up but I will give you a key. I would appreciate it if you would keep an eye on him too. I can't watch him all the time. Don't be afraid to correct him if he is doing something you know is wrong. I have decided all three of us should meet in the big shed every morning at 8.30. Mr Oliphant will be there too sometimes but he's going to take things easier. We'll discuss the work for the day and you will know what Rodney is supposed to be doing. You have my permission to guide him when I am away from the gardens. I intend to deliver the vegetables for the hotel myself instead of having both my mother and the new chef darting here, there and everywhere helping themselves. I have to make a profitable business of this and that includes keeping my own accounts and paying bills and your wages, so I shall need your cooperation. How do you feel about that?'

'It is a great relief, Miss Palmer-Farr. I have seen Rodney do some strange things when Mr Oliphant was not looking. I was not sure whether I should interfere.'

'Well now you know, Paul. And another thing — if we are to work together please call me Rosie, or Rosemary.' She grinned. 'You may need to call for me across the gardens. Using my first name will not stop me telling you off if you make a mistake,' she warned. 'I need to make a success of this venture. We are all in this together. If things go well I shall increase your pay, if not, we may all be looking for another job. Right?'

'Right. You can count on me Miss . . . er, Rosemary.' Paul smiled and Rosie was glad she had spoken frankly. He looked less worried and later she heard him whistling as he weeded between the rows of young plants. He looked about fifteen so Rosie was surprised to discover he was a year older than herself when she collected the wages sheets from the hotel office. He had not yet learned to drive so John Oliphant started him off in the van, going up and down the drive, before and after work. Rosie felt he would be a steady driver once he gained confidence.

'It will be handy if I can send him to collect things, or do some deliveries now and then,' Rosie said. She had done some accounting and a smattering of economics at college and she was determined to pay attention to the business side of her little enterprise. During the summer and autumn she did her bookkeeping in the evenings so she didn't have much free time for visits to Bengairney. Both Sam and Alex missed her lively company.

'Your grandfather says Rosie is taking her business very seriously and she's working hard,' Megan told them, 'but she still makes time to cook him a hot meal and he helps her to make soup when they have a surplus of vegetables.'

* ★ ★

It was the following spring when Steven heard there was a cottage and twenty-five acres of land to sell near the village of Darlonachie.

'That's near Martinwold,' Sam said, 'Do you think Mr Turner will be interested in buying it?'

'I don't know,' his father replied. 'You can ask him while you're milking at Martinwold this weekend. I don't want to bid against him when he's been good enough to take on both my sons as students. If he's not interested it could be an investment for us. It would save renting a couple of grass parks for summer grazing and it would raise some capital if we get the chance to rent another farm.'

Sam mentioned the sale to Mr Turner when he came into the dairy at Martinwold that Saturday.

'I heard Jimmy Roland was selling a couple of fields off Mid Lochie,' he nodded. 'Is your father interested in buying?'

'He is, but he doesn't want to bid against you, Mr Turner.'

'I hope you and Alex grow up to be as decent men as your father,' Murdo Turner said. Sam considered he was already grown up. 'Tell your father I wish him luck. The

Rolands sold one of their cottages last year for two thousand pounds but it was in better condition than this one. Jimmy Roland is having a hard time. That son of his is useless. I feel sorry for old Jimmy but he should tell the lad to clear out if all he's going to do is run up debts with gambling and women.'

Sam didn't say anything. It was common knowledge Mr Turner had quarrelled with his own daughter over the debts her husband was running up. Dr Wright-Manton had spilled the beans himself while he was drunk in the Darlonachie pub.

Steven, Sam and Alex went to see the land and the cottage the following Tuesday.

'The land is pretty good,' Steven decided, 'but it would benefit from some well rotted manure. It would be worth ploughing one of the fields for corn for a couple of years, then sow it back to grass.'

'Yes,' Sam said, 'the new grass seed mixtures would be more productive. We could plough the other field for corn the following two years.'

'We'd need to buy it first,' Steven reminded him. 'I'll call on Jimmy Roland. We'll put in an offer but I'll tell him we need an answer before this season's grass parks come up for auction.'

The tenant of the cottage couldn't show

them round until half past three. She was a young woman with a small child and she seemed flustered to find them waiting for her.

'We need to get home for the milking,' Steven explained. 'I believe you're a school teacher?'

'Y-yes I am. We-we only moved here in January. Now we'll have to move out.' She looked pale and tired and her voice shook.

'Does your husband work in the area?' Steven asked to put her at ease.

'I . . . he . . . I'm a widow. M-my husband was killed last September. He was an engineer. A lorry skidded and ran right into Tim's car.'

'I'm so sorry to hear that,' Steven said. 'You put the kettle on and make yourself a cup of tea,' he added kindly. 'We only want a quick look. We're more interested in the land. The cottage hasna had much done in the way of repairs, has it?'

'I painted the living room and the bedroom as soon as we moved in. I tried to paint the kitchen and the bathroom but all those black specks have come through already.' Sam noticed her defensive tone and the colour mounting her cheeks.

'My father meant the landlord hadn't done much general maintenance,' he said.

'Maintenance?' she echoed. 'I've been

43

flushing the toilet with a bucket for a fortnight. Young Mr Roland said he would get a plumber to sort it but he's never been. He didn't even look at it himself.'

'Please Mummy, can I make myself some tea? I'm famished,' the little girl asked, 'and some bread and strawberry jam?'

'In a minute, Ginny, when I've attended to these two gentlemen.'

'It's all right, Mrs . . . ?' Steven began.

'Green — Penny Green.' She flashed him a harassed smile. 'Ginny is nine. She's always hungry by the time we get home. I was lucky to get a job in teaching so quickly and Mrs Struthers, the headmistress, has been very understanding. She told me about this cottage being vacant. Now I shall need to search for somewhere else. I doubt if there'll be anything so convenient, or at such a low rent.'

'Don't do anything hasty,' Steven advised. 'If we are fortunate enough to buy the land we would be letting the cottage anyway — although I'd be ashamed of it in this state. It needs repairs to the door and windows for a start.'

'I could take a look at the toilet for you, if you like?' Sam offered.

'Would you?' Penny Green asked eagerly. 'I'm afraid the water cistern is up in the loft.

There's a chain through the ceiling for flushing.'

'Do you have a ladder?'

'Yes, I bought one. I thought of using the loft as a bedroom but . . . ' she shrugged. 'The ladder is in the coal shed. I'll get it.'

'I'll bring it,' Alex offered, 'while you show Dad round.'

'There's not much more to see,' Steven said, 'but you do keep it clean and tidy, Mrs Green.'

'I try. Do you mind if I attend to Ginny?' She smiled down at the child waiting hopefully. 'Can I offer you all a cup of tea?'

'No thanks, we haven't much time. Alex is doing his student year at Martinwold Farm so they'll be expecting him back. You go ahead with Ginny's jam sandwich,' he said.

Ten minutes later Sam climbed down from the loft, grinning with satisfaction. 'That's the toilet sorted. The pin holding the ball cock had rusted through. Alex found me a bit of wire in the Land Rover. That should hold it in place until we — or someone else — gets a proper pin.'

'What a relief. I don't know how to thank you,' Penny Green said.

'No big deal.' Sam smiled. 'You've a good big loft up there and the roof seems to be sound enough, but I'll bet it's cold in winter?

There's no sarking under the slates.'

'It was freezing when we moved in. That's why I only use it for storage. I do hope you will manage to buy the land.' She blushed. 'I only pay a low rent. Would you charge a lot more?'

'If we're lucky enough to buy the land and the cottage,' Steven said, glancing round, 'I'd want to maintain this place in a better state. I'm not saying we should spend a lot of money on it, but I hope we would manage some improvement. Would you be willing to pay more rent?'

'Within reason. Could we negotiate?'

'Of course.' Steven smiled. 'Let's hope Mr Roland is open to negotiation too.'

'Mr Roland senior is very reasonable,' Penny said, 'but his son . . . ' She shuddered 'He's horrible, and he's greedy.'

'We hope to deal with his father. Good day to you, Mrs Green. I hope we shall meet again.'

'What did you think, Dad?' Alex asked when they were back in the Land Rover. 'The land looks similar to Martinwold land — a decent loam, and it's level. The burn down the edge of both fields means we wouldn't have any worries about water for the cattle.'

'No, that's a big plus, Alex,' Steven agreed. His younger son was full of enthusiasm. 'I almost wish they hadn't included the cottage. I'd be ashamed to let it out in that state.'

'What do you think the land is worth?' Sam asked. 'A hundred pounds an acre? A hundred and twenty? It's not like buying a farm. There's no buildings included.'

'We'll discuss it with your mother when we get home,' Steven said 'but I reckon we could afford to offer £100 an acre and £800 for the cottage. It would take as much again to make it decent for that poor woman — or any other respectable tenant.'

'That's £3,300 then,' Sam said.

'We'll offer £3,000 and be prepared to negotiate. We could go up to four at a pinch, but that wouldn't leave anything for repairs, or any emergencies for us, such as a major machinery repair, or the need to buy extra fodder if we get a bad season. Remember we've agreed to pay for the new shed at Bengairney too.'

'But we wouldn't need to rent as much extra grass.'

'True,' Steven agreed. 'The cottage might be worth something some day. Prices are increasing since decimalization.'

Steven called on Mr Roland the following day. After a bit of hard bargaining, in which Steven told him he'd be ashamed to offer a tenant the cottage in that state, they settled on £3,500.

'I'll see our solicitor without delay and put in a firm offer,' Steven said. 'I'd like it signed and paid before all the grass parks are let. I've already taken twenty acres at Highfold Farm. The auction was earlier this year.'

'I'll get my man onto it before that lad o' mine gets back from his holidays,' Roland agreed. 'I dinna ken how you manage two sons. Reece goes through money like water.'

'Our lads know they need to watch the pennies if they want to farm.' Steven felt he and Megan had been lucky with their family, but then he remembered Sam's friendship with the Blade girl.

Megan knew Steven's mind was on their latest acquisition as they lay in bed.

'Is the cottage so dreadful?' she asked, 'or are you sorry for the young widow?'

'A bit of both.' He turned and drew her close. 'Remember how worried your parents were when we wanted to get married before you finished your teacher training? The same thing could have happened to us and you'd have been left with young Sam.' He kissed her and passion flared between them. Neither of them considered they would ever be too old for love.

'Are you sleeping?' Megan whispered later.

'No,' Steven chuckled. 'Are you wanting a repeat performance?'

'Steven . . . ' Megan warned, stifling a smile herself. 'I was thinking about Mr Patterson. He drew the plans for my parents to modernize Honeysuckle Cottage. He knew about grants for improvements.'

'So he did! That's a good idea, Meggie. I'll visit Mother tomorrow evening. He usually goes round for his meal.'

Angus Patterson seemed pleased Steven wanted his advice. 'I still like to hear what's going on,' he said. 'Young Archie Pattinson could help. He lives in the next road. The postmen kept getting our letters mixed due to similar names and him being an architect. He brought my letters round several times and we got talking. Shall I ask him to contact you? I know there is a grant for improving sanitation. Archie will tell you the details.'

'Thank you.' Steven nodded. 'The bathroom and kitchen are a mess. I'd like to make them decent but we don't want to spend too much.'

'Archie will advise you,' Mr Patterson assured him. 'How is John Oliphant since his wife died?'

'Better than we expected,' Steven said. 'He still helps at the gardens at Langton Tower and young Rosie is good to him. Tania visits him at weekends and he comes to us for his Sunday dinner. He's bought himself a little freezer so Megan stocks it up. He never grumbles.'

'I'm sure he appreciates having a loving family. I've appreciated your mother's kindness to me over the years since my wife died.' He smiled at Hannah.

Archie Pattinson, the young architect, called to see the cottage the following week when Penny Green would be home to show him and Steven round. He made several suggestions.

'Even with a seventy-five per cent grant we can't afford to build on a second storey,' Steven said.

'And a big house would be too much rent,' Penny said.

'All right.' Archie smiled down at Ginny, who was gazing at him wide-eyed.

'My daddy made us a lovely kitchen with lots of cupboards and pretty tiles,' she said hopefully.

'In that case I shall see what I can do,' Archie promised. He agreed to send Steven a rough draft of two suggestions. 'Or you could simply repair the flat roof,' he said, 'but whatever you decide, the electric wiring needs renewing. If it were my house, and given the present grant available, I would put two dormer windows in the roof and enlarge the existing skylight for a bathroom. Downstairs I'd demolish the lean-to and build one decent sized kitchen. Most people have an electric washing machine so there's no need for a wash house and a coal bunker would replace the coal shed.'

'Streamline things you mean. Sounds a good idea to me,' Steven nodded, 'but I need some idea of the cost. Send me the plans and estimates for the dormer windows idea.'

Steven returned to Bengairney feeling optimistic. The grants were more than he'd expected and any improvement should be a good investment.

'We would have to lay out the money to complete the renovation,' he told Megan, 'but if we get on with it we should be able to claim the grant before we need to start paying out for the new shed.'

They sent a bunch of heifer stirks to graze the two Mid Lochie fields for the summer. There was no herdsman to check on them as there was with rented summer grazing so Sam and Steven took turns to check them most evenings. While Alex was working at Martinwold he was nearer, so he took his bicycle back with him so that he could take a turn at inspecting the cattle too. One evening in May he discovered an animal was missing.

He walked to the next field in search of it. He was surprised to find a digger parked on the other side of the burn in the field still belonging to the Rolands but it was being used for dredging the burn and the operator was piling the spoil in their field as well as on the Rolands' side. Their animals would need to scramble over to get to the water if it continued all the way beside their fields. The missing stirk was lying alone beside the far hedge. Alex knew instinctively there was something amiss. He got her onto her feet. One hind leg was swollen and she made no effort to move away when he ran his hand over her other legs. He left her in peace and cycled back. He met Mr Turner crossing the Martinwold farmyard. Alex told him about the lame animal and the digger.

'Didn't they consult your father before they started dredging?'

'He would have mentioned it. I'm going down to the phone to tell him so he can see for himself in the morning.'

'Use the phone in the office, Alex. Steven will want to know about the stirk being lame.'

'I'll go straight after breakfast,' Steven promised. He trusted Alex's judgment. He would have made a good vet. 'I'll take Joe in case we need to bring the lame animal home in the trailer.'

The following morning the digger was already at work and Steven went to speak to the driver.

'Reece Roland told me to dredge the burn to stop the low fields flooding but he didna say he'd sold those fields,' the man said.

'I can't object to you dredging but I would like you to leave gaps to give the animals access to the water. They're some of our best young stirks. I don't want any more of them getting injured.'

'I saw a wee beast lying beneath the hedge,' the driver said. 'It looked mighty dead tae me but I havena injured any o' them.'

Steven was dismayed to find the stirk was dead. He bent to feel the swollen leg. It was hard and stiff. He was more worried when he saw two others limping. As Alex had said there was no blood or obvious wound. He sent Joe to bring the Land Rover and trailer closer.

'We'll need to take this one home with us, Joe. I'd take the two lame beasts as well but I don't think we could get them gathered up on our own.'

'We could try,' Joe said. He was always willing, but the young animals took off in a wild gallop round the field and the lame ones tried to limp after them.

'There's a third one beginning to limp,' Steven said, 'and its leg is swollen. Chasing them will cause more stress. We'll get back home and I'll phone the vet to see if he has any suggestions for treatment.'

It was Iain McNaught who answered the telephone. He sounded serious when Steven described the lame animals.

'I think I'd better come and take a look. Have any of your animals had Blackleg?'

'Not as far as I know.' Steven frowned. 'I've never heard of it.'

'I'll come right away. Lucky you caught me before I set off on my rounds.' Steven was worried. Iain McNaught was young but he was a clever vet. He examined the dead animal in the trailer, his expression serious.

'I'd like to see the others in the field. Are they on the land you bought?'

'Yes. Why?'

'I don't want to alarm you but I ought to check the rest.' When they reached the field Steven was more than alarmed to find another stirk already dead. Two others were lying down, panting and obviously unwell.

'I'm afraid it is Blackleg,' Ian said grimly after he had made a careful examination of the two lame animals. 'I doubt if we can save these two. The rest need vaccinating without delay.'

'Dear God. It must be a bad disease,' Steven said.

'It is. I brought some vaccine in the car as a precaution,' Iain said, 'but you'll need to round them up to jag them and you might find more are affected before you're finished.'

'But how can they have got such a disease?' Steven asked in consternation. 'We rear our own replacements. We haven't bought any animals in for years.'

'The animals don't infect each other. It's caused by a spore-forming bacteria like anthrax. It can live for years in the soil. It's proper name is *Clostridium chauvoei*. The animals ingest the bacteria. They're usually dead within twelve to forty-eight hours so you don't always notice they're ill until it's too late.'

'It was Alex who noticed the first one last night. He thought she had a temperature and her leg was swollen.'

'He's observant and a good stockman. Don't be surprised if you lose more of them. My advice is to vaccinate now. These animals are in good condition and they're young. They're the ones most often affected. I see you're dredging the burn. It's possible the spores have been lying dormant until the soil was disturbed but I couldn't swear to that. I'm afraid you'll need to vaccinate all your young stock every year from now on — at least for a good number of years.'

'Good God! All of them? Every year? That's going to cost something.'

'Yes, I'm afraid it is, but prevention is the only solution and it's better than risking losing fine young stirks like these.

'Aye, you're right there.' Steven sighed heavily. 'These are all pedigree. The registration fee is another loss now they're dead. We'd better get back and get the vaccine from you, Iain. The sooner we get them done the better. I can't afford to lose many more or we shall be out of business.'

'I'm sure it will not come to that for Bengairney,' Iain McNaught said, 'but I know you are proud of your stock and I don't blame you for being upset.'

'Aye, I'll ask Roland if he knew about Blackleg when I see him.'

'He does. He vaccinates all his young stock every year. He must have had it at some time. It's a routine to him now. Pity he didn't mention it.'

'Aye, I wish to God he'd warned us,' Steven said.

It was a bad time at Bengairney. By the time all the young animals had been vaccinated six of them had died. Steven felt so helpless he wanted to weep at the sight of them lying dead. But grown men didn't weep, except inside. Megan understood and she held him tenderly in her arms when they were alone in bed.

'You can't blame yourself, Steven,' she said. She felt upset and anxious about the loss herself but she knew these things happened in farming. They were a reminder that men did not know everything and life could be uncertain. Sam and Alex were shocked and upset by so many deaths. It was the first time either of them had seen such a disease strike out of the blue.

'Bad though it is,' Steven said, 'if neither of you live to see anything worse you'll be lucky. When your mother and I were starting farming some of the cows got contagious abortion. It nearly put us out of business before we'd begun. Tuberculosis was another menace before the herds became attested. A lot of good animals were slaughtered and there's no guarantee it can't flare up again. That's why all the herds still have to be tested regularly. We must always be vigilant.'

'We'll not forget this,' Sam said. 'The wee Butterfly stirk was one of our best families.'

'And what about Viola?' Alex demanded. 'I reared her myself from when she was born. Dad said I could take her and her offspring with me if ever I set up on my own.'

'It's part of farming and we have to move on,' Steven said. He felt sick inside but it was no use making his sons even more upset.

Sam brooded. In two years' time there would be six fewer heifers to sell, or to bring into the herd to produce more milk. It was a big loss but it was not just the money; he had hated seeing healthy cattle stretched out cold, killed by a disease which could have been prevented if they had known of the danger lurking in the soil.

'For God's sake, cheer up, Sam!' Lidia snapped. 'You've hardly spoken since you picked me up.'

'I told you what happened,' Sam said. 'It's enough to make anybody glum. Those animals were frisking around one minute and lying dead the next. Mum and Dad are upset too.'

'Well if you think I'm going to put up with your moods you can think again. Forget about the bloody farm for once. I'm not interested in hearing about cattle dying.'

'And I'm not interested in watching you bat your eyelashes at every Tom, Dick and Harry on the dance floor.' Sam's temper flared. 'I don't feel like dancing tonight. Shall I take you home now or do you want to beg a lift with one of the fellows who keeps ogling at you?'

'I don't need to beg!' She flounced away from him. Sam took her at her word and went home. Their relationship was often stormy but Sam had thought Lidia would share his sadness. His grandfather was right. She had looks and glamour but no substance. She was not the sort to lend support to a working farmer, as his mother had done all her life. He was better without her.

The following lunchtime Lidia telephoned all sweet and gushing with sympathy.

'No, I'm not taking you to the films tonight,' Sam said, unimpressed. Lidia whispered endearments and apologies.

'I'll pick you up on Friday.' Even as he put the phone down Sam despised himself. In his heart he knew Lidia was not the kind of woman he wanted to spend his life with but she could be so damned alluring. He knew it was shallow to keep going out with her. When he was away from her he had no illusions about either Lidia or himself. He knew now she had singled him out after his birthday party when she had seen his home and assumed his family was wealthy.

Steven was surprised how quickly the improvements were going ahead for Midloch Cottage. Archie Pattinson had completed the plans and applied for a grant on their behalf, but he still came to the cottage on the pretext of inspecting the progress.

'Maybe he's attracted to Mrs Green,' Megan said.

'But he's a young architect and Penny is a widow with a child.'

'A young and attractive widow. Remember Ruth already had Avril when Lint met her. It didn't stop him falling in love.'

'That's true,' Steven nodded. 'Well it's young Pattinson's affair. He took care with the plans. He thinks we might decide to retire there ourselves one day so he made sure there would be room for a further extension.'

Both Megan and Steven put the cottage out of their minds. The foundations for the new shed were being laid and the steel posts and girders had arrived ready for erection. Samuel was paying great attention to the measurements and position, making sure everything was as they had planned.

'Everything seems to be going up in price,' Megan remarked, 'and I don't like all this unrest and talk of strikes and electricity blackouts.'

3

At Langton Tower Rosie was enjoying making her own decisions. There was a happy atmosphere with Paul often whistling or humming a popular song, while Rodney worked away with a smile on his face. Her mother had agreed with her idea of placing a daily order for fruit and vegetables for the hotel. Rosie delivered them to the kitchens and things were working well, except for the new chef.

Catherine had hired two chefs from London when the hotel first became established. They had preferred the privacy of the converted stable cottage, which adjoined the walled garden. It was now in Rosemary's grounds, along with the orchard and the paddock with the back drive running through it so she was pleased when the new chef had insisted on having a room in the hotel above the kitchens with food, laundry and heating as perks. His name was Louis Lambert, which he pronounced Lambère. He had begun to walk around the gardens at odd times and his attitude irritated Rosie.

'I swear I'll hit him on the head with my

spade if I catch him helping himself to herbs and fruit again without putting them through the hotel's accounts,' she said to Paul one morning.

'I have seen him prowling round when I arrive early. I was afraid you might think Rodney or I had stolen the first ripe tomatoes, and some of the early strawberries.'

'You should have told me, Paul. Tell him he has no business in this part of the grounds if you see him again. You have my authority to be as blunt as you like.' Paul's thin face flushed and Rosie knew he would not quarrel with the chef if he could avoid it.

'I don't like that man,' she muttered, 'he can't keep his hands to himself — and I don't mean the vegetables.'

'I noticed. You should take care, Rosemary.' Paul sounded so grave she wanted to laugh, but it was no laughing matter. The chef was sly and she hated the expression in his eyes when he looked her up and down like meat on a slab.

'I am careful. He's worse when I go near the kitchens. He always appears even though he's finished work. Since he came I prefer to take stuff to Honeysuckle Cottage and cook in Papa Oliphant's kitchen.'

'There is a solution,' Paul suggested, 'but it would cost money.'

'What sort of solution?'

'No one needs access to the Stables Cottage since the last chefs went away. You could erect tall iron gates at the entrance to the gardens. They could be locked at night. I come by the back drive from the main road and through the orchard. The back entrance is nearer to my house and the village. Rodney cycles the same way.'

'It's years since I've used the back drive. I always seem to be heading in the other direction for Honeysuckle Cottage, or on to Bengairney. Gates would be a splendid idea to bar the access from the hotel. I must see how much they would cost.' Her blue eyes gleamed. She detested Lambert creeping around. He tried to slide his hands down her arms when she was passing him a tray of vegetables. Once he had crept up behind her in the kitchens and tried to stroke her neck.

Rosemary discussed the idea of erecting gates with her father and with John Oliphant. Douglas Palmer-Farr couldn't understand why she wanted to spend precious capital on something unproductive.

'I want to lock out the chef. He's sly and I don't trust him. He helps himself to produce without accounting for it. I can't stand him creeping about.'

'I don't see any objection so long as you

can afford to do it,' Catherine said. 'You have your own telephone line and I notice you use one of the rooms at Stable Cottage for your office. It is sensible to be separate. It's a pity the garden traffic needs to use the front drive. It is not convenient when we have a lot of cars for a conference.'

'Rodney and Paul use the back drive.'

'There was a transit van making deliveries two days ago,' Catherine argued, 'and last week there was a lorry delivering bags of fertilizer.'

'Oh dear.' Rosemary sighed. 'You'll be even less happy then when I tell you I intend to keep hens again, and a couple of beehives.'

'Bees? You can't keep bees. They might sting the guests and keeping hens would mean vans bringing poultry feed.' Catherine frowned. 'Although I admit we have missed the fresh eggs since Chrissie died. The guests liked the idea that we produced our own.'

Rosemary was busy with the summer produce and delivering surplus vegetables to local shops. She had received quite a few inquiries from local gardeners for young plants to grow on in their own gardens and she was considering expanding these sales. Her vegetables and salads were always fresh and there was plenty of demand without delivering too far.

'You seem to be managing the gardens very well, Rosemary Lavender,' Catherine said one evening. 'Do you think you will have made any profit?'

'Yes, I reckon so. Not a huge profit but we have extended the vegetable garden. It cost quite a bit to hire a rotavator for a day, but the man made a good job. It will give us more scope.'

'I see. Where did you intend to put the beehives if you get them?' Catherine asked. She had begun to recognize her own determination in her daughter. She had learned long ago to plant the seed of an idea, leave it to germinate, then foster its growth when everyone had had time to consider.

'Down the far edge of the paddock, near the orchard but out of the shadow of the trees,' Rosemary replied and Catherine knew she had been right; Rosemary had not given up the idea. 'They would never come near your guests and they only sting if they're disturbed. I've been to two lectures on bee keeping and I've read about it. I'm going on a short course in the spring. I've budgeted for two hives and the bees. We have mended the large hen house and the pullets will be delivered next spring.' She smiled the engaging smile which transformed her pixie face. 'Just think Mum, your guests will love home produced eggs and honey for breakfast. You'll build up a reputation irrespective of that horrible chef. Local honey is supposed to help build up immunity to infections so it will be good for Paul. He's proving a real treasure and I'm amazed at the things he knows.'

'Paul is not my concern,' Catherine said. 'Your schemes mean more traffic.' She was resistant to her daughter's enthusiasm. 'I am trying to persuade your father to improve the back road so that you can direct all your traffic that way. You would need to put up a large sign at the back lodge directing vehicles to Langton Gardens.'

'I see. What did Daddy say? How would he improve it? What would it cost?' Rosemary gnawed her lip. She had another idea growing in her mind for any spare cash she could accumulate.

'He said I was being premature and he is refusing to spend money on a proper road until he is sure you are going to keep on with the gardens.'

'Of course I mean to keep on with the gardens. Anyway the traffic will be much the same whoever is in charge of them,' Rosemary said, 'but I can't afford any money towards improving the back road yet. It hasn't been used for proper traffic for years.'

'I think your father would be willing to

bring in several loads of gravel and a roller to make an even surface but he refuses to spend money on having it tarred.'

'Plenty of gravel and a heavy roller would make a big improvement. Lots of farm roads are made that way. It doesn't have to be posh so long as it is level and dries quickly.'

'I'm glad you agree,' Catherine said with satisfaction. 'Your father will pay for the improvement but you will be responsible for maintainance. Shall I tell him to go ahead then and you'll keep all your garden traffic away from the hotel drive and forecourt?'

'All except Papa Oliphant. He doesn't come every day now. He needs his car.'

'Very well. Louis grumbles because you have shut him out of the gardens.'

'He was helping himself too much, and not just to the herbs,' she said. 'Selling produce is my business. You will have to tell him that, Mum. And another thing, I can't get near the kitchens without him coming down and watching me all the time, however late I wait. I'm thinking of doing up the kitchen in the Stable Cottage and cooking there. I won-dered if you'd mind if I took my bedroom furniture? I could live there if I had my bed.'

'You want to move out?' Catherine asked in dismay.

'I'd still be popping in and out but I'd like

to be a bit more independent.'

'Are you still cooking a meal for John Oliphant?' Catherine demanded. 'His family should be looking after him now that Chrissie has died.'

'He refuses to take any money for all the jobs he does around the garden and he appreciates a good bowl of soup. You know I've always enjoyed his company. If I was at the Stable Cottage we could eat together and it would save me taking it down to Honeysuckle Cottage. Mrs Caraford attends to his laundry and cleaning and Tania stocks his wee freezer at weekends. Sometimes she stays overnight and takes him down to Bengairney for his Sunday lunch.'

'I suppose you will do as you like, as usual. At least you've stopped running down to the farm as often. How do you propose to move your bedroom furniture?'

'Paul and Rodney will help me move things in the van. Thanks Mum.' Rosemary grinned. 'I need to do some scrubbing out first so it will have to wait until we're a bit less busy.' If she could get the bedroom painted before she moved the furniture, the other rooms could wait.

She didn't mention that she would be visiting Bengairney very soon. They were hosting a Young Farmers Stock Judging competition before Alex went back to college. Both Alex and Sam had insisted she must be there. She would be able to do as she pleased if she was in the Stable Cottage.

* * *

'Shall I pick you up to night, Papa Oli? It's the stock judging competition at Bengairney.'

'Eh, young Rosie, I think I'm getting a bit old for such things, don't you?' John Oliphant said, shaking his white head and smiling.

'Of course not. You've always enjoyed looking round the cattle. The Bengairney herd is becoming well known so I expect there will be people taking the chance to see the stock, apart from members of the club. Maybe Mr Turner will be there,'

'Aye, he might, he's always taken an interest in Sam and Alex. It's a shame he has no son, or grandson, to follow on at Martinwold. All right, I'll be ready.'

'I've been trying to persuade Paul to come too.'

'Aye, it wouldna do the laddie any harm.'

Paul decided he would go to Bengairney when he heard John Oliphant was going. He had a thirst for knowledge, but after spending long periods in hospital he had no desire to spend time at university. In fact both he and his mother were grateful to John Oliphant for encouraging him to work in the gardens. Any time he spent studying now was related to plants or garden design.

'I think I might be a bit nervous around cows,' he confided to Rosie that afternoon.

'Don't worry, the cows for the competition will be haltered for leading round the ring. I'll not desert you to a crowd of strangers or take you where you're in any danger. I'll pick you up first, then we'll collect Papa Oliphant. You'll enjoy meeting the Carafords. They're a lovely family.'

'If you say so,' Paul said, 'but I get the impression Alexander would like to flog me anytime I'm in your company.'

'Of course he wouldn't.' Rosie grinned. 'We've known each other all our lives. He's a bit protective, that's all.'

'Possessive, I'd say,' Paul suggested.

'We're good friends, nothing more.' She tossed her mop of blonde curls and frowned. Alex was inclined to be jealous whenever he saw her in the company of eligible males and Paul was quite handsome if you admired fair hair and blue eyes and finely chiselled features. He had grown taller since he first came to the gardens, but he was still very slim. She smiled to herself. It wouldn't do Alex any harm to see her with someone else.

Sam would never even notice, she thought gloomily. Lidia Blade was sure to be there.

When they arrived, three of the committee members were handing out cards for the judging competition. Lidia was flitting around like a colourful butterfly; Rosie had to admit she was the most glamorous girl there. She was not helping with anything, though, and her expression grew sullen when Sam continued to groom the cattle, making sure they looked their best for the judging. There were four classes of four animals so Joe Finkel would be leading one, along with Steven, Alex and Sam.

Dean came over to speak to them and she introduced Paul. 'Dean will be master judge tonight so we all have to try and agree with his order of choice.'

'I hope someone agrees,' Dean said with a laugh. 'Is she a tough boss?'

'She's a hard taskmaster.' Paul glanced at her and winked. 'I'm enjoying working in the gardens. I may decide to have a nursery of my own one day, or perhaps try garden design.'

'I see.' Dean looked at him. They all knew it had been touch and go whether or not he would recover from leukaemia but he looked well and healthy.

'It's good to have ambitions,' Dean said. 'I used to get frustrated, but you have to keep hoping and planning. I wish you luck, Paul.' Dean turned to Rosie. 'Are you going to have a go at the judging tonight, Rosie, or have you forgotten about cows these days?'

'I'll never forget about the animals.' She looked at Paul. 'Farming was my first love you know. 'So yes, Dean Scott, I am having a go at the judging so you'd better agree with my choices.' Her blue eyes glinted with laughter. There were often heated arguments after each class when people disagreed with the judges' selection. At the end of the four classes the points were added up. There were prizes for junior and senior club members, as well as a class for open judging, which was the one Rosie would be entering. She tried to persuade Paul to have a go but he shook his head.

'I wouldn't know which cows have good legs and top line, milk veins and udders — and all the stuff you and Dean were discussing.'

Everyone chattered over the refreshments. Some were still discussing the judging and asking Dean to justify his reasons if they had not agreed with his choice. Mr Turner and John Oliphant had gone indoors for a seat and some of Megan's home baking. Tania and Struan came to join them.

'Speaking about gardening,' Struan said,

when Rosie had introduced Paul, 'you can come and design ours any time you like. Farmers are notorious for neglecting their gardens — at least that's what my father reckons. Mother says it's just an excuse.'

'We don't do garden design,' Rosie said 'but Paul has had a brilliant idea for the forecourt to the hotel with a fountain in the centre and a rockery round about for small plants and spring bulbs. Even Mother is impressed. If you're serious we could come to Shawlands and look at yours in about six weeks' time. It might be a project for the winter. If Paul can suggest something to suit you we could grow the plants ready for planting next spring and autumn.'

'Goodness, Rosie, you're a devil for punishment,' Tania teased. 'Grandpa says you're moving into the Stables Cottage as soon as you've done some decorating?'

'That's the plan, if I can get my bedroom furniture moved with my little van.'

'Grandpa was telling Alex and Sam they should help you move your furniture. It would be easier for them with the Land Rover and trailer.'

'I shall not refuse any offers of help,' Rosie said with a grin.

'Good. Oh listen, they're announcing the winners of the stock judging.'

The winners of the Young Farmers' Club junior and senior classes were announced first amidst cheers and a few friendly groans.

'The open class, as well as best score overall, is Rosemary Palmer-Farr,' the chairman announced. Blushing, but smiling Rosie went up to claim her prize.

'You're wasting your time being a gardener, Rosie,' the chairman said with a grin. He raised his voice and held her hand in the air. 'Tell her, boys, she must rejoin the club now she's home from college. We need her for the stock judging team for next year's Highland Show.' There were several cheers as Rosie walked back to Paul and Tania. Sam came running after her, seized her in his arms and swung her off her feet.

'You only had two places different to Dean. That's brilliant!' He hugged her close, then blinked, startled by the feel of her soft curves as he held her against him. His eyes darkened and he kissed her firmly on her surprised mouth. Over his shoulder Rosie saw Lidia glaring furiously at her. She stiffened and struggled to break away but Sam held her tighter, oblivious of their surroundings.

'Let me go!' she hissed. 'I will not be used, Samuel.' She pushed against his chest.

'Used?' Sam stared down at her. 'Rosie . . . ?' He relinquished his grip. 'What do you mean?'

He looked bewildered.

'Don't use me to make Lidia jealous. She's glaring as though she'd like to drown me in the cattle trough over there.'

'B-but I was congratulating you. I'm proud of you. Here's Dad coming.' He moved aside and Steven shook her hand and kissed her cheek.

'You did well, young Rosie. You always did remember everything I taught you about the crops and the animals, but I thought you might have forgotten now you're gardening.'

'I'm glad somebody agreed with my opinions,' Dean said coming up behind him.

'You did a good job, Dean,' Steven assured him.

'You're the one who coached us so it's not surprising we look for the same type of animal.'

'I hadn't thought of that,' Steven said. 'At the end of the day it is one man's opinion against another's, but the stock judging has always been good fun.'

Alex came to join them. 'You did well, Rosie. Congratulations.' He eyed Paul. 'Did your friend have a go?'

'No. Paul, meet my old school buddy, Alex Caraford. Alex, this is my right hand man, Paul Keir.'

'I thought it must be,' Alex said, 'So you're

interested in more than gardening, then?'

'I am indeed.' Paul's eyes gleamed with amusement. He did not miss Alex's innuendo. 'Your grandfather and Rosie persuaded me to come, but gardening is my main interest.'

'Right.' Alex nodded. 'You coming in to speak to Mum, before you leave, Rosie?'

'We've already had a chat. I brought you some Victoria plums. I know they're your favourite. I'll collect Papa OIiphant, then we'd better head home. You'll be going back to college soon, Alex?'

'Yes, I wish I was finished and home for good but I'd better get my diploma or I shall never hear the end of it from big brother.'

'Quite right too,' she nodded. 'We're ready to leave when you are, Papa Oliphant,' she called popping her head round the kitchen door where several men were seated round the table.

'Oh you're leaving, Rosemary? The plums are beautiful,' Megan said, 'but I would like to pay for them now you're in business.'

'I owe you more than a few plums,' Rosie said, 'but you can buy the jam plums if you're sure you want them.'

'Indeed I do. When will they be ready?'

'I'll bring them down in about ten days or so. They are in the orchard so they're later than the desert plums in the walled garden.'

'If you have plenty my wife might like some,' Mr Turner said. 'She used to make a good plum chutney.'

'Rosie makes a good plum chutney herself,' John Oliphant said.

'We have plenty at present. Will you ask Mrs Turner to give me a ring and tell me how many she would like?' Rosie said with a smile. She pulled a printed card from the back pocket of her smart brown trousers. 'This is my telephone number. I'm separate from the hotel.' Alex and Sam both raised an eyebrow. It was hard to believe their little tomboy with the patched jeans was an efficient business woman now. Sam wondered why he had never realized Rosie was an attractive and desirable young woman. Where had he been looking? It had shaken him tonight when he held her soft young body in his arms. She was no longer the skinny child he had carried down from the loft after she had run away from boarding school and almost died of exhaustion and hypothermia. Tonight he had been far too aware of her womanly curves. He'd had a further shock when Rosie had hissed at him in fury. They had never quarrelled in all the years they'd known each other. He felt hurt by her reaction.

'Do you think that fellow, Paul, has his eye

on Rosie?' Alex asked, interrupting his thoughts.

'I hadn't thought about that . . . '

'It wouldn't bother you anyway,' Alex muttered. 'You've got Lidia. She's glaring our way now. She didna even make an attempt at the judging and the other girls say she never helps with the teas.' Sam scowled and ignored Alex's comments but he knew his younger brother was right.

'You did a good bit of business tonight, lassie,' John Oliphant remarked as he climbed into Rosie's car. 'I remember the surplus plums going to waste at one time. It vexed Chrissie.'

'I know. Both the local grocers have agreed to take our spare fruit this year on a sale or return basis. So far they have sold everything I've taken.'

'I was surprised at Mr Turner wanting plums. He didna seem quite himself tonight.'

'He always looks healthy to me. He has an outdoor glow.'

'Aye, but it wasna his looks. He seemed . . . sort of abstracted, a bit vague at times. He's always been so alert. He used to ride out on his horse every morning, summer or winter, but he was telling me he's sold his hunter.'

'Perhaps he feels he's too old to ride every

day,' Rosie suggested.

'Aye maybe. He's five years younger than I am so he'll be seventy next year. Here we are, home again. I'm glad I went tonight. Thanks for the lift, lassie. Good night, young Paul.'

Rosie drove further along the road to the village where Paul lived.

'You're very quiet, Paul,' Rosie said. 'Are you very tired?'

'No, not at all.' Paul leaned forward and folded his arms on the back of the passenger seat so he was closer to her. 'I enjoyed meeting your friends. Everyone was very pleasant. I heard one of the girls suggesting they should invite you as a speaker to tell them about setting up in business on your own. I think they admire your courage.'

'Goodness! I hope they don't ask me. I've barely begun and I couldn't have made a go of things if Dad hadn't let me have the gardens. He's had the new boundaries drawn up and he's putting them into my name so I'll feel more secure. I'm luckier than most people.'

'No more so than all those boys there tonight who expect to step into their father's shoes and take over a farm.'

'I suppose you're right,' Rosie agreed. She drew the car to a halt in his drive. 'Alex and Samuel may not have it so easy, though.

Bengairney is rented and there are two of them.'

'At least they are prepared to work hard. I didn't get the impression they were all like that. I liked Struan Ritchie, though, even though he is better off than most of them.'

'Struan is Tania's boyfriend. His parents own their farm so I suppose they are more on a level with Mr Turner, except that Struan's parents and grandparents have been land-owners for several generations, while Mr Turner had to make his own way. You're right, though, Struan is a nice person. He's never arrogant and he doesn't brag.'

'I was right about Alex too. He would like you as his special girl.' He gave her a sideways glance, 'But it's Sam for you, isn't it, Rosie?'

'S-Sam? N-no, how can you say that, Paul? You only met him tonight and — ' She broke off, floundering.

'And onlookers see most of the game,' Paul quipped with a smile.

'I've always regarded Alex and Sam as the brothers I never had — or at least sort of cousins.'

'Maybe you did once, and still do with Alex, but not Sam. I could see that at once.'

'I-I don't know what you mean, Paul.'

'When I was ill, even though I was young, I knew I might be going to die. It made me see

— I mean really see — everything more clearly. You observe details. When you look at an overcast sky you don't see clouds, you see many shades from white to grey to silver and there's almost always a gleam of sunshine peeping through somewhere. You don't look at a green field, you see a myriad individual grasses in every shade of green, swaying in the breeze, or sparkling with dew in the early morning. Does that sound silly to you?'

'No. No, Paul, it doesn't. It makes me realize how shallow the rest of us often are, and how much we miss.'

'Yes. Your secret about Sam is safe with me and I'm here if you ever want to talk. I hope things work out for you one day. Give him time. He's older than I am in years but he doesn't know what he wants from life yet, apart from being a farmer of course.' Rosie looked at Paul, realizing how perceptive he was. She sighed.

'There's no hiding anything from you, Paul Keir, I must remember that.' He grinned at her.

'Thanks for the lift, boss. See you in the morning.'

'Yes. Paul, it's too dark to see your garden very well but it does look beautifully laid out. Had you anything to do with that?'

'Yes, Mum and I together anyway. Why

don't you come to tea on Sunday afternoon and we'll show you round?'

'I can't invite myself to tea, Paul!' Rosie laughed.

'You're not, I'm inviting you. Mother would be pleased to meet you. In fact I think the two of you will get on well. She loves her plants and she will feel easier when she's met my boss.'

★   ★   ★

Rosie enjoyed her Sunday afternoon with Paul and his mother. The house was built in local red sandstone and stood back from the road with a large garden all round and no near neighbours.

'It was my parents' home,' Mrs Keir told her. 'I grew up here. When my husband was working at the bank in Edinburgh we bought a bungalow on the outskirts but my parents left the house to me and my sister. Pauline and her husband live in Australia so we bought her share in the house. I am so thankful that we kept it. When my husband died, Paul was having his second lot of treatment and he was very ill. It felt as though my whole world was crashing around me. This place was my haven.'

'It must have been terrible,' Rosie said with real sympathy.

'Paul often came to stay here with his grandparents. When he was recovering I decided to bring him down here, hoping the country air might help. We were so much happier here so I sold our home in Edinburgh. I thank God every day for Paul's recovery. My husband and I had made improvements to the interior of the house but the garden was mainly grass. Paul spent hours outside dreaming up changes, sketching plans, discussing different flowers and shrubs.'

'It is lovely now,' Rosie said. 'It is like going on an adventure. I turn a corner and see a rockery; I go through an archway and there is the rose garden. Then down this meandering path and here we are at a pond. Paul told me you were responsible.'

'The planning is all Paul's. We employed a man to do the hard landscaping and heavy work, then I planted the shrubs and flowers. I enjoy it. Each week there is something new, a wee surprise, another plant I'd forgotten about. It has been my saving grace.'

'I think I can understand that.'

'This was the last change we made. The burn running across the bottom corner allowed Paul scope to widen it and make the small pond and this rustic bridge.'

'It's so beautiful.' Rosie stood looking

down into the water. 'Ooh there's a fish! See the ripples.' Mrs Keir glanced at her young companion. Her smile and sparkling eyes made you want to smile back. It lifted the spirits. There was nothing autocratic about her, in spite of her background. She was just as Paul had described her.

It was a crisp autumn afternoon with the white clouds sailing high in the sky. The house martins were darting hither and thither, then gathering together on the telephone wire with an incredible amount of chirruping. Any day now they would start their long journey to warmer places. There were fields at the bottom of the garden and a small copse a few hundred yards away.

'I do love this time of year,' Rosie said, stretching her arms wide as though to embrace the world.

'I agree,' Jeanette Keir said with a smile. 'You are an outdoor person, aren't you. If you don't mind me saying so, Rosemary, you're not at all as I imagined. I can understand now why Paul is so happy working with you.'

'He seems to have a natural instinct for plants. He must have inherited that from you I think. He tells me he would like to be a garden designer some day.'

'I am pleased to hear he is so positive about the future. The doctors are very pleased with

him but deep down I still have this fear . . . '
She smiled at Rosie. 'I must try to be positive
too, and plan for the future. We're fortunate
in that we are well provided for but it takes
more than money to bring health and
happiness. I am so pleased you took time to
come today. I have enjoyed meeting you.'

'I'm glad I came. Your garden has opened
my eyes to Paul's real talents. We are going up
to see the garden of a friend soon. I shall be
able to recommend Paul's suggestions now.'

'Thank you. Er, if . . . if your friend would
like to see any of Paul's ideas here, he would
be welcome to come and look.'

'I will tell Struan that. Thank you.'

The following Sunday afternoon found
Struan, Tania and Mr Ritchie wandering
around the garden with Rosie and Paul, while
Mrs Keir insisted on making afternoon tea
for them.

'We don't wish to put you to any trouble,'
Mr Ritchie said and Rosie thought what a
nice old gentleman he was.

'It is no trouble,' Mrs Keir assured him
with a smile. 'I am pleased to have visitors. I
have not done much entertaining since my
husband died.'

'Then I am sorry my wife could not come.
She does not keep good health these days.'
Tania caught Rosie's glance and raised her

eyebrows heavenwards. Privately Rosie had begun to wonder if Mrs Ritchie's imaginary ailments were her way of clinging to her son. She had made it plain she considered Struan and Tania too young to marry.

'She certainly has no intention of moving out of the farmhouse,' Tania had confided to Rosie a few weeks earler. 'Not that I want to get married until I've worked for a while and earned some money of my own, but there was a lovely bungalow for sale a couple of miles away from the farm. Struan and his father went to see it, but she refused to look, let alone consider buying it. I try hard not to let her come between us but I can tell she expects we should wait about ten years and even then we should all live together.'

Mr Ritchie was impressed with the Keirs' garden and he felt some of Paul's ideas could be adapted to suit Shawlands.

'It might improve your mother's health, Struan, if she had a pleasant garden like this to walk around.'

'Maybe,' Struan was doubtful.

'You will be hoping for grandchildren to live there one day, Mr Ritchie?' Paul asked with a smile.

'I hope so. I keep telling Struan he must make an earlier start than his mother and I did.'

'In that case you would need to plan for grassy area near the house where children could play, and perhaps have a sandpit and a swing. I used to have such things here when I stayed with my grandparents.'

'You must come over and give us your ideas, my boy.'

'Mr Ritchie, you do know we do not undertake landscaping?' Rosie said, 'at least not yet, but as you can see Paul has excellent ideas. He could draw up plans. If you decide to go ahead I suggest you pay Paul for his designs. He has passed his driving test now so he could come to you from time to time to supervise the landscaping work if your own men do the labouring for walls or paths.'

'Yes, yes of course.' Mr Ritchie looked at Struan. 'I'm sure we could come to some arrangement, couldn't we?'

'We have the men and the digger if Paul tells them what to do. We could employ our local builder for a patio or walls,' Struan said. 'Tania and I would like to be consulted too.'

'Yes, of course.' Mr Ritchie turned to smile at Tania.

'My business is the plants,' Rosie said. 'I hope you would let us supply and plant the shrubs and flowers if Paul takes time out to supervise the work?'

'Of course we will, Rosie,' Struan said, then

is disarming grin. 'Tania might know a
tree from an elderberry bush, but I
bt if I'd be much good. Potatoes and
rots are my contribution to gardening.'

'So you would like an area for fruit and
vegetables then?' Paul asked.

'He would if he's expecting me to live there
and cook for him,' Tania said with a grin.
Rosie glanced at Mr Ritchie and was relived
to see a twinkle in his eye. He turned to Mrs
Keir as she came to tell them tea was ready. 'I
like a girl with a bit of spirit,' he said. 'I hope
they don't wait too long to marry. I'd like to
see my grandchildren. If I could persuade my
wife to move to a smaller house I think she
might keep better health but she is adamant
she cannot contemplate such an upheaval.'

'Sometimes upheavals are thrust upon us,'
Mrs Keir said. 'We do find the strength to
cope when we have to.' She knew nothing of
Mrs Ritchie's imaginary ill health.

★　★　★

The days were getting shorter but Rosie was
determined to move into Stables Cottage.
She had worked hard at rubbing down the
dark brown woodwork, so that she could
paint it white. Catherine grumbled at the
time she spent at it. She worked alone most

evenings and whenever she had time at weekends. Tania came to lend a hand with painting the woodwork and John Oliphant spent hours painting round tiny window panes.

'So long as I don't have to climb ladders or spend all day on my old knees, I'm fine,' he assured the girls, 'and you'll feel better if the whole place is fresh before you move in, Rosie.'

Rosie knew he was right. She was beginning to feel proud of her little home. She and Tania drove into Dumfries to choose curtains for the bedrooms and material for the living room curtains.

'I didn't know you could sew,' Tania teased.

'I can only do straight lines,' Rosie grinned. 'I'm going to borrow Mum's electric sewing machine, although she doesn't know that yet. I can work on the curtains at my leisure in the evenings. There's no one to look in and there are shutters on the downstairs windows. What is Mrs Ritchie saying about Paul's ideas for the garden at Shawlands now it's taking shape?'

'She doesn't seem interested until Mr Ritchie asks me for an opinion. Twice she has asked what it has to do with me. Mr Ritchie tells her Struan and I will live there one day and perhaps have children, then she claims her health wouldn't stand up to children about the place. I do wonder if she was ever young and what sort of things she did with Struan when he was a child. He says he spent most of his time outside with an old odd-job man they used to have. He's dead now but Struan still speaks of him with affection. He says he learned all sorts of useful things about the farm and animals from him.'

'I can sympathize with Struan,' Rosie said 'It's hard enough managing my mother, but at least she never plays on people's sympathy.'

'Can you keep a secret, Rosie? I'm dying to tell someone . . . '

'Of course I can. I love secrets!' Rosie gave her eager smile.

'We're going to announce our engagement at Christmas. Struan has bought me a ring.'

'Oh Tania, that's wonderful news!' Rosie hugged her friend exuberantly. 'I wonder what Mrs Ritchie will say to that?'

'Struan said he didn't want her interfering so we haven't told anyone else yet, not even Mum.'

'I'll not breathe a word.' Rosie's eyes sparkled.

'We're not planning to get married for a couple of years but we're hoping this will make Mrs Ritchie realize we are serious. Thank goodness his father understands.

Struan says if his mother still pretends she is too ill to move out of the farm we'll look for a house nearby.'

'Speaking of illness,' Rosie said, 'I think your grandfather's chest is bothering him. He's breathless if he walks from the bottom of the gardens to here without stopping for a break. Paul noticed it too. We're going to make a small arbour when we can get some rustic fencing but meanwhile we've put a seat beside the path. Papa Oliphant will be able to sit and view the rows of vegetables and talk to the boys while they work.'

'You're very good to Grandfather, Rosie,' Tania said. 'We appreciate it, you know. I'm sure Sam would cut you some lengths of wood to make the rustic poles. Dad bought a new chainsaw last year.'

'That would be a great help,' Rosie said. 'We plan to cover it with honeysuckle and a couple of rambler roses.'

'I'll tell Sam it's for Grandfather,' Tania promised. 'I called to see him on my way here. I've put a casserole in the oven — I'm having my lunch with him today instead of our evening meal. Struan and I are going to a performance at the Theatre Royal in Dumfries tonight so it would have been a bit of a rush and Grandfather enjoys a chat, as I'm sure you know.'

'I do.' Rosie nodded. 'He is one of the best friends I have, and just as I would have wanted my own grandfather to be if I'd ever known one of them.'

The following weekend Sam arrived with the Land Rover and trailer to move Rosie's furniture to Stables Cottage. Alex had returned to college so Tania had asked Struan to come and help lift the awkward pieces of furniture. They carried some of the things down the back stairs of Langton Tower but Chef Lambert came out of his kitchen to grumble about the noise and nuisance. They had to move the wardrobe down the front staircase as it was wider and this time it was Catherine who fussed in case they bumped her precious wallpaper. Rosie raised her eyebrows heavenward. She was wearing a broad blue bandanna to hold her hair back. Sam thought it made her eyes look bluer than ever, just like a summer sky. Since the night of the Young Farmers' Stock Judging he had been quiet in Rosie's company. He had told Lidia for the second time that there was no future for her with him but she refused to listen, alternating between trying to entice him into her bed and threatening to harm herself if he refused to see her.

He was aware that things had changed between himself and Rosie. He longed for their old youthful camaraderie, but deep down he had realized he wanted her for more than a playmate. He had felt a deep affection for her and a desire to protect her for as long as he could remember but she was no longer a child and the realization that he was no longer the most important person in her life had come as a shock. Both he and Struan admired the transformation she had made to the Stables Cottage.

'If I'd had plenty of money I would have made the large room upstairs into the sitting room with French windows and a balcony opening onto the stone staircase outside.'

'It's hard to believe this was once a loft and stables. It has a lovely view,' Tania said.

'It was Paul's idea for a balcony,' Rosie said. He had insisted on coming to help carry smaller items into the cottage and they exchanged a warm smile.

'You seem to have an eye for such things, Paul,' Struan said. 'Father is pleased with your ideas for our garden. Even Mother approves.'

'Ideas cost money,' Sam muttered. Rosie and Tania looked at him in surprise, knowing he had plenty of ideas himself in relation to the farm. Sam flushed, ashamed that he was being so churlish to a fellow like Paul Keir, who had had little else but ideas to occupy him during the years spent in hospitals or convalescing. He was making up for it now though, spending every day in Rosie's company. Like Alex, Sam was beginning to wonder how close they were.

'Tania said you wanted some rustic rails to make a rose arbour, Rosie,' he said as he was leaving. 'If you come down on Saturday and tell me how thick you want them and the length, I'll cut them to suit.'

'That would be super, wouldn't it Paul? But I can't come next weekend. Can we arrange it later?'

'OK.' Sam shrugged. He wondered what Rosie was doing that weekend. He could remember a time when she came to Bengairney every Saturday, Sundays too if she could.

4

Rosie enjoyed the privacy and peace of her own home but she made sure the iron gates were locked when Paul and Rodney went home. She would not give Chef Lambert any opportunity to prowl around. She was delighted when her father fell into the habit of dropping in most mornings for a cup of coffee and a chat. If she was busy in the gardens he made the coffee and brought out a mug for each of them, strolling beside her as she supervised the work or discussed her plans. On wet mornings he and John Oliphant made themselves at home in her large bright kitchen and waited for her return.

Douglas Palmer-Farr often worked late into the night on his translations and Rosie knew he had been busy for months with work for a foreign diplomat as well as his regular assignments. He was good at his job and he often had to turn down work if he couldn't fit it in. He was well paid for a lot of the confidential work he undertook. He also received a small income from investments left in trust by his parents. He told Rosie the income had increased since decimalization but Catherine insisted nothing was keeping pace with the rise in the cost of living. The turnover for the hotel was on a different scale but so were the overheads.

Sam eventually arranged a Saturday morning when they were both free to liaise over the rustic poles needed to complete the arbour around John Oliphant's seat. The days were getting too cold to sit outside for long now so there was no immediate rush to finish it but Rosie was annoyed when she arrived at Bengairney to find no sign of Sam. She knew he was booked to do the relief milking at Martinwold but he had told her he would be home early. The door was not locked so Rosie called a greeting to Megan and Tania. No one answered. Rosie then remembered Tania and Struan had gone up to Edinburgh for a reunion with some of their fellow students; they were spending Friday and Saturday nights with friends. She went through to the kitchen. She was surprised to see the remains of breakfast still in evidence, porridge plates stacked beside the sink. She knew her Aunt Megan's routine as well as her own. Something urgent must have called her outside to make her leave an untidy kitchen. She closed the door and hurried outside. She met Joe Finkle coming across the yard bringing straw to bed the calves.

'Where is everyone, Joe? Is something wrong?' Joe had worked for Steven since he was a young prisoner of war.

'Hello, Miss Rosemary,' Joe smiled at her. 'Samuel work at Martinwold this weekend. He is not back. Mr and Mrs Caraford, they go off in their car, in great hurry. I was eating breakfast. Maybe something happened . . . ?'

'An accident you mean, Joe? But what's keeping Samuel?'

'Maybe accident is at Martinwold?'

'An accident to Samuel you mean? Oh no . . . ' Rosie felt her face paling.

'I not know, but Mr Steven never drive like, z-zoom in the car.'

★ ★ ★

The previous evening Murdo Turner had joined Sam in the milking parlour at Martinwold, chatting and discussing treatment for a sick cow which was not responding to the antibiotic the dairyman had given her for mastitis.

'I'll telephone Patrick Fisher for advice when I go in,' he said. 'I'm glad you saw her, Sam. She's one of our best animals.'

Ella Turner heard him come into the house via the farm office but when she called him for his evening meal an hour later he didn't answer. She went to see what was detaining him. She found him slumped in his chair, his face grey. There were beads of perspiration on his forehead.

'Murdo? You're ill.' Murdo Turner met his wife's eyes but the pain was too intense for him to answer. Swiftly she reached for the phone and dialled the home of her daughter and son-in-law, Niven Wright-Manton. He was a heart consultant and he would know how to treat her beloved husband. Natalie answered.

'It's your father, Natalie. I think he's having a heart attack. Please ask Niven to come. It's urgent, I know it is.' She described Murdo's symptoms and heard her own panic reflected in Natalie's voice as she related them to her husband. Doctor Wright-Manton's eyes narrowed. He did not get on with his father-in-law. He had expected to semi-retire on his wife's money when he married Natalie Turner, only child of a wealthy farmer and landowner but so far her old man had kept a tight hold on the purse strings.

'Hurry, Niven! Mum says it's urgent. She doesn't panic easily.'

'It will be a touch of indigestion,' he said. Six months before he had recognized the symptoms of heart trouble in his father-in-law but it suited him to keep his knowledge to himself.

Ella Turner had mentioned niggling anxieties to Natalie several times since and they had confirmed his suspicions.

As a young man, Niven had been a good doctor and had risen quickly in his profession, but he had begun to indulge in his own pleasures with drink and women, hence the divorce of his first wife. It pleased him to know he could still diagnose illness when he saw it, even though he had no intention of doing anything about it.

He reasoned he would be better off if Turner died. The farm would have to be sold and Natalie could always get round her mother for money. On the other hand Ella Turner was only two or three years older than himself. She kept herself trim and smart. He wouldn't mind having a little fling with her or even —

'Niven!' Natalie shouted, 'Mum needs you! Dad can't speak for the pain. She says his face is like putty.'

'I heard her from here,' he drawled. 'Tell her I'll come over when we've had our meal.'

Ella Turner slammed down the receiver. Her hand trembled as she dialled for an ambulance.

'The ambulance will be here soon, my darling. Oh Murdo, you were right about Niven. He doesn't care for anyone but himself.' Her voice shook as she put her hand on her husband's brow and felt it damp and clammy. He was not a man who complained over trivialities. Every instinct told her this was serious. Even if it was not, the least Niven could have done was come over and reassure her. She had always taken his side when Murdo had criticized him. She knew her husband was a good judge of character but she had hidden her own doubts because Niven was their son-in-law.

The ambulance men were efficient. Ella insisted on travelling beside her husband, holding his hand in both of hers. He was worse now and she wondered if he knew she was there. They were about to leave when Natalie drove up, alone.

'We need to get going, it's urgent,' one of the men said slamming the door.

'I'll follow you in the car, Mum,' Natalie called, her voice wobbling. She had known her mother was not exaggerating and the ambulance man had confirmed her fears. Niven was too idle to be bothered.

'Damn him, he should have come anyway,' she muttered aloud. As a consultant he would have known what to do and the staff would have paid attention. She didn't realize Dr Wright-Manton had become the least respected of any member of the hospital staff. She telephoned from the hospital to say her father's condition was serious and neither she nor her mother were allowed to see him while the doctors were working on him.

'Please come, Niven. You would know better than anybody how to help him.'

'I can't come. I needed a couple of glasses of wine to keep me company since you chose to desert me,' he said petulantly. 'Now I'm enjoying a glass of scotch. Can't drink and drive.'

'You knew I might need you. You could have resisted the drink for once,' Natalie snapped. She had not touched her own meal. She felt tense and tired, and disillusioned with Niven.

The doctors did their best but at three in the morning they had to admit defeat.

'Your husband suffered a massive heart attack, Mrs Turner,' the doctor in charge said. 'We did our best to save him but it was not possible. I'm so sorry.' Ella Turner looked white and strained but she hung onto her composure. It was Natalie who lost control, blaming the doctors for not doing enough, and crying hysterically.

'Perhaps if Doctor Wright-Manton had seen him earlier . . . ?' the doctor suggested, wondering why the chief was not with his wife now.

'I'd like to go home,' Ella Turner pleaded, looking at Natalie, willing her not to say any more. It was bad enough that the two of them knew how callously Niven had behaved. Natalie opened her mouth to protest, then closed it with a snap. She took her mother's arm and guided her to the car. When they reached Martinwold it was Ella who went to the kitchen and switched on the kettle. During the next few hours she and Natalie were as close as they had ever been before, or would be again. Neither felt like eating. As a new day had dawned Ella knew there would be a lot to do.

'I'll phone Niven,' Natalie said. 'He must be up by now.' The telephone rang a long time before Wright-Manton stirred himself to lift the receiver.

'You're drunk!' Natalie snapped in disgust as his slurred voice came over the wire. 'You're supposed to be on call at the hospital today.'

'So what? They can manage without me for once.'

'You keep saying that. You haven't even

asked after my father,' Natalie snapped.

'I'd forgotten about your old man. So what's the news?'

'You should have been here last night, then you would know. He-he's d-dead.'

'Is he now?' Niven Wright-Manton pushed himself upright. 'I shall be able to retire altogether now then. Once you get the bloody farm sold and get your hands on the money. We'll enjoy — '

'You're despicable,' Natalie put the phone down, cutting off her husband's bark of laughter.

Ella Turner was cradling a cup of cold tea and remembering the conversation she and Murdo had had a few weeks earlier after he had been at the stock judging at Bengairney.

'If ever I'm ill and you're worried about anything to do with the farm,' he had said, 'you can rely on Steven Caraford and trust his advice, Ella. In fact you could depend on both Steven and Megan if ever you need help. Megan was always a grand lassie when she lived here with her parents.' Ella had always liked Megan and her family but she wondered now whether Murdo had had some sort of premonition that he was not as well as he should be. She had been surprised when he sold his beloved stallion. He had always enjoyed a morning ride ever since he had been able to afford a horse of his own. Other little incidents came back to her. Tears trickled down her cheeks. Never again would Murdo sit opposite her and chat as they ate breakfast together.

'Oh Mother, don't cry,' Natalie said. Her mother was always calm and in control.

'I-I'll be all right.' Ella struggled to stem her tears. 'There's things to do. We need a-a death certificate to register the death. Maybe Niven will — '

'Niven!' Natalie pinched up her mouth. 'I need to get home and see what state he's in.' She knew he would drink even more if she was not there to try sobering him up. 'I'll come back as soon as I can. You try to get some sleep.'

Even in a situation as serious as this Ella Turner realized she would never be able to rely on her son-in-law. He seemed to control Natalie's life too. She was on her own. Her world had crumbled overnight. She sat staring into space, thinking of her husband and their life together. She remembered Murdo telling her, years ago, soon after Natalie married, that he had written a letter leaving instructions if he should die first. More recently, he had told her she should consult Andrew MacNicol, their solicitor, if anything happened to him.

'Natalie has never been much use in a crisis,' he had said without rancour. 'As for that man she married, he can't manage his own affairs, even if he is a doctor. You'd need someone reliable like Lindsay Gray or Steven Caraford.'

Ella pushed back her chair and went upstairs to their bedroom to get Murdo's keys. He had always been methodical. She knew the letter was in a file in his desk. There were the birth and marriage certificates, even a list of his favourite hymns. She bit back a sob and tried to hold her tears in check as Murdo's words echoed in her mind.

If you read this letter, my dearest Ella, remember everything is in here and my will is with Andrew MacNicol and Son.

However long we live, my love, it doesn't look as though we shall get a grandson, or even a granddaughter, now Natalie has married that man. If Lint had been our son-in-law, as we hoped, I would have had faith in him taking care of everything. I confess I can't look ahead and visualize giving up the farm as long as I'm able to carry on. Forgive me, Ella, if I'm selfish but you know it is my life. I do not want to burden you with it but if that should happen Steven Caraford is the best man to help you. He has integrity and he'll never let you down.

Steven had returned from the war and was farming a smallholding at Gretna when the letter was written, Ella reflected. He and Megan were newly married. Even then Murdo had respected and trusted Steven.

She remembered when Steven and Sam Oliphant had played together at Martinwold as boys before they had been forced to join the army. It had amused Murdo the way he was always asking questions, eager to learn and desperate to farm. Ella rubbed her eyes. She felt exhausted. Shock and lack of sleep, she supposed. She shuddered. How could she face the future without Murdo? He'd been her rock. He had made the decisions. She began to tremble with dread for the future and all the things which would need to be done. The animals would have to be sold, and the land. Their workers were all in tied houses; they would lose their homes. They would be shocked and unsettled too. Would they continue to work for her until a sale could be arranged? How would she know if things were being done properly?

'Oh Murdo,' she moaned, 'if only we'd finished our bungalow and moved — ' She stopped short. Had that been another premonition? Six months before she had been surprised when Murdo arrived home with three sets of plans and asked what sort of house she would like when she retired. He had given her a hug and kissed her gently. The tears started again. They had spent weeks deciding which of the plans they preferred. She would move there alone now. Her tears made damp splotches on the letter. She found her handkerchief and blew her nose hard. It was no use. She couldn't sit here and cry all day. It was almost eight o'clock and the men would be getting on with their work. They would have to be told of Murdo's death. She shivered. Death was such a final word. She rarely went into the farmyard; she had left all of that to Murdo. She didn't even know which of the men would be working that weekend.

Almost of its own volition her hand reached for the telephone. It was Megan who answered. Ella had intended to be calm and in control. She was not going to cry, even though she felt as though her heart was breaking, but the words tumbled out; she could almost feel Megan's shock and dismay coming over the wires.

'Oh Mrs Turner,' Megan whispered. 'I'm so sorry, so very sorry. C-can we help? Is there anything we can do?' The instant sympathy, the spontaneous offer of help affected Ella and tears streamed down her face again.

'I-I feel so — so useless,' she whispered. 'C-could you and Steven c-come over? Please, Megan . . . I — '

'Of course we'll come, Mrs Turner. We'll come right away.' Megan said. She was shocked herself and she could understand that Mrs Turner would be shattered. She had wanted to ask, When? And where?

Steven was finishing his breakfast. He stared up at her in disbelief.

'Surely Natalie will be with her mother,' he said, but he jumped to his feet. 'Mrs Turner would not have phoned unless she needed us, Meggie. I'll change my clothes. We'd better get over there. Sam will be finishing the milking at Martinwold. I don't suppose any of the men will know yet. We must help all we can for Mr Turner's sake.'

Megan was shocked at the sight of Mrs Turner's white face and red-rimmed eyes. She always looked serene and well groomed but today she looked haggard with fatigue. She recounted the events of the previous evening. 'Niven refused to come,' she repeated twice. 'Natalie had to go back to him. M-Murdo thinks . . . thought, he was drinking too much. She said I should go to bed but I c-can't do that. Will you help

108

me, Megan?' She looked up with childlike trust. If it had been anyone else Megan would have hugged her, offering comfort and reassurance, but the Turners had been her parents' employers for years and Megan had grown up in awe of them.

'Steven and I will help in anyway we can, Mrs Turner, but maybe Natalie is right. You had no sleep last night.'

'No, no, I can't sleep — not yet. I . . . will you take me to the hospital, Megan? I must see about the death certificate. Register the death. There's the minister . . . and the undertaker.' Her voice rose in panic.

'I will drive you,' Megan said, 'but I'm not sure how much we can do when it is the weekend. First will you let me make you something light and nourishing to eat? We may need to wait. You don't want to feel faint.'

'I'm not hungry.' She looked and sounded like a bewildered child, Megan thought. Natalie should have been here with her mother at a time like this, and her husband too. 'I will wash my face and change my clothes. Perhaps a little scrambled egg? Will you have some too, Megan?'

'I will drink a cup of tea with you. Steven and I had breakfast before we left.' Steven was thankful Megan had come with him. Mrs

Turner seemed so unsure and dependent. Mr Turner had always tried to shelter her from problems. He felt a surge of anger that neither Natalie nor her husband were here to support her now.

'Would you like me to tell the men, Mrs Turner?'

'Oh Steven, would you do that for me? I-I know it is cowardly, b-but I can't face them yet.'

'I will go and speak to them now. They will be shocked and saddened, as we are.' He barely knew what to say to Mrs Turner in her present state. She had always seemed so elegant and calm, more reserved than her husband. Now she seemed like a lost child and his heart filled with pity.

Steven caught Sam as he was hosing down the collecting area where the cows gathered before going through the milking parlour. He broke the news.

'Dead? Mr Turner? No! It can't be true, Dad. Can it?' His face looked young and pale with shock. He met his father's steady gaze. 'Oh my God.' He looked around him at the gleaming parlour and the big cubicle shed. 'This is his life.' He bit back a sob. 'Everything will have to be sold. The herd will be scattered all over the country.'

'I'm afraid so,' Steven said. 'I promised to

break the news to the men.'

'Gosh, Dad, it will affect them badly. Their jobs, their homes . . . '

'Aye it's a sad day. Mr Turner was well liked and respected by everybody, except maybe his son-in-law.' Steven's mouth tightened. 'He hasna been down to see Mrs Turner. Natalie should be with her. They're heartless.'

'No wonder she and Mum were never friends. It's strange Mrs Turner should seek help from Mum and you, don't you think?'

'I suppose so.' Steven nodded. 'The Turners have known your mother since she was a child, known both of us really. Your Uncle Sam was my best friend. I don't think the Turners have any close relatives. Is everything in order here?'

'The work is finished until the milking this afternoon,' Sam nodded, still trying to take in the news and all it would imply to everyone connected to Martinwold, including himself. 'There's a sick cow in one of the loose boxes. Mr Turner was going to phone the vet. There's one to serve. I was going to ask which bull to use . . . ' He broke off. 'It's terrible, Dad. What shall I do? Who will make decisions now? It will take ages to organize a farm sale for a place this size. Do you think the new owner will keep on any of the men?'

'They'll all wonder that,' Steven sighed. 'It's a sad business with no family to carry on.'

'Madam Natalie will be a wealthy woman now.'

'She will. Meanwhile we'll do our best for his animals. You'd better get back to Bengairney and phone the vet. Explain what's happened. I'll see him if I'm still here. You'll need to cook your own breakfast. We came away in a hurry. Joe will need a hand.'

'OK.' Sam was home before he remembered he had promised to meet Rosie that morning. She had cleared the table and was washing the breakfast dishes when he entered the kitchen. He told her what had happened.

'Oh Sam, how awful!' Her blue eyes darkened with shock. 'It must have been sudden. His wife?'

'Dad says she's shattered. Mum is with her.'

'But what about her daughter? And her son-in-law?'

'I don't know. I feel shocked too but I'm still famished. Is that porridge still hot?'

'I'll stir it over the hot plate if you like?'

'Thanks, Rosie. I must phone the vet first.'

'Shall I cook you bacon and egg?'

'Please. I'm sorry about the fencing but I

don't think I'll have time today.'

'There's no rush.'

★　★　★

'Do you think we should book a light lunch at Langton Tower for the mourners after the funeral, Megan?' Mrs Turner asked. Megan was astonished at being consulted but Mrs Turner's assurance seemed to have deserted her.

'It saddens me that she has to depend on someone like me,' she said to Lint when he phoned to check on the time of the funeral.

'She's fortunate to have you, Megan. You're kind and reliable. Surely Natalie and Wright-Manton are helping too?'

'They're only at Martinwold to sleep. I don't think Mrs Turner would eat if I wasn't there.'

The following day Dr Wright-Manton was finishing an extremely late breakfast when Megan arrived.

'We're moving in here after the funeral. You'll not be needed. Here, get on with your work,' he said, pushing his dirty dishes towards her.

'He acts as though I'm his servant,' she told Steven when she arrived home later than she had intended. It had been a stressful day.

113

The funeral was expected to be large and Natalie had bought herself a smart black suit and a new black hat. She had called at Martinwold late in the afternoon to show her mother.

'You'll need a new black outfit,' she announced but she didn't offer to drive her mother into town to buy one. She already had a smart black coat and hat which Megan had assured her were suitable, but Natalie's criticism renewed her uncertainty. It was Megan who had to drive her to Dumfries for clothes she neither needed nor wanted.

'Megan, will you invite Dean Scott and Avril to come to the funeral tea? I may not get an opportunity to speak to them myself. Lindsay will come with you and Steven and your family, perhaps?'

'I, er, I don't know. It is a time for families and close friends to be together so . . . '

'Megan, my dear,' Ella Turner laid a hand on her arm, 'I don't know how I could have got through without you and Steven. You have proved the truest of friends when I needed help, just as Murdo knew you would. He was a good judge of character. I value your support.' Her manner was calmer and Megan blessed her GP for prescribing a mild sedative to help her cope. She was more like the Mrs

Turner of old in spite of the dark circles beneath her eyes and her pale, drawn face. She seemed to have made a resolve to face the future bravely and with her usual dignity.

Andrew MacNicol, the solicitor, telephoned the night before the funeral.

'It is important that Murdo's will should be read without delay, Ella, after the funeral, and in the presence of you and your daughter.'

'Surely it's not so urgent, Andrew?'

'It is. Murdo left various bequests. You will feel easier, too, when you hear the provisions he has made for you. It is essential that your daughter understands how the will affects her. I shall be there to answer any questions.' Privately he thought he would be lucky if it was only questions he got thrown at him. He had known Natalie Turner all her life and had seen her throw tantrums when she was far too old for such behaviour. Aloud he added, 'If you don't mind I would like my son to be present since he will be taking over the firm when I retire in a few years' time and he was there when Murdo added more conditions to his will. He is an executor, along with James Ross, your accountant and Patrick Fisher.'

'Patrick? Our vet?' Ella echoed in surprise.

'I think you will see he had reason for his choice.'

Alex was genuinely upset at the death of the man who had taken such a fatherly interest in him during his student year at Martinwold. He had come back from college early that morning. John Oliphant was glad he was travelling with Steven and Megan and the boys. The death of his former boss had shaken him — Murdo Turner had been five years younger than himself. Lindsay was driving Dean and Avril and they collected Tania.

It was always difficult to know how many people would require refreshments after a funeral. Some fellow cattle breeders had travelled long distances to attend. Catherine was in her element dealing with the crowd who congregated at Langton Tower. There was ample food and plenty of choice to please everyone. Megan and Avril agreed Catherine had made an excellent job. Mrs Turner came up to their table as they finished eating.

'Thank you, Megan, for arranging everything so beautifully. Murdo would be pleased we have given him a good send off.'

'I can't take any credit, Mrs Turner, but I am glad you are satisfied.'

'Indeed I am. Mr MacNicol would like to read the will soon. We wondered whether there is a private room where we could go? He has asked for you and Steven, Samuel, Alex and Dean to join us for the first part of the reading,' her voice softened, 'and you too of course, John.' They all looked at her in surprise.

'I could ask Catherine about a room,' Megan offered. Catherine and Douglas were standing together, discussing the identities of various guests, when she approached.

'They could use my office for that,' Douglas offered. 'They will be quiet and private in there and there's some comfortable leather chairs. I will ask one of the maids to bring in extra seats if required. It looks as though some of the mourners are settling down for a chat and a few drinks,' he said nodding towards a group gathered round the bar.

Andrew MacNicol thanked Douglas and proceeded to gather together the people he required.

'Are you sure you intended me to come, sir?' Alex asked.

'I am sure, young man. I shall not keep you long. Are you rushing home to milk your cows?'

'No, I'm driving back to college.'

'Very well. We'll proceed as soon as we're all gathered together.' He frowned across at

Dr Wright-Manton filling up his whisky glass. To his knowledge it was the third time he had filled it since arriving at the hotel and MacNicol guessed he had had a drink or two before leaving Martinwold.

As everyone gathered in Douglas's office Natalie scowled at the Caraford family and John Oliphant. Her eyes widened as Dean Scott joined them, followed by the current Martinwold workers, all fidgeting uneasily with their caps as they clustered together near the door.

'Surely Father has not made bequests to all this lot,' she muttered. 'He paid them well enough when they worked for us.'

'I will begin with the smaller bequests made by my late friend and client, Mr Murdo Turner,' Andrew MacNicol began, standing behind Douglas's large desk, with his son seated beside him.

'The first bequest is for £3,000 to Miss Lizzie Buchanan who worked at Martinwold for thirty years before her retirement last year. She is in hospital recovering from an operation.

'To Mr and Mrs John Oliphant, £3,000 in appreciation of many years of loyal service in charge of the dairy herd at Martinwold. A bequest of £1,000 is made to three young men Mr Turner considered his best farm students.' He beamed over his spectacles.

'He assured me he would have been proud to have any one of you as his son — Dean Scott, Samuel Edward Caraford and Alexander Caraford.

'The remaining bequests are a small reward of a hundred pounds for every complete year of service to any man in Mr Turner's employ at the time of his death.

'There is a condition attached to these bequests. The money will not be paid until one year from the date of death, and it will be paid only if that person has remained a loyal and conscientious worker at Martinwold during that year, supporting whoever is in charge of Martinwold until it is sold or taken over.' Mr MacNicol cleared his throat. 'Obviously that would not have applied if my client had lived long enough to arrange disposal of the farm during his lifetime.' He glanced at the papers again then peered over his spectacles. I think that covers all the minor bequests. If you young men and Mr Oliphant would care to leave us you may go now. I shall be in touch as soon as probate has been granted.'

Steven and Megan got up to leave too but Mr MacNicol waved them to remain seated. Dr Wright-Manton levered himself out of a large leather chair and moved towards a side table on which stood a silver tray with a

119

crystal decanter half full of whisky and one glass. It was clearly for Douglas Palmer-Farr's own use but Niven helped himself. Mr MacNicol and his son stared at him, and then at Natalie, but she shrugged and said nothing. Niven got belligerent when he'd had several drinks. Mrs Turner looked uncomfortable. Andrew MacNicol had thought Murdo had judged his son-in-law too harshly when he drew up his will, but he understood and agreed with him now. He cleared his throat.

'May I remind you, Dr Wright-Manton, this is Mr Palmer-Farr's private office. You are helping yourself to someone else's whisky. We are only here as a concession on account of Mr and Mrs Caraford's friendship with the owners.' Natalie jerked her head up. She gave Megan a baleful glare. Megan and Steven exchanged glances. They had never considered themselves on such terms.

'He'll not miss a glass or two,' Wright-Manton drawled. 'He can afford it.' He took a generous swig of whisky. 'It's a damned good malt!' He turned back to the table and topped up his glass before returning to his seat.

Andrew MacNicol's mouth tightened. The man was ignorant, and as greedy as Murdo had warned him. Any sympathy he had had for Natalie and her husband flew out of the window. The atmosphere in the room grew tense.

Megan wished she was back home. Natalie glowered in their direction. Mr MacNicol began to explain his client's last wishes in detail.

'Ella, I spoke to the firm handling the new bungalow. It could be ready for you to move in, in a couple of months. It will be — '

'A couple of months! It will have to be quicker than that!' Wright-Manton protested. 'We are planning — '

'As I was saying,' the solicitor interrupted with a pointed cough, 'it will be up to you, Ella, whether you move then or stay at Martinwold for the year.'

'A bloody year!'

'I should be obliged if you would refrain from interrupting,' MacNicol said coldly and turned back to Mrs Turner with an apologetic smile. 'I advise you to wait until everything is settled to your satisfaction.' He gave Ella an encouraging smile. They both knew Murdo had not anticipated it would be needed so soon.

'Murdo had given a great deal of thought to financial matters in recent years. Few working farmers thought about retirement or pensions when he was young so he has made provision by investing most of his available capital in an annuity. This will ensure you have an adequate monthly income for the rest of your life, Ella.' MacNicol caught his son's eye and the quirk of his eyebrow. It was a generous sum, especially now there would only be Ella to keep, but he had no intention of letting Wright-Manton know that. 'I believe you had planned to take your favourite pieces of furniture to your new home but I must emphasize that everything not required by you personally, must remain in situ. Do you understand, Ella?' He sounded a little anxious.

'I understand,' she said quietly. 'We had decided to take the antique pieces and leave the rest. I shall do as Murdo wanted.'

'Excellent.' He fixed his gaze on Natalie and her husband. 'So you *all* understand, the remaining carpets, curtains, light fittings — all of these must remain. They must not be removed for sale or for any other purpose. I have arranged for Mr Vincent, the auctioneer to do an inventory and valuation of the household items as well as the farm stock.'

'That will not be necessary,' Wright-Manton began.

'I assure you it is. Now Ella, you will also receive one third of the moveable estate. This consists mainly of the value of the remaining furniture at Martinwold and the farm stock and machinery.' He paused and looked down at his papers.

'Now Mrs Wright-Manton,' Natalie sat up straighter, her eyes expectant. 'Your father has left to you the property known as Burwood House and — '

'Burwood?' Wright-Manton echoed. 'It's already ours! We already live in the bloody house. What the hell . . . ?'

'You may live there, Dr Wright-Manton, but you do not own it.' Andrew MacNicol had expected to feel some sympathy for the young couple, but he found himself almost enjoying the expression on the doctor's face. 'Mr Turner bought the property to ensure his daughter had a home of her own when she married you. He retained the deeds in his own name. I understand he has continued to maintain the property, including paying a man to cut grass and tidy the gardens. Is that correct?'

'You know bloody well it is, but he could afford it.'

'He could afford it because he worked hard all his life. He instructed his executors to transfer the deeds to Mrs Natalie Ellen Wright-Manton. You will be responsible for upkeep in future, Mrs Wright-Manton. In addition you will also receive a third of the value of the moveable estate. The exact amount cannot be determined until Mr Vincent has completed his valuation.'

'A third!' Natalie gasped. 'That can't be right.' Her voice was rising. 'He must have left me more than that.' She glared accusingly at her mother.

'Don't worry, old girl,' Wright-Manton smirked. 'We shall have the farm to sell. We'll sell the house separately. That will fetch a pretty penny.' Mr MacNicol frowned and hung onto his patience but his son broke in abruptly.

'I am afraid you are mistaken, Dr Wright-Manton.' He stood up. 'Shall I take over from here, Father?'

'Very well.' Andrew MacNicol nodded and sat down. He reached for his glass of water.

'My father has dealt with most of the moveable assets which belonged to our client but as you know there remains the land and houses of the farm known as Martinwold, including Martinwold House. Mr and Mrs Caraford, you have been very patient and I thank you. What I have to say concerns you and with your cooperation we shall endeavour to fulfil our client's most earnest wishes.

'Mr Turner had great respect for both of you. Moreover, Mr Caraford, he assured us you are trustworthy and the best person to

carry out his wishes, along with your wife.'
Steven flushed but he didn't know what to
say or what they were expecting him to do.
Megan was uncomfortably aware of Natalie
glaring furiously in their direction.

'It was our client's greatest regret that he
had neither son, nor grandson, to carry on his
life's work at Martinwold Farm. He could not
contemplate the prospect of his pedigree herd
and the farm being sold and broken up. It is
for this reason he made his proposition. It
was his wish that you should be given the
opportunity to purchase the farm, for a fixed
sum of £60,000.'

Steven and Megan gasped. It was worth far
more than that but it was well beyond their
reach. There were 360 acres, of good land
and several cottages. Never in their wildest
dreams could they expect to buy such a farm.
They felt comfortably well off with £10,000
in the bank and a well stocked rented farm.
Steven shook his head in bewilderment, but
Drew MacNicol went on. 'You will have one
year to decide whether you can raise the
money. If you decide to go ahead you will
have a further year to pay the sum in full.'
Again Steven shook his head, knowing it was
impossible.

'I must urge you to take time and consider
carefully, Mr Caraford,' Mr MacNicol Senior

interrupted. 'It was our client's dearest wish to keep the farm together if at all possible and he had faith that you and your sons could do that. He hoped Martinwold would continue for generations to come.'

'This is ridiculous,' Wright-Manton bellowed, getting to his feet. He was very unsteady. 'The property belongs to us. It must be worth — '

'Please sit down and let me finish,' Drew MacNicol said coldly. 'Mr Caraford, apparently Mr Turner trusted you and your family implicitly. He probably knew you would be cautious so we are instructed to keep Martinwold as it is for one year to give you time to consider. Whatever you decide he hoped you would manage the farm on behalf of Mrs Turner and arrange a sale if that is your decision. You will be paid a manager's salary. He was most anxious that things should be made as easy as possible for his wife. I should add he did not anticipate this situation arising for many years yet. He expected your sons would be working with you and he knew they were both keen to farm.' Again, Wright-Manton got to his feet unsteadily.

'I pot — p-prot-test. The fool was out of his mind. We sh-shall con-cont — '

'I must ask you to remain silent, or leave

the room,' Drew MacNicol said sternly. 'It may interest you to know, Dr Wright-Manton, that your late father-in-law's aim was to prevent you benefiting from his hard work. Whatever Mr and Mrs Caraford decide, the farm is no concern of yours.'

'Of course it's our concern, you silly bloody — '

'Dr Wright-Manton! If you cannot be civil please leave.' Natalie tugged his sleeve and pulled him back into his chair. 'As I was saying, whoever buys the farm the proceeds are to go to a charity named by our client.' He held up his hand as Wright-Manton began to bluster and swear. 'One of his aims in purchasing an annuity was to give his wife security for life. This removed a large part of his moveable estate from your grasp.'

Natalie's face had grown pale with shock. Charity! How could her father have been so mean? They were already more than the five thousand pounds in debt, and her husband sought every possible excuse for evading his duties at the hospital these days. She was afraid he would make a serious blunder and be struck off. Then where would they be? She had not realized until a year ago that Niven's drinking had become a serious problem. One of his colleagues had advised her to seek help. Until then she had thought he knew how to enjoy the good things in life. Now she knew it was at other people's expense, including hers.

'What about Martinwold House?' she asked hoarsely.

'It is included with the farm. I must add there are certain conditions regarding the purchase of Martinwold. I shall let you have the details in writing, Mr Caraford, but the main condition is that if you do buy the farm you, or your family, must keep it for at least ten years. If you were to sell it with vacant possession before then, all profit over the £60,000 purchase price, plus the cost of any improvements you may have made, must be repaid and go to the same charity. The exception to that is Martinwold House. When Mrs Turner has finished with it, if you cannot afford to live there yourselves, you may sell it along with the five-acre paddock at the back. There will be no other exceptions. However if you purchase the farm with the intention of continuing to farm there you will also retain stock and machinery to the value of the remaining third of the moveable estate, as valued by Mr Vincent.'

'That's not fair!' Natalie burst out, almost sobbing with fury. 'What have they done to deserve anything! It should all be mine.'

'We are carrying out your father's wishes, Mrs — '

'Whims, bloody insane whims!' Wright-Manton shouted.

'Meanwhile,' Drew MacNicol went on firmly, ignoring the interruptions, 'for Mrs Turner's sake, as well as the staff and the animals, it is essential that we know whether you feel able, and willing, to take over the management of Martinwold Farm immediately. Mr Caraford?'

'I . . . yes, I think I can do that,' Steven said, his mind racing, 'but I would like to discuss it with my wife.'

'Yes, I understand. Mr Turner has done his best to guarantee the cooperation of the Martinwold staff by making each bequest dependent on them continuing to work for a year. Mr Fisher is one of the executors. He has undertaken to help you in any way he can. According to our client, your wife,' he smiled at Megan, 'deals with your own farm accounts. He hoped you would take over the Martinwold accounts for a year in return for remuneration, Mrs Caraford. There are one or two other points we can discuss later.'

'Yes, of course,' Steven agreed but he felt he was being swept along on a tidal wave. Ella Turner sent him a pleading look. He summoned a smile. 'I promise I shall do my best, whatever happens,' he said quietly.

'You're a good man, Steven.' He didn't feel

good. He felt trapped, out of his depth. The Wright-Mantons were shooting daggers in their direction.

As Mr MacNicol ended the formalities Wright-Manton struggled to his feet intent on refilling his whisky glass but Drew MacNicol hurried from behind the desk and took him firmly by the arm, beckoning Steven to take his other arm.

'What you need, my man, is some strong black coffee,' MacNicol said coldly, ushering him through the door. Catherine had been hovering in the hall. The group at the bar had dispersed.

'I will order you some coffee at once, Dr Wright-Manton,' Catherine said obligingly, ignoring Steven and smiling at Natalie who was trailing behind them looking peevish, leaving her mother in Megan's company.

'I fear there's going to be terrible trouble,' Mrs Turner said. 'They are always so short of money. I don't understand it. Niven has an excellent job and his children are adults and independent.' Mr MacNicol Senior was walking behind them.

'I will call on you in a day or two, Ella, but you must try to ignore Dr Wright-Manton's complaints. Take my advice and stop giving them money. I believe Wright-Manton is well on the way to becoming an alcoholic. It will do no good if you subsidize his craving.' Ella Turner looked at him in dismay. 'Murdo hinted as much several times but I thought he was prejudiced.'

'I gather things had deteriorated between them.'

'He refused to come when I telephoned to say Murdo was ill.' Her voice shook as she remembered. She could never forgive her son-in-law for that.

'The sooner he gets help the better,' Mr MacNicol said. He considered telling Ella that his old friend had made provision for their daughter if she divorced Wright-Manton, or found herself a widow, but he didn't believe she could keep the information to herself when Natalie put her under pressure. It was time the girl faced facts and accepted responsibility for her actions.

5

The months sped by. Steven was conscientious in his management of Martinwold and having worked there as students both Sam and Alex were familiar with the fields and the stock. They got on well with the workers and understood their routine.

'It would be more efficient if we could work both farms together,' Sam said but Steven was still undecided about buying. 'We shall never get such an opportunity again,' he persisted. He couldn't understand why his father didn't seize the opportunity.

'We're only tenants here, at Bengairney,' Steven reminded him. 'The landlord would never agree to us combining the two farms.' Sam was silent. He had tried to explain that to Lidia since she had insisted on rekindling their relationship. As far as he was concerned everything had been over between them but Lidia had heard all manner of rumours since Mr Turner's death and the possibility of living in a house like Martinwold had fuelled her ambitions of grandeur. She refused to listen to reason. Several times she threatened to harm herself when Sam refused to see her.

He couldn't believe she would do so but he had seen her fly into hysterics more than once. He was afraid she might act on the spur of the moment if he pushed her too far. He felt sickened by the situation but he didn't know how to extricate himself.

Alex was even keener to buy Martinwold than Sam. He came home from college every weekend and he worked hard, taking his turn with milking at Bengairney while Sam continued relief milking at Martinwold. He worked out figures for bank interest and rent, projecting their income, and schemes for repaying the money.

'Figures on paper are only half a story,' Steven insisted. 'You two boys should talk to Rosemary. According to your grandfather she's turning into a proper young business woman and she doesn't do anything without considering every angle.'

'But Dad, the gardens are small in comparison,' Alex protested.

'Exactly. We have more to lose with all of us in the same boat. Farming is equally dependent on the weather, though, and diseases can strike out of the blue and wipe away our income,' Steven reminded him. 'We're talking about half a lifetime, maybe more, before the money will be repaid,' He was tense and abrupt. It worried Megan. He was fifty-one and she felt it was not a good age to be taking on so much responsibility, even without the worry of a huge loan.

'You can't project what our income will be,' she told Alex. 'Remember how we lost those young heifer stirks? They would have been coming into the herd now as milking cows, and we'd have had their calves to rear as well as extra milk to sell. You boys should stop badgering your father. He'll reach the right decision when he's ready.'

'But what if it's not the right decision for us?' Sam said. 'It's our future as well, remember.'

'Your future is all your father and I have thought about since the day you were born,' Megan said 'We've always done our best for you.'

'I know, Mum, I'm sorry,' Sam muttered.

'It's just that it's such a great opportunity,' Alex persisted, 'especially with two of us.'

'And what if you both want to get married?'

'We'd go on farming both places as a partnership,' Alex said.

'You have so little experience of life.' Megan sighed. 'I've seen brothers who are the best of friends until they each get a wife.' She was thinking of Lidia. 'Before you know it you are splitting up, or getting divorced and selling up everything your father and I have worked for all our lives.'

'But Mother — '

'That's enough. Give your father time to reach his own decision, and Samuel, think on what I've said about wives. You need someone who will stand beside you through thick and thin in a business, especially farming.'

Megan felt it was a welcome distraction when Tania and Struan broke the news of their engagement the week before Christmas.

'That's wonderful, Tania.' Megan hugged her and then Struan. 'Welcome to our family, Struan,' she said with a smile.

'Aye, ye're more than welcome into the fold, laddie,' Steven said, 'but I don't feel old enough to have a daughter getting engaged.'

'Oh Dad, don't you say that. Struan's mother is always saying we're far too young to think of marriage. We are twenty-two you know, in fact Struan will be twenty-three in January and that's only a few weeks away. We're not planning to get married for another couple of years. We want to give everyone time to get used to the idea.'

'Tania means my mother but she's too polite to say so,' Struan chuckled and drew Tania close to drop a kiss on her cheek. Megan beamed at them. Oh to be young and in love. She sighed and caught Steven's eye.

'We must have a family party and invite your parents, Struan. Have you any other relatives you would like me to invite? I know your sister and her husband live abroad.'

'There's no one else,' Struan said. 'We might have a problem persuading my mother to come though. She often calls off at the last minute but we shall not allow her to spoil things,' he added with determination. Steven looked at him with respect. He liked Struan. He was cheerful and easy going but there was a firmness about him which reflected character and reliability. He would have said Samuel was pretty much the same but recently he had been tense and irritable, even unreasonable.

'We'll have a Boxing Night buffet,' Megan said. 'How would that suit? Or if your mother doesn't like being out at night we could make it a lunch party.'

'I'm sure evening will be fine,' Struan said. 'It suits everyone better if the work is finished.'

'I'll invite Rosie for Boxing Day,' Tania said. 'She will bring Grandfather and take him home again. She has persuaded her parents to invite Paul Keir and his mother for Christmas dinner at Langton Tower this year. The hotel is closed for Christmas Day so they're having a family dinner for once.

Granny Caraford will be staying over for Christmas, won't she?'

'Yes, I think so. I was dismayed to see how frail she is getting when I called last week.'

'She seems to have lost her confidence for going out since Mr Patterson died,' Steven agreed.

'Samuel can drive down to get her on Christmas morning,' Megan said. 'After all, she gave the boys her car so they ought to chauffeur her.'

'Shall we ask Dean and Avril and the children?' Tania asked.

'Yes, of course, and Lint if he's not on call,' Megan nodded. 'The twins will be home from university too. I expect Alex and Rosie will be pleased to see their old chums again.'

True to character Struan's mother took to bed after dinner on Christmas Day saying she was too ill to contemplate going to Bengairney, and her son was far too young to be getting engaged.

'That's all right then, dear,' her husband said. 'You can stay in bed if you think you'll feel better lying down. Lizzie will be here if you need anything.' Lizzie was their live-in maid-cum-cook and housekeeper and Struan often wondered how she put up with his mother's whims but she had no family or home of her own.

'Of course Lizzie will be here, but you'll be here too.' Mrs Ritchie said.

'Oh no, I can't miss my only son's engagement party and Mrs Caraford and Tania are excellent cooks. Anyway we're all the family Struan has. He needs my support.' Struan stared at his father in surprise. He had humoured his mother for as long as he could remember. Mr Ritchie winked at him and Struan realized that for once his mother would not get her own way. He smiled. Mr Ritchie smiled back like a schoolboy up to pranks. 'I've humoured her too long and too often,' he said. 'It's her duty to be there tomorrow.'

'But I need you,' Mrs Ritchie wailed. 'I might need the doctor.'

'We'll see what tomorrow brings, dear. You may feel right as rain. If not I'll ask Doctor Jones to admit you to hospital for some tests to get to the bottom of your troubles.'

'I don't need to go to hospital,' Mrs Struan insisted; patches of angry colour rising.

'Whatever you say, dear. Tomorrow is another day. We'll go to the Carafords together and celebrate with Struan and Tania.' His voice was firm and Struan knew his mother would go to Bengairney.

Reluctantly Lidia had gone north to her own family for Christmas when Mrs Caraford did not issue an invitation to Bengairney. Tania and Rosie agreed it was like having the clouds lifted. They were both in high spirits and there were kisses all round, with and without the mistletoe. Only Sam seemed quieter than usual. His kiss was gentle but he couldn't resist holding Rosie in his arms longer than was strictly necessary. She felt her knees tremble and in her heart she knew Sam was the man she loved. It was a happy occasion and Steven felt it had been like an island of calm amidst waves of indecision and worry.

★ ★ ★

Strangely it was Natalie and Niven Wright-Manton who forced a decision. They were impatient for their share of the money.

'It's months since my father died,' Natalie declared, storming into the solicitor's office on a cold March morning. 'It's a miserable pittance but I demand it now. The farm, the house, it should all be mine. I was his only child.'

'It was your father who insisted on waiting a year before his affairs were wound up, Mrs Wright-Manton,' Mr MacNicol reminded her.

'The Carafords will never be able to buy

Martinwold. It's all a pretence to say they are considering it. The price of cattle might have gone down in another six months.'

'If you are needing the money I will consult the other executors and talk with Mr Caraford, but if prices rise you will have no further claim if you insist on payment now.'

'I do insist,' Natalie snapped, 'I can't believe you let my father make such a stupid will. Mother made sure she's got plenty and she's an old woman. It's not fair!' Mr MacNicol thought she was going to stamp her foot as he remembered her doing on several occasions in the past. 'And what happens to the new bungalow when she dies?' Natalie demanded.

'I'm afraid you will need to wait and see about that, Mrs Wright-Manton,' Andrew MacNicol said. 'Your father arranged an adequate income for retirement but he didn't expect your mother to be left a widow, so soon. Ella is an attractive woman. She may marry again. I'd advise you and your husband to make provision for your own future rather than waiting for your mother to die.' The more he saw of Natalie Wright-Manton the more he disliked her; he wondered how a couple like the Turners could have bred such a daughter.

He watched her flounce out of his office

then he telephoned Bengairney to arrange an appointment with Steven Caraford.

'I could come to the farm to see you, Mrs Caraford, if that would be more convenient?'

'It would suit my husband better, if you don't mind, Mr MacNicol. Steven and the men are getting ahead with the spring sowing while the weather holds, and there is a batch of heifers calving at Martinwold. He likes to see them as often as he can.'

'I understand.' He explained about Natalie wanting her share in cash. 'I wanted to consult your husband before I speak to the other executors.'

Mr MacNicol knew most of the dairy farmers stopped for afternoon tea before they started milking so he arrived at Bengairney just after three.

'I thought we could talk while you take a break,' he said to Steven, then smiled at Megan, 'and of course I know by now what an excellent baker your wife is.'

'We could arrange to sell one of the tractors as soon as the spring sowing is finished,' Steven said. 'If we do buy Martinwold we would streamline the machinery and the labour between the two farms. If we don't buy it, everything will be to sell anyway.'

'I presume you have not approached Mr

Slater, your bank manager yet, then?'

'I mentioned it soon after Mr Turner died,' Steven said. 'He was noncommittal. We need more figures and a plan for a future strategy before we have a formal meeting. We shall do that before my younger son returns to college after Easter. Alexander's head is bursting with calculations. On paper it all looks feasible but neither of our sons have had much experience. It's the unexpected problems which can cause catastrophes. We need to budget for all eventualities.'

'Weather? Politics?'

'Amongst other things — accidents, illnesses, diseases. Politics are changing. At one time the hierarchy of the National Farmers' Union met with the minister of agriculture each year and ironed out a policy according to what the country needed. Everyone understood farming is a long term business. These days the British government can't make decisions without consulting Europe. I reckon it will get worse.'

'I hadn't considered that aspect,' Mr MacNicol mused. 'Your sons are the new generation. They'll adapt to changes, just as we had to adjust to the war and all the restrictions after it. Mr Slater's uncle has a farm in the Borders and he spent a lot of his boyhood holidays there so he understands some of the difficulties. It is possible he may want to come out and look around the two farms to assess what sort of manager you are. I think he will be impressed.'

'I didn't know he had farming connections,' Steven said. 'Speaking of Mrs Wright-Manton though, I see no problem in selling enough stock and machinery to raise the sum the auctioneer calculated after his valuation if the executors agree.'

'I will speak to them and let you know.'

'Fine, I'll make an appointment with the bank so we can decide the best way forward for everyone. Would Mrs Wright-Manton wait another month?'

'It will do her no harm to wait,' Mr MacNicol said.

'If we do buy Martinwold the house would have to be sold,' Steven said. 'Would you be prepared to handle that?'

'Of course. I don't see any difficulty in getting a buyer for a house like that. I wouldn't have minded living there myself but my wife wants a bungalow like Mrs Turner's.' He smiled at Megan. 'I expect you understand that, Mrs Caraford?'

'I do indeed,' Megan nodded.

'If Mr Slater agrees to lend us the money to buy Martinwold,' Steven said, 'I would like to sell enough stock and surplus machinery to pay out both Mrs Wright-Manton and Mrs Turner. I prefer to know where I stand.'

'I can assure you Mrs Turner is more than willing to wait the two years for her share, and longer if you need more time. She is very grateful to you and your wife and she is not short of money, I assure you.'

'Paying both shares would mean a drastic cut in stock numbers, which in turn means less milk to sell and less income until we build up again. That will take three to six years for our young stock to make up the numbers.'

'I leave the planning to you, Mr Caraford, but I am delighted you are coming round to the idea of keeping Martinwold. I can't tell you how keen Murdo Turner was for you to do so. He was convinced you and your boys would keep up his standards.'

'I can understand he wouldn't want to sell it himself,' Steven said, 'but it is still a big decision and I have a feeling interest rates are going to rise along with inflation. I don't want to end up paying more in interest than I would pay to rent the land.'

'I understand. We have the first woman leader of a British political party now so we shall have to wait and see what Mrs Thatcher can do if the Tories get in at the next election.'

'She can't do much worse,' Steven commented, but he had no crystal ball to warn him of the changes which lay ahead for British farmers. The Milk Marketing Boards guaranteed a monthly payment for milk but they were the envy of European farmers.

★ ★ ★

At Langton Tower Rosemary had had a better winter than she expected and the spring season was promising. Paul's ideas for the garden at Shawlands had earned Mr Ritchie's approval and both he and Struan were more than willing to leave the plants and planting in Rosie's hands. Now they were well into spring and the greenhouses were full of young plants in varying stages. John Oliphant enjoyed sitting on a stool pricking out seedlings in the warmth of the greenhouse.

Douglas Palmer-Farr looked forward to his daughter's company over coffee every morning. She was young and cheerful and optimistic. Her enthusiasm was irresistible when she shared her ideas with him, even though he had little knowledge of gardening.

'I know you don't know what I'm talking about half the time, Daddy,' she told him one morning with a laugh, 'but I love having you to myself, listening while I sort out my ideas.'

'I look forward to our morning break, Rosie,' Douglas admitted. 'I'd never have believed you could make this cottage into such a cheerful happy home for yourself.'

'I've grown very attached to having my own wee house,' Rosie said, 'with no one to interfere.' They both knew she meant her mother. Although Catherine meant well she tended to take over and expect her ideas to be carried out. 'I do appreciate you letting me have the gardens too. I know Mum still doesn't trust me to make a go of things but we're doing quite well for a beginning and I have lots more plans.'

'You enjoy growing things, don't you, Rosemary?'

'Yes. I always loved watching the fields being sown at Bengairney and all the stages when the soil was covered in tender green shoots, then later when the barley swayed in the breeze like a silvery sea, and turned golden for the harvest. Nature is such a wonderful thing, Daddy.' She sighed. 'Mum never understood how much I loved everything about the farm, or how I hated going away to that horrid school.'

'I know.' Douglas shuddered, remembering how close they had come to losing her. 'I've never told you how glad I am you forced us to bring you home, have I, my love?'

'So you didn't blame me for running away, Daddy? I know Mum will never forgive me for throwing away her idea of a wonderful opportunity. She's always casting up about Sir Henry Braebourne's family and their private education, but I've no regrets.'

'Neither have I, my dear, neither have I. You are more precious to me than all the money or success in the world. Sometimes I think we only got to know each other after you returned home. I enjoyed supervising your studies and I'm proud of you. Whatever you do in life I believe you'll do it well. Never be afraid to follow your heart, Rosemary. Take life by the scruff of the neck and enjoy it.' He grinned at her. 'Are you going to tell me you need fifty thousand pounds for some hare-brained project now?'

'Of course not,' Rosie chuckled. 'But I'm glad you have faith in me, Daddy.' She sighed. 'I am going to tell you I must get some work done though.'

'All right, I'll walk down to the greenhouses with you and have a chat with John if he's around. He's always been a fount of knowledge, but he doesn't realize it.'

Local demand for fresh fruit and vegetables as well as young plants was increasing now that people understood Langton Tower Gardens was an independent and expanding business with sales to the general public.

'We're lucky we have plenty of land to expand,' Rosie told Paul. 'I think we should turn over another two acres of the paddock and grow a crop of potatoes to clean it.'

'I reckon we could sell them easily enough,' Paul agreed, 'and the ground would be ready for whatever we need next year.'

'Yes, we could lengthen the rotation and try to avoid disease. I know sprays are becoming all the fashion but I'd rather manage without them if we can.'

'You said we might try a couple of the new varieties of apples too,' Paul reminded her.

'Mmm, so I did. I think I ought to take on more help for next spring. I can't expect Papa Oliphant to keep helping out.'

'He enjoys the company and doing what he can,' Paul said. Rosie smiled at him with affection. He was a thoughtful and caring young man. If she'd had a brother she would have liked him to be like Paul, though without the shadow of the leukaemia which still clouded his horizon. Tania and Struan often persuaded her to accompany them to the local dances if they were going and they were happy to include Paul too.

'I don't want to tag along and play gooseberry to you and Struan,' Rosie said, half serious, half laughing.

'There's no fear of that,' Tania said, 'You're never short of partners. Sometimes I think you bring Paul along as a protector. Sam often asks for a lift. He says it's because Alex has their car away at college but he could always borrow Dad's if he wanted. I think he's avoiding Lidia. He's always asking if you're coming with us.'

'I don't know why he bothers,' Rosie said, bending down on the pretext of pulling a weed to hide her sudden rush of colour.

'Lidia clings to him like glue,' Tania admitted. 'She's worse than ever. She's always phoning. Avril and Dean think she means to have him; Struan agrees with them,' she added.

'I thought he was going on a Young Farmers Association exchange visit to escape?'

'That was before the Martinwold affair came up. Dean says he's too soft with her or he would tell her where to go, but it bothers Sam when she gets hysterical and threatens to do all sorts of weird things.'

'Sam wants to have his cake and eat it if you ask me,' Rosie muttered. 'He likes to be seen dancing with the prettiest girl in the hall.'

'Do you think so?' Tania said, looking at her young friend. 'You and Sam used to be such good friends. You would never let Alex

149

or I, or Avril's brothers say anything wrong about him. He always looked out for you, too, far more than he ever did for me,' she added with a rueful smile. She frowned. 'You and Sam haven't fallen out, have you?'

'No, we've grown up, that's all. People change.'

'Mmm, I suppose some people do. Struan and I haven't changed.'

'Of course you have,' Rosie chuckled.

'How? We were always good friends, all through school.'

'But you're more than just friends now, aren't you, Tania?' Rosie smiled and Tania blushed.

'I wouldn't change Struan for the world. Can you keep a secret, Rosie?'

'You know I can. I never told anyone about your engagement, did I?'

'No, but this is a bit different. I-I suppose I'm telling you because I feel a bit guilty, and yet I feel . . . I feel so elated.'

'You'll have to spill the beans now, Tania,' Rosie chuckled.

'I . . . we slept together when we went to Edinburgh for the reunion weekend.'

'Gosh!' Rosie blushed. In many ways she was still very naïve. 'Did you . . . ? I mean — '

'It was wonderful,' Tania breathed, 'especially the second night. The rest of our friends all seemed to be doing the same and it seemed to be, well sort of expected that we would share a room.'

'I see.' Rosie felt very young and gauche.

'That's why we decided to get engaged. Struan gets exasperated with his mother refusing to consider moving.'

'At least she attended your engagement party at Bengairney.'

'She did but only after Mr Ritchie said he was coming with or without her.'

★ ★ ★

It was a hectic summer for all the Carafords. To Sam and Alex's great relief their parents had at last agreed to buy Martinwold. They still had more than a year before they needed to find the full amount, but once Steven had reached a decision he was impatient to start planning. Mr Slater, the bank manager, insisted on meeting them all.

'It is a big responsibility and it needs serious consideration,' he said, looking at Samuel and then at Alexander. 'You young men must realize your parents are doing this for your sakes. Are you prepared to work hard and share the responsibility, and the personal sacrifices which a project like this involves?'

'We are,' Sam said.

151

'We know Mother and Father are doing this for us,' Alex said.

'And what happens when you both want to get married?'

'We hope Father and Mother will be in charge for a long time yet,' Samuel said. 'Alex and I have talked it over. We want to keep on renting Bengairney and run the two farms together as far as we can, with Father in charge. If either of us gets married we would have to live in one of the cottages and draw a wage to live on out of our share of the profits, but neither of us have any plans to marry yet.'

'Fair enough.' Mr Slater's expression relaxed a little. 'You seem to have thought things through.' He looked at Megan. 'Thank you for the coffee, Mrs Caraford. It is a long time since I tasted homemade scones. They remind me of the holidays I spent with my grandparents. They had a farm in the Borders. It belongs to my uncle now, although he is almost ready to retire.' He turned back to Steven. 'I would like to take a walk round both the farms if it is convenient?'

'Yes, of course,' Steven agreed, glad Mr MacNicol had warned him the banker was more than just a man for figures and balance sheets. He was proud of the way he farmed Bengairney and he was doing his best to continue farming Martinwold as Mr Turner had done.

A fortnight later Mr Slater brought a more senior banker down from Edinburgh to see them but they did not look round the farms. The financial plans were agreed.

Steven had not looked forward to telling Penny Green and her young daughter he needed to sell their cottage with vacant possession. He waited until late Friday afternoon when she had finished teaching so that she would have all weekend to consider his news.

'I can offer you another cottage to rent,' he offered. 'It is the one next to Joe Finkel and his wife, Emily. You know Joe from your visits to the farm, don't you, Ginny?'

'Yes,' she nodded. 'But we love living here, next to the fields. I can see the animals from my bedroom window every morning.'

'I do understand you need to sell, Mr Caraford,' Penny Green said. 'Can I have a little time to consider?'

'I wanted to give you as much notice as possible.'

It was a surprise when Penny arrived at Bengairney on Sunday afternoon.

'Would it be all right if Archie, that is Mr Pattinson, came in too?' she asked.

'We-ell, yes,' Steven said, frowning a little.

He disliked trouble but the cottage had to be sold whatever arguments the young architect might put forward. He had noticed Pattinson's car was often at the cottage, although the improvements had been finished long ago. 'What about Ginny?'

'She has gone off with your sons to look at some of the animals.' Penny Green smiled. 'She loves being in the country. She wants to be a vet.'

'I'm sorry I have to uproot you both,' Steven said, 'but we do need to sell your cottage. The two here, on Bengairney, belong to the landlord so I can't sell the one which is vacant.'

'That's why Archie has come too. We wondered if you would consider a private sale?'

'Bring him in, but I need vacant possession to get the best price.' He repeated this to Archie Pattinson once they were seated in the small room which Steven used as an office.

'I can understand you will get a better price if the house has vacant possession, Mr Caraford, but you see, Penny and I have decided to get married. Now this has cropped up we are thinking of bringing things forward if we can do a deal with you. I feel we can offer a fair price but we would like a bit more ground. I thought perhaps the corner of the

154

field which runs by the side of the garden and comes to a point at the road side? I reckon it is about three quarters of an acre. We would like to include that if you're willing to sell to us. We both enjoy gardening you see. Also we would want to build on an extension.'

'I'd have no problem with that, but as I said — '

'We can offer a good price if you would agree to a private sale. That way Penny wouldn't have all the upheaval of moving. We shall have a good deposit between us when I've sold my own house. Penny sold the house where she lived with her first husband, didn't you darling?'

'Yes. Billy's life insurance covered the mortgage. We had done a lot of improvements so I got more than we paid for it. I invested the money. I didn't want to buy another house until I was sure Ginny was happy and I was settled in a job.'

'Things are different now,' Archie Pattinson broke in. 'The house would be in joint names. Would you take five thousand for it, including the extra land?' he finished.

'Five thousand pounds . . . ' Steven said and lowered his eyelids. That was more than they had paid for the tumbledown cottage and twenty-five acres when they bought it. They had spent quite a bit on the improvements, but they had got a grant towards the cost.

'I-I'm afraid that's about our limit,' Archie Pattinson said. 'We might manage another two hundred . . . ?' He looked at Penny. 'We do want to buy it. We hadn't expected you would sell it, at least not for some time.'

'Right,' Steven said, hiding his delight. 'I think we could come to an agreement for five thousand. I will meet you there to discuss the corner of the field and mark it out then it will be up to you to see your solicitor and put in a formal offer. We can give you a month. If you can't raise the money I shall have to advertise it for sale.'

'Oh I'm sure we can get it all agreed before the end of May,' Archie said, his face splitting into a wide smile.

'Very well. I will erect a stock proof fence across the corner area.'

'I thought for a minute he was going to lift Penny off her chair and hug her there and then,' Steven said later to Megan. 'I hope things will work out for them. They're offering a big price.'

'Well it's a better price than we had expected,' Megan said with a smile, 'but I must admit it is a nice situation and I don't think Archie Pattinson is anybody's fool so they must like it.'

'Mmm, I hope they can handle the finances as well as they think.'

'I expect they will. I didn't realize Penny had sold a house before she came down here, and you say Archie has his own house to sell, even if it is mortgaged.'

'That would be one hurdle over,' Steven said.

'The next will be Martinwold House. Mrs Turner will have moved out by the end of next week,' Megan reminded him. 'She thinks we ought to put it up for sale straight away now that we're buying the farm. She is pleased we're doing what Mr Turner wanted. I do wish Natalie had helped her more, though. She's hardly been near and when she does come she upsets her mother with her criticism, or demanding things she thinks should be hers. Mrs Turner ends up either getting angry, then regretting it, or bursting into tears. Natalie can have a very vicious tongue at times.'

'Nothing new there, then. She was the same when we were youngsters. She was a selfish little snob. I'm glad she's got her share of the money. We sold the older cows in the herd to raise it so with any luck we should build up again in two to three years if we keep all the calves. Thank goodness Mr Slater understood calves have to be born and grow to adults, then another nine months before they have a calf and begin to milk.'

'Mrs Turner asked me not to tell Natalie anything about our arrangement for paying her share in quarterly instalments. I suspect she's afraid Natalie will ask her for a loan.'

'A gift you mean!' Steven said with a harsh laugh. 'Knowing Natalie and that man of hers they would have no intention of repaying it.'

6

Rosie was surprised to see Lindsay Gray accompanying her father as they strolled towards her, chuckling together over some anecdote. Lindsay was her mother's half cousin and the only relative Rosie had ever heard her mention. Although he was a surgeon he used to come to Langton Tower before he married. He had enjoyed helping John Oliphant in the gardens then. Ruth's death had been a cruel blow to him, but he had been happy for Avril when she and Dean married and made their home with him at Riverview.

John Oliphant was keeping an eye on Rodney and the two men stopped to chat. Rosie knew they would never get a more willing worker than Rodney but he did need supervision. A month before she had almost wept when he hoed up a whole row of young peas, not even realizing they were not weeds.

'Hello Rosemary,' Lint greeted her with a smile. 'I see you are hard at work but things are looking well.'

'Hello Uncle Lint. How are Avril and the

children? And the twins? Is Callum enjoying being at Oxford?'

'He is. He has decided to study medicine after all. Craig never had any doubts of course. Changing the subject though, Rosemary, I have been admiring John's seat and the arbour. He tells me it makes a good windbreak now the plants are creeping over it. He says you made it for him.'

'I have to take care of my main supervisor.'

'Of course,' Lint agreed with an answering smile. He remembered Rosie had always had the most infectious of smiles even as a toddler, except when Catherine had sent her to boarding school with such disastrous results. 'I think a seat like that would be a good idea for Mrs Caraford. Avril has been racking her brains wondering what to buy for her birthday. She is too frail to work in the garden these days but she always loved being out in the fresh air. Would you be able to make one?'

'I think so,' Rosie said. 'We bought the seat and made the rustic shelter to fit around it then we planted the honeysuckle and rambler rose as a windbreak.'

'It smells wonderful when the honeysuckle is in bloom,' John Oliphant said, looking up at Lint. 'It reminds me of the honeysuckle Chrissie planted round the gate when we first moved into the cottage. If Avril decides to go ahead tell her to ask Sam to cut the rustic posts to the right lengths. After all Hannah Caraford is his grandmother as well as hers.'

'We'll fix it up one way or another,' Rosie promised. 'Ask Avril to telephone me with the seat measurements when she's decided. We'll make the panels here then it will not take so long to erect them in Mrs Caraford's garden.'

Avril telephoned the following day giving Rosie the measurements for a teak garden seat.

'We thought a small one would be cosier,' Avril said, 'big enough to seat two people. My father says you have made a good job of Mr Oliphant's, Rosie. In fact he says you're making a splendid business with the gardens.'

'Papa Oliphant approves,' Rosie agreed with a chuckle. 'He keeps an eye on things and he uses his seat every day unless it's raining. You do know they're not meant to be wind and waterproof?'

'Oh yes, but Granny C wouldn't be out in the rain these days anyway.'

'Perhaps we should ask her what sort of flowers she would prefer? She might fancy a rose. The Zephirine Douhin has no thorns and it's a very pretty pink, but the honeysuckle spreads and makes the cover as well as a perfume.'

'Could I leave it to you to plant the honeysuckle straight away, Rosie? Then we could add a clematis or a rose, or whatever Granny C would like. I phoned Sam about the rustic fencing. He'll get in touch with you himself.'

'That's fine. I'll wait for him to phone me, then,' Rosie agreed. 'I expect they're all busy helping out at Martinwold but I hope he's not too last minute.'

In fact Samuel did not waste any time. He arrived at the gardens in person the following Saturday just before lunchtime. He could see Rosie and Paul Keir working in one of the greenhouses. They looked at ease together and a burst of laughter told him they were sharing a private joke. He and Rosie had once shared a rapport like that, he thought, but Rosie had changed since she returned from college and set up in business on her own. She had grown more serious and efficient; they no longer shared the easy relationship they'd once enjoyed. He remembered how they had discussed anything and everything without awkwardness or embarrassment. Rosie had always stated her opinion and backed it up with reasons. Beneath the mass of wild blonde curls she had an intelligent brain and a mischievous sense of humour. It dawned on Sam that Rosie and Lidia were the only two girls he knew well, apart from Tania, of course. They were complete opposites. Lidia was always groomed with her face made up, her nails manicured and painted, yet her conversation was trivial, about clothes, and furnishing a big house and having a maid to cook and clean. Their relationship had cooled now she realized Martinwold House was on the market for sale.

He made his way round to the open door of the greenhouse.

'I thought you didn't work on Saturdays,' he said, startling both Paul and Rosie.

'And good morning to you too, Mr Caraford,' Rosie answered, her brows rising at his tone. Sam flushed, realizing he had been both curt and rude.

'I don't work at the weekend,' Paul said in his amiable manner, 'but I knew it would take Rosie all day on her own to finish pricking out the last of the seedlings. I'll go now if you want to talk,' he added, looking at Rosemary.

'Not at all,' Rosie said, tossing her head. 'Samuel can say whatever he has to say whether you're here or not.' She cast a defiant look at Sam.

'I, er . . . I only came to see if you were free to come and supervise the sawing of the rustic poles this afternoon — the ones for

Granny Caraford's seat. Mother said I should invite you down to lunch before we start but I got held up moving some young cattle so I'm later than I intended.'

'I see,' Rosie said frowning hard at the tray of seedlings.

'I can finish these off,' Paul offered, 'if you want to go and wash your face and change.'

'Wash my face?' Rosie looked at Paul, her blue eyes indignant.

'Mmm,' he murmured, his eyes dancing with laughter. 'Streaks of mud down one cheek aren't the new fashion, are they?'

'Mud?' Rosie scowled and wiped her cheek with her sleeve.

'Wrong side,' Paul said, trying to keep a straight face. Sam stepped forward and wiped her cheek with his hanky.

'I'm used to seeing Rosie with mud on her face,' he said, grinning. 'She's more like the girl I used to know this way.' Rosie blushed. It was a long time since she and Sam had been on teasing terms.

'Go on, Rosie,' Paul urged. 'It will not take me long to finish here and you know you were worrying about getting the seat fixed in time for Mrs Caraford's birthday.'

'That's true,' Rosie admitted. 'Are you sure your mother invited me to lunch?' she asked Sam.

'Of course I'm sure. Anyway when did you ever need inviting to Bengairney? It's always been your second home.'

'That was when I was a child,' Rosie said. 'Polite adults wait to be asked.' Sam wondered if she was referring to Lidia. She invited herself at the most inconvenient times. Thank goodness he hadn't seen her for the past three weeks. He knew she was waiting for him to call her after their latest quarrel but she would wait for ever as far as he was concerned.

'All right,' Rosie said, interrupting his thoughts, 'I'll go and get ready, but if you're still looking as grim when I return, Sam, I shall stay at home.'

'I'm not grim!' Sam said in surprise. 'Am I?'

'You look like you're under a thunder cloud,' Rosie declared. 'Paul, I haven't seen my father this morning. If he comes into the gardens before you leave, tell him where I've gone will you? I'll leave a note for him on my kitchen table in case you're not around.' She hurried away.

'Does Mr Palmer-Farr come to the gardens every day?' Sam asked. 'I didn't think he was interested in outdoor pursuits.'

'The translations are his work but Rosie is the light of his life. He never misses a day.

There's a wonderful bond between them,' Paul added. 'I barely remember what my father looked like now, though my mother tells me we were close when he was alive.'

'I suppose we don't appreciate what we have, while we have it,' Sam said slowly. 'My parents discuss everything together. I expect that's why we feel so secure. I never thought about it before. I never got the impression Rosie was very close to her parents.'

'She told me about the boarding school fiasco. I guess it made her father realize how much she meant to him. You have known Rosemary since she was a baby according to Mr Oliphant?'

'Yes, Granny and Grandfather Oliphant often brought her with them to Bengairney. She loved the farm and the animals. Later she used to cycle over. Her mother never seemed to have much time for her.'

'I don't know Mrs Palmer-Farr well but I don't think she's the maternal kind. My own mother thinks Rosie would have responded to affection like flowers to the sun.' He smiled. 'I don't suppose running a hotel this size leaves time for home life,' he reflected.

'Maybe not. My own parents think Mrs Palmer-Farr puts her business before everything else, including her husband and Rosie. We're all surprised the way Rosie runs these gardens, but I don't think she'll ever be as hard as her mother. Does Rosie visit your home often?'

'Quite often,' Paul said, watching Sam out of the corner of his eye and allowing himself a little inner smile. It wouldn't do any harm for the popular Samuel Caraford to experience a bit of the green-eyed monster. 'Mother enjoys Rosie's company when she comes for Sunday lunch. They're both interested in gardening and country life.'

'As you are too, of course,' Sam said.

'I wouldn't say that,' Paul mused, concentrating on his task. 'I drifted into the gardening when I was recovering. My main interest is in designing and landscape but I have found it absorbing learning about the plant side of things and Rosie is very good at passing on information. I've learned a lot and I'm very grateful but I don't envisage working as a gardener all my life. Now that my medical reports are so good and I'm feeling more energetic I'm beginning to consider my future and what I want to do with my life.'

'I see.' Samuel realized he had never had a proper conversation with Paul Keir before. He had never taken the trouble to get to know him. 'Grandfather Oliphant reckons you're indispensable so Rosie would miss you if you moved on.'

'Oh I'm not thinking of *leaving* Rosie,' Paul assured him. 'I've still too much to learn. I went on one or two specialist courses last year and I intend to do the same again if we can fit them in.'

'I see,' Sam said again. It seemed Paul and Rosie were much more than work colleagues, then.

'Hi, I'm ready if you are, Sam,' Rosie called from the gates at the end of the path. 'Paul, I'll lock the gates. You'll be going the other way out, won't you?'

'Yes, of course. Anyway I've got my key with me today.' He grinned at her, noting she had changed into a smart blue blouse he had never seen her wear before. It matched her eyes, and she had brushed her fair hair until it fell in shining waves around her small face. 'You look good enough to eat now,' he called, then, mischievously to Sam, 'or at least to kiss . . . ' Sam glowered at him and hurried up the path to join Rosemary and drive her away from Paul Keir. Paul chuckled as he watched them go.

Lunch at Bengairney was as cheerful as it had always been for as long as Rosie could remember. Alex was home from college for the weekend and he and his father were in a hurry to get back to the fence they were erecting across the corner of the field, which

Penny Green and Archie Pattinson were buying along with the cottage.

'Tania is at my father's today,' Megan said. 'She's gone to tidy up a bit and bring his washing for me, though I must say he does keep the house clean and tidy, for a man.'

'He does,' Rosie smiled. 'It is his nature to be tidy. He's the same around the gardens, especially in the greenhouses and he often tidies the garden sheds if it's a wet day. He looks forward to Tania's company at the weekends though.'

'I know.' Megan smiled. 'Between the two of you he says you keep him young in spirit, if not in body.' She refused Rosie's offer to clear away and shooed everyone on their way to carry out their plans for the afternoon.

'We have been cutting some fence posts for Dad and Alex to use,' Sam said, 'but we thought you would want the thinner ones.'

'I do for the panels but I need four stronger ones for the corners to hold everything firm. Did you notice the one Paul and I made for your grandfather? It has criss-cross posts on each panel for the sides, back and top.'

'That will make more work won't it?'

'Yes, but it's more rustic-looking and prettier when the climbing plants grow over.'

'OK, you're the boss.'

'Mmm? That makes a change.'

'Does it?' Sam stopped and stared down at her. 'I always thought we were good friends.'

'Come on, let's get on with the job,' Rosie said, unwilling to meet Sam's earnest green eyes. She was afraid he might see too much.

'We'll do the thinner posts first, then,' Sam decided. 'Did you bring a measuring tape?'

'Yes, and a diagram. The ones on the top, or outer side of the crossover are slightly longer. Like this. See?' Sam came close and leaned over her shoulder, draping an arm around her as they looked at the paper together. Rosie stiffened. Sam frowned. Since when had they been so awkward in each other's company, he wondered. He had a sudden flashback to the limp young body he had carried upstairs the night he had found Rosie half dead with cold and exhaustion. His mother had wrapped her in a large bath towel but it had fallen open a little as he carried her up the stairs and he had been amazed to see small buds of breasts forming on her thin chest. He had covered them hastily, but had realized then that Rosie was leaving childhood behind. Strange that he should think of that now, but he had always thought of Rosie as belonging to him since then and it was a painful shock to realize he could be wrong. He moved away from her and started up his chainsaw.

They had almost finished the thinner poles and Rosie had them laid out in neat piles of the same lengths.

'You're very methodical,' Sam remarked with a grin. 'We've done well. Two more of these, then the four corner posts. They're the thick ones over there. They're all the same length, eh?'

'That's right. You've worked hard, Sam. I'm grateful.' Rosie smiled at him, her old infectious smile and he felt his heart leap. Neither of them heard footsteps approaching.

'Samuel Caraford, you always give me every excuse under the sun about being too busy to see me but you've plenty of time for the little gardener, I see.'

'Lidia?' Sam turned at the sound of her voice. His heart sank. Rosie looked up in surprise from placing the last thin pole with the rest. He didn't look all that pleased to see his girlfriend, she thought, and wished she didn't feel glad about it. She was unaware their relationship had been more off than on for a long time now, at least as far as Sam was concerned.

'Hello Lidia,' he said, stifling a groan. 'You don't look as though you've come to help.' He eyed her pink pleated skirt and the white three-quarter jacket, belted around her narrow waist. Rosie thought it was a wonder she had negotiated the rough ground through the stack yard in those high-heeled shoes with their fashionable square toes. Her spirits fell as she raised her eyes to Lidia's made-up face. Surely the long dark eyelashes couldn't be real? She blinked, wishing the other girl would disappear and let them get on.

'We're nearly finished,' she said. 'Four more to go.' Lidia sniffed and ignored her.

'How come you find time for her when you're too busy to see me?' she demanded, glaring at Sam as he moved to put another post across the saw bench, reaching for the tape from Rosie.

'These posts are for Sam's grandmother,' Rosie said, 'for her birthday. At least they will be when we've made them into an arbour and erected it in her garden.'

'I wasn't speaking to you,' Lidia snapped. Sam raised his eyebrows and his green eyes sparked with annoyance.

'We'd better get on with the job.' He lifted the saw and sliced through the post. 'I'll lift these four, Rosie. They're heavy. In fact Alex and I will take them down to Granny Caraford's tomorrow and set them up ready for you to fix the panels.'

'Oh Sam, would you? That would be a great help. I don't like to give Paul too much

172

lifting or hard digging and we are rather busy.'

'Oh Sam, would you?' Lidia mimicked in an exaggerated simper. It brought angry colour to Rosie's cheeks but before she could speak Lidia snapped, 'It's all right for some folks.'

Sam ignored her and placed another pole in position and cut it to size. He set the chainsaw aside on a pile of logs while he carried the last two poles nearer to the saw bench. Lidia watched as he laid them down. She kicked the logs, scuffing the toe of her shoe. She swore. Afterwards Rosie was never quite sure what happened.

The log pile wobbled. The chainsaw slid sideways. Lidia grabbed for it. It was heavy, much heavier than she had expected. She grasped the other handle, unaware it was the throttle control.

The chain sprang into life. Sam lifted his arm instinctively. The moving blade sliced across it then sank to the ground. Blood spurted from his arm. Lidia jumped back in horror. Sam reeled, clutching his arm against his chest and sank to his knees. Rosie sprang to his side with a gasp.

'I-I didn't mean to . . . ' Lidia gasped. 'I didn't know it was so heavy.'

'We must stop the bleeding. I th-think it

must have severed an artery.' Rosie looked up at Lidia. 'Phone for an ambulance!' she ordered. 'Hurry!'

Sam felt faint, from shock and the sight of so much blood. 'Lie down flat, Sam,' Rosie urged and raised his arm. 'I need something to make a pad.' She looked around. 'Don't stand there gawping. Run!' she shouted at Lidia. 'Phone! Now! Bring a towel to staunch the blood! There's no time to lose.' She choked back a sob.

'B-but I didn't mean — '

'Go,' Rosie yelled. 'He's b-bleeding to death.' She jerked her blouse from her jeans with one hand and tore it open, sending the tiny pearl buttons popping everywhere. Her hand shook as she struggled to form a pad; she wished she'd asked Lidia for her belt to make a tourniquet. Sam was lying still, his face white, his eyes closed. Rosie tried to keep his arm raised, remembering the wound should be higher than his heart and his head. She bent over him. She couldn't stop her tears.

'Oh Sam, please don't die,' she whispered. 'Oh dear God, help him.' She looked down into his beloved face. Sam felt a tear fall on his cheek. He opened his eyes. He saw two small, firm breasts in a pink lacy bra — or at least he thought he did.

'Rosie . . . ?' He wished he didn't feel so groggy. The sky was going round and round. His eyelids were lead weights.

'Oh Sam,' Rosie whispered. 'I love you so much. D-don't die . . . '

It was Megan who came running from the house with two clean towels.

'Oh my goodness!' She paled with shock as she handed a towel to Rosie. 'Lidia was gabbling hysterically. I phoned for an ambulance.'

'I think the saw has cut an artery,' Rosie whispered. She pressed the towel against the wound and held it hard against her chest with one hand while holding Sam's arm up with the other. 'I think we're supposed to keep the wound higher than his heart to stop the blood pumping.' It was half statement, half question.

'I'll do that.' Megan said, but her voice was trembling as she knelt beside Sam and looked down into his white face.

'Rosie . . . ' he whispered, forcing his eyes open with an effort, then wishing he hadn't. 'Don't leave me . . . '

'I'm still here, Sam. I won't leave you. The ambulance will be here soon.'

'What a mess. You're covered in blood, Rosie.' Megan's voice was shaking.

It seemed an age to Rosie as they waited

for the ambulance but in fact it was quick. The crew had been delivering a patient to his home in Darlonachie Village and the hospital had managed to make contact while they were settling the man into his bed. The crew were calm and efficient, assuring Rosie she had done a good job.

'Rosie. Rosie . . . ' Sam protested as they lifted him onto a stretcher.

'Hush, laddie. You'd best come with him, lassie,' the man said, looking at Rosie. 'We need to get a drip set up and get some fluid back into him. We don't want him getting upset.' Rosie looked at Megan, knowing it was his mother's place to be with him.

'You go,' Megan said softly. She draped the spare towel round her shoulders and Rosie became aware that she was barely decent. Her cheeks burned, but the ambulance men had no time to notice such things. Their attention was one hundred per cent with their patient and she was thankful.

'I'll follow in the car, Rosie,' Megan said. 'It's you Sam needs. I'll bring some of Tania's clothes for you to change at the hospital.'

'That's right, lassie. You keep holding his arm up. You may well have saved the laddie's life. A good thing ye were there. Here's a blanket to put around you,' he added as Rosie began to shiver with reaction.

7

Later Megan and Rosie waited together at the hospital.

'I thought Lidia would be here,' Megan said. 'Her car had gone when I got back to the house. Tell me what happened, Rosie?'

'I-I didn't see,' Rosie said. 'The saw fell off the pile of logs and Lidia grabbed it, I think.' Megan looked at her but she didn't pursue the matter. The main thing was that Sam was alive. The doctors said he was young and strong and they would do their best to save his arm.

It was evening by the time Megan and Rosie arrived back at Bengairney. Tania had returned home and she was cooking the evening meal for Alex and her father.

'We saw the note you scribbled, Mum,' she said. 'Is Sam going to be all right? Dad is worried sick. We all are.'

'Yes, he's going to be all right but he'll be in hospital for a while,' Megan said. 'Thank God Rosie was so sensible.'

'I didn't feel sensible,' Rosie admitted with a quiver in her voice. 'I'm sorry I needed to wear your clothes, Tania. I'll wash them and send them back tomorrow.'

'There's no rush, Rosie,' Tania said. 'They're too big on you. You must have shrunk.'

'You look exhausted, lassie,' Megan said, eying Rosie. 'I expect it's the shock and reaction. I think you should stay here tonight. We'll phone the hospital for news first thing tomorrow. You'll feel better for a hot meal and a good night's sleep.'

'Oh I couldn't do — '

'Of course you must stay, Rosie,' Tania said. 'I'll lend you some pyjamas and I made plenty of food for all of us. What's the point in you going home to brood alone. Struan will be here later. We'll get out the Monopoly board. Alex will have a game with us too. It will be better than being alone.'

'All right. Thank you,' Rosie said, knowing Tania was right. 'Can I just telephone and tell Daddy what's happened? I didn't see him this morning before I left and if he goes round to my cottage and finds it empty he might be worried.'

'You do that,' Megan said. 'Has Lidia phoned to inquire for Sam, Tania?'

'Lidia? Was she here? I thought Sam had made the break this time.'

'Well she was here this afternoon,' Megan said, 'but she didn't wait for the ambulance. I thought she would want to know Sam is going to be all right.'

When Steven and Alex came in after milking they settled down to eat their meal.

'I cut the two remaining posts the same length as the other two thicker ones,' Alex said. 'I'm assuming they are the four for the corners, Rosie?'

'Yes they are. Thanks, Alex.'

'They will need setting in well if they're going to hold up the rest. I'll dig the holes and set them up tomorrow. They're for our grandma after all.'

'You'll not have much time,' Steven said. 'You'll be driving back to college tomorrow and you said you were going in to see Sam in the afternoon, but I agree we shouldn't leave them to Rosie.'

'It would be a great help,' Rosie admitted. 'Sam said he would fix them but he was going to ask you to help him, Alex.'

'I'll drop off the thin poles at your place tomorrow, before I go to see Sam. Are you coming too, Rosie?'

'Er no. G-give him my good wishes.' Alex gave her a quizzical look, wondering why she seemed flustered. He didn't know she was squirming with embarrassment. Why had she blurted out her love for Sam? She uttered a silent prayer that he would have no recollection or she'd never be able to look him in the eye again.

'It's a blessing you were there,' Megan said. 'Lidia kept sobbing, 'I didn't mean to do it.' I had to shake her before she told me to phone for an ambulance.' Tania looked across at Rosie and raised her eyebrows. Rosie knew she would have some questions to answer when they were alone.

★ ★ ★

At Langton Tower Douglas Palmer-Farr was hoping to finish the translation before he went to bed. It had been an interesting manuscript relating to Ancient Greece but it had been more difficult and complicated than his usual work. Catherine knew he would work on until the early hours. He liked the peace and quiet at the end of the day and into night. She took him in a cup of tea and poured them both a tot of whisky.

'Rosemary Lavender telephoned to say she is staying the night at Bengairney,' she told him. 'Samuel Caraford has had an accident. He's in hospital.'

'That's not so good,' Douglas said, looking up and pushing his work away from him for a short break. 'Rosemary thinks a lot of Samuel I think. She could do worse; they're a decent family. Maybe I should go down and lock the door to her cottage if she's not coming home tonight. She never locks the cottage during the day.'

'You drink up your tea and relax for a while,' Catherine said. 'I could do with a breath of fresh air. I'll check the cottage is locked.'

'Thank you, darling. I'd like to finish this before I turn in. You'll need the key for the gates. Rosemary always locks them. My key is hanging up there beside the fireplace.'

'I've always thought she's a bit paranoid about hotel guests and staff wandering around her gardens,' Catherine mused, 'and yet she doesn't mind Paul Keir or John Oliphant wandering in and out of her home, or even that fellow Rodney.'

She collected the key and took her jacket from the hall cupboard. It was almost dark but when her eyes became accustomed it was easy enough to find her way down the path to the cottage without her torch. Sure enough the door was not locked. She was groping for the light switch to find the key when she was seized. A soft, fleshy hand clamped over her mouth, and a strong arm pinioned her arms, holding her pressed against her captor. Surprise robbed Catherine of reaction, but only for a moment. She struggled.

'No use fighting me, you stuck up little bitch. Miss Palmer-Farr will be no better than the lowest kitchen maid when I've had my way wi — '

'You!' Catherine mumbled, recognizing the voice of her chef, as well as the smell of onions and garlic, but his hand was clamped over her mouth. Indignation leant her strength. She kicked his shins. He swore. His grip loosened and she bit his hand, jerking her head free.

'Lambert!' Her voice was hard and cold as steel. He gasped. His arm fell away. Catherine reached for the light switch and turned to face him. 'How dare you! What do you think you're doing intruding in my daughter's home?'

'I have an assignation with her, Madam,' he said, gathering his wits. 'Your daughter is not the innocent child you and her father think. She's a — ' Catherine slapped his face. Fury boiled up in her.

'You're a liar, Lambert. Rosemary Lavender never could stand the sight of you. Now I know why. Pack your things and get away from here. You're sacked.'

'You can't do that!' The chef's ruddy face paled. Then he rallied. 'We have four couples for breakfast in the morning. Your blue-eyed young chef is on holiday in case you've

182

forgotten. You can't manage without me.'

'How wrong you are, Lambert. Breakfast for eight is a simple task to me. Remember I started this hotel. Now go.' He turned to leave, opened his mouth to speak then changed his mind, but his eyes narrowed and he muttered as he went. Catherine trembled with reaction. She was surprised when he headed towards the orchard. Then she realized he'd driven round about and hidden his car. She shuddered. What if Rosemary had returned alone . . . ?

Catherine hurried back to the hotel. She never disturbed Douglas when he was concentrating on his work, just as he never interfered with her management of the hotel. Tonight, though, she didn't even wait to remove her jacket before she burst into his office. Her hair was dishevelled and her eyes were huge in her pale face.

'What's wrong?' Douglas asked, looking up in surprise. Catherine told him.

'Supposing he had caught Rosemary Lavender on her own? Oh Douglas, I knew she didn't like him. I should have guessed he was part of the reason she wanted her own place.'

'You've told him to go? Without notice?'

'Yes. He doesn't deserve notice.'

'We must pay him for whatever time he's

worked. I'll come with you to see him off.' Douglas's tone was grim, his mouth tight. The very thought of the man laying a finger on his beloved daughter made him boil with anger. He rubbed his throbbing temple.

'Catherine? You said a young maid left, without reason. Do you think Lambert could have been the cause? I remember you liked the girl. You couldn't understand her behaviour.'

'Trudy Fellows? Something like this may have occurred. She was young and innocent. She wouldn't know how to deal with a man like Lambert. There was Anne Winkworth too. She worked a week's notice while Lambert was on holiday. She was young and pretty. I remember Mrs Dixon's tone at the time, 'I don't blame the lassie for leaving. I wouldn't want my daughter in that kitchen.' I didn't understand. She worked between the kitchen and the dining room herself.'

'I'll speak to Lambert myself,' Douglas said. 'Get his cheque ready and tell him we shall send on his P45. Perhaps you should ask Mrs Dixon what she knows about Lambert. She is staying in the staff quarters at present, isn't she? I'll wait for Lambert in the kitchen. He will want to gather up his own tools.'

'He will. I'll not be long. I don't want to give him the opportunity to take what doesn't belong to him, or to sabotage anything.' She yawned. 'I'm for bed as soon as he has gone. I shall need to cook the breakfasts in the morning, but that's not a big deal. Mrs Dixon will help.'

'When we have dealt with Lambert I'd like to finish this translation before I come up to bed. I'll try not to disturb you.'

'You never do disturb me, Douglas. You must sleep as long as you need in the morning.'

'I will, sweetheart.' He drew her closer and kissed her on her mouth. 'Try not to worry about Lambert. I'll deal with him. Now, see if you can get any ammunition from Mrs Dixon. We don't want him claiming unfair dismissal.' He gave her a squeeze but his smile was strained as he watched her disappear in the direction of the staff quarters.

Catherine returned to find Douglas still pacing about the kitchen, waiting for Lambert.

'He'll not be long,' she said in a low voice. 'I've just seen him humping a huge holdall into his car. Mrs Dixon says he was responsible for the two maids leaving and she suspects Lucy Shaw left on account of him last year. He can't keep his hands or his eyes to himself where young women are con-cerned, she says. Peter, the young trainee chef

I employed, has had words with him about pestering the girls. Lambert threatened to get him dismissed if he didn't mind his own business. I wish to God they had come to me. Mrs Dixon says Lambert gave the impression he was on very favourable terms with me.'

'We have no proof of anything but Lambert is not to know that. Let me deal with him over this, Catherine.'

'Thank you, darling. I'll lay out his tools. It will save time.'

Lambert was disconcerted to find Douglas Palmer-Farr in the kitchen and he soon realized he had better go quietly instead of demanding compensation for dismissal, as he had intended. He paled when he discovered the Palmer-Farrs knew about his penchant for young maids. Douglas threatened to report him to the police if he sought employment within a hundred miles of Langton Tower.

'He's guilty as hell,' Douglas said as they heard Lambert drive away. 'Otherwise he would have objected.'

'Yes, I fear there's more to this than we know,' Catherine said in a troubled voice. She had prided herself on getting to know her staff, looking after their welfare, and having their loyalty in return. 'I shall call to see the two young maids who left,' she said. 'They were good workers and pleasant girls and I need to know they are all right.' She stifled another yawn. 'If you don't mind, darling, I'm off to bed.'

'Right. I'll get back to my office. I should be finished in a couple of hours or so. Rosemary will need to collect her key in the morning. Tell her I'll be down for a coffee with her later in the day.'

'Will do.' Catherine shuddered. 'I dare not imagine what might have happened if she had found Lambert waiting for her. He meant business and he sounded savage.'

'Thank God she didn't run into him,' Douglas said. 'Good night, darling.' He blinked rapidly and rubbed his temple as he went back into his own office. He sat down at his desk but the words seemed to jump about on the page. He sat with his eyes closed and his head in his hands, willing himself to relax and concentrate on his work but his mind kept returning to Rosemary and the sly looking Lambert. Her instincts had been proved right. He opened his eyes and forced himself to concentrate. He couldn't remember when he had last felt so tired, or when it had ever been such an effort to concentrate. He had always enjoyed his work.

It was later than he had expected by the time Douglas dragged himself up stairs, shed his clothes and stumbled into bed in a state of utter exhaustion. He resolved he would go to see the doctor on Monday: it was time he faced facts and stopped procrastinating.

★   ★   ★

The following morning Megan telephoned the hospital. Sam was as well as could be expected but he had had a restless night. The doctor thought there could be infection in the wound.

'Oh dear,' Rosie said. 'What if it's from something I did?'

'You saved him from bleeding to death, lassie, or at least losing even more blood and being a lot weaker than he is already,' Steven said.

'Sam's as strong as a horse,' Alex said. 'Don't you worry about him, Rosie. I'm more concerned about you, Dad.' He looked at Steven. 'How will you manage Martinwold and Bengairney without both of us? I think I ought to leave college and come home to work.'

'No Alex! You can't do that,' Megan protested. 'You've only a few more weeks. As soon as you've done your final exams you'll be home for good. I shall help your father with the milking. It's a lot easier than it used to be now there's no buckets to carry. I'm sure Joe's wife will help me feed the young calves.'

'I've been wondering how we're going to manage,' Steven said. 'You're sure you don't mind turning out to the milking again, Megan? That would solve the problem here at Bengairney. As far as Martinwold is concerned, thank goodness Mr Turner had the foresight to give his men an inducement to stay until we get sorted out. The only problem will be the relief milking when Pete has his weekends off.'

'I'll take Sam's place,' Alex said. 'It's only every second weekend and Pete's a good fellow. I reckon he'll cooperate. If I come home on Friday nights I shall be here for the morning milking on Saturdays. I'll go back to college after supper on Sunday evenings.'

'And when will you do all your studying?' Megan asked. 'You've been doing so well and none of us know what the future holds. You might need your paper qualifications yet.'

'I'm well up to date with everything, Mum. Don't worry about it. Now, Rosie, I'll hitch up the Land Rover and trailer and drop off the poles at Langton Tower.'

'I'd appreciate that, Alex.'

It was mid morning by the time Rosie arrived home and discovered her door locked.

She looked at it in surprise then searched under the doormat, then under the two pots of pansies. There was no key. Daddy must have locked it, she thought. Of course she had not intended staying away overnight when she left yesterday. She shivered, remembering Sam lying there white-faced and bleeding. She went in at the front door of Langton Tower but there was no sign of her mother. Her father was not in his office either but that was not surprising as he rarely worked on Sundays, and never before midday. One of the maids came down the wide staircase carrying her basket of cleaning materials.

'Have you seen Mrs Palmer-Farr, Amy?' she asked.

'Oh yes, Miss. She is finishing up in the kitchens and preparing for the dinner this evening. Six of the guests are staying on until tomorrow.' Rosie raised her eyebrows in surprise but she walked down the hall and pushed open the door leading to the kitchens. True enough Catherine was giving the gleaming surfaces a final scrutiny.

'Hello Mum, what are you doing in here on a Sunday morning?'

'Ah, Rosemary Lavender,' Catherine came towards her and hugged her. Rosie was astonished. Her mother had never been a demonstrative person, even when she was small and needed comfort. 'We should have listened to you. Now I understand why you detested Lambert.'

'Lambert?' Rosie gazed at her wide eyed. 'What about him?'

'We dismissed him. He left last night.' She shuddered. 'After you phoned I went to lock up the cottage. Lambert was lurking inside, waiting for you to return.'

'Lambert was in my home?' Rosie's face flushed with anger and her blue eyes sparked. Catherine told her the rest of the story. Even in her anger Rosie couldn't help but laugh at the thought of the greasy little chef pouncing on her mother. What a mistake that would be.

'It was no laughing matter,' Catherine said, but she smiled too. 'I shudder to think what he might have done to you. I am bigger than you and he was stronger than he looked. You must lock your door in future.'

'I do lock it when I go to bed. I hadn't intended to be away overnight.'

'Ah yes. How is Samuel? What happened? I'll make us a cup of coffee and you can tell me.'

'All right,' Rosie agreed, sighing. The morning was passing, but she was grateful to her mother for dealing with the odious Lambert. 'I'm not surprised to hear he made a nuisance of himself with the young maids,' Rosie reflected. 'I hope he didn't do anything awful to them.'

'I intend to call on the two who left. I feel responsible for their welfare. It's almost midday. Will you stay and have a light lunch with us, Rosemary Lavender? Your father must be awake by now. He must have been exhausted by the time he came to bed because he stepped out of his clothes and left them lying beside the bed. I've never known him do that. He is always particular about folding his trousers and hanging up his jacket. Boarding school training, I suppose. Will you waken him dear while I put together a ham and chicken salad?'

'All right,' Rosie acquiesced with a smile. 'I didn't see him yesterday. After lunch I do want to get to work putting the rustic panels together so that the arbour is ready for Mrs Caraford's birthday.'

Minutes later Rosie ran downstairs, white faced and almost incoherent.

'Whatever's the matter? Rosemary Lavender?' Catherine demanded, her voice sharpening with panic at the sight of her daughter's eyes, wide with shock.

'It's Daddy. I-I c-can't waken him,' she gasped in a hoarse whisper.

'What? What do you mean? He can't

be . . . ' Catherine was already on her way to their bedroom. Rosie followed with dragging footsteps, her heart pounding. She had seen dead animals often enough. There was no mistake. Her beloved father looked so peaceful with the familiar smile lifting the corners of his mouth. It was hard to believe, but she knew he was dead.

'Oh Daddy . . . ' she whispered. She felt a lump of ice was taking possession of her chest.

Her mother was kneeling beside the bed, holding one of his hands in both of hers and pleading with him to waken up.

'You can't leave me, Douglas. I c-can't manage without you,' she murmured, her head bowed over their clasped hands. Rosemary watched them. This was a different side to the mother she thought she knew, a softer, more dependent side. Her face was white and she looked distraught.

'D-do you want me to telephone the doctor?' she asked, her own voice husky with tears.

'The doctor?' Catherine looked up at her askance.

'He will need to — to come, Mama.' Her mother bowed her head again over the hand she held so despairingly. Rosie looked at her parents then crept from the room.

All her tears for her beloved father were

frozen inside her. There would be no more discussions, no more little jokes, no more comforting presence. She walked down the wide staircase in a daze. In their private sitting room she lifted the telephone and dialled the doctor's number. She had left the door open. Crossing the hall, Mrs Dixon heard her conversation. She stopped, rooted to the spot. Mr Palmer-Farr couldn't be dead — he couldn't. Rosie came out of the room and the woman saw by her face that her worst fears were confirmed.

'It canna be true?' She had been with them for ten years. The Palmer-Farrs were good employers.

'Yes, Mrs Dixon, m-my father must have died in his s-sleep.' Rosemary looked at the older woman's shocked expression and remembered there were guests in the hotel. They would expect the usual care and attention, at least until tomorrow. Rosie realized it was beyond her mother to consider anything except her father's death. 'C-can you manage?' she asked. 'I — we . . . cannot take it in.'

'No wonder, lassie. Your father was fine last night. He dealt with Lambert.' She clapped a hand to her mouth. 'There'll be the dinner to cook tonight. Thank God we've only six guests until tomorrow. Shall I telephone Finn? He's young but he's a capable chef and he's always obliging. I know he'll come in. He'll be as relieved as the rest of us to hear Lambert has gone. But the master . . . ' she shook her grey head in disbelief.

'I will leave the kitchens to you,' Rosie said. 'Come to me if you have any queries. Mother is — ' She broke off and looked at the older woman, her blue eyes still dark with shock.

'I understand, lassie. We'll all do what we can to help.'

⋆   ⋆   ⋆

It was well over a week before funeral arrangements could be made. Rosie had hated the idea of a post mortem but the doctor had explained that as he had not attended him as a patient for several years, it was necessary. Sudden deaths had to be reported to the coroner. Rosemary depended on Paul to supervise the work in the gardens while she attended to any queries which came from the hotel side and she helped her mother make arrangements for the funeral. Her eyes had a haunted look in her white face but she was outwardly calm. Inwardly she felt frozen, unable to shed the tears which were like a heavy weight dragging her down.

'The lassie is too calm,' Mrs Dixon said to Finn.

'It's a good thing she is. We need someone to keep things going. I would never have believed Mrs Palmer-Farr would go to pieces the way she has. I hope it will be all right when she learns my brother is coming to take Lambert's place.'

'Miss Rosemary seemed to think it was a good temporary arrangement all round. He'll be needing work when he returns from his year in France and we have a three-day conference booked for the end of the month. We shall need two of you for that.'

'John is good. My parents have a guest house in Blackpool so we were brought up to work hard. My middle brother trained as a hotel manager. He owns a small hotel on the south coast.'

'It's in the family, then,' Mrs Dixon nodded.

'It is that. We have a group of businessmen for a long weekend before the conference?'

'Aye, we do. We'll all have to do our best. Right now though Miss Rosemary has asked me to get several rooms ready. Mr Gray has been here most days since Mr Palmer-Farr died. He's a relation of Mrs Palmer-Farr and he was a surgeon. He thinks there will be people coming from a distance for the funeral and they may want to stay. Miss Rosemary says some of them were at university with her

196

parents. She doesn't know them. In fact she looked bewildered by it all. 'Why can't we just lay him to rest in peace?' she said.'

Rosie was grateful for Lindsay's help and advice, in dealing with her mother.

'She depended on your father more than people realized,' he said. 'He was a brilliant academic, you know, but he was always modest about his own achievements. Languages came naturally to him. He gave Catherine the reassurance she needed right from the beginning of their friendship at university. She had never known security from her parents and Douglas gave her a sense of belonging and self worth. She was the business woman here but your father was the quiet strength and support she needed to succeed.'

'I have never seen my mother show emotion before,' Rosie said. 'She is distraught. She has no interest in the hotel. I don't know whether I'm making the right decisions or not.'

'You're doing well,' Lindsay assured her. 'We're all proud of the way you've coped, Rosemary. We know how you will miss your father too, but may I give you a little advice? Don't let your mother become too demanding, or too dependent on you. After the funeral she must get back to taking up the threads again. The hotel is her business.

However hard things are, however deep our grief, life does go on.'

'Yes,' Rosie said, meeting his eyes, 'I know.' No one knew that better than Uncle Lindsay, she thought. He had loved Ruth dearly but she had died just the same. Avril too had grieved for her mother. They understood how bereft she felt.

Rosie was astonished and dismayed at the crowd of people who attended the funeral. At the church all she saw was a blur of faces and they all seemed to be strangers. The Palmer-Farrs had been well known and respected in the area for generations and many of the local gentry and landowners were present. Douglas was a young man and his death was a shock to those who had been fellow students with him at boarding school or university. Many had been drawn to pay their last respects. Lindsay had expected this and had given Catherine a mild sedative to help her face the day's ordeal. Standing beside Rosemary she seemed calm and more like her usual competent self as she greeted the people who had come to Langton Tower for the lunch, which Chef Finn and his elder brother, John, had prepared.

Rosemary was relieved to see Megan and Steven. Her eyes widened when she saw Sam behind them with Tania. She had thought he was still in hospital. He looked pale in his dark suit with his arm in a sling. For a moment her mind went back to the day of the accident and she prayed he did not recall any details.

She didn't know he had insisted on getting home to attend the funeral, or that he wanted to hold her close and comfort her. He had never dreamt there would be so many people but he remembered Rosie's father had been well connected with the local gentry, and there were many other people he had never seen before.

'I've never seen so many toffs,' he muttered to Tania. 'We're out of place here.'

'I know,' she whispered back. 'Half the county seem to be here but Lindsay insisted we should come for the meal for Rosie's sake. He says she will need her own friends more than ever now. Anyway there's Avril and Dean over there. Look. Callum and Craig are with them. They must have come home for the funeral. What smart young men they are. Avril must be proud of her twin brothers.'

'Thank goodness,' Sam said. Most of the people there were his parents' generation but there were four or five well dressed younger men and he eyed them as they greeted Rosemary. He was unaware that he was as good looking and well dressed as any of them, even if he didn't have their air of assurance.

As they drew nearer his heart sank. Rosie looked so different in her smart black suit and court shoes. Her cloud of blonde curls was brushed neatly to frame her oval face. Her expression was tense and to Sam she seemed like a stranger, elegant, aloof, typical of the way Sam thought of the gentry. He didn't know how hard Rosie was struggling to keep her emotions under control to get through this ordeal of greeting everyone as her mother had insisted they must. As he drew close, Sam saw she was thinner and he thought he glimpsed a vulnerable look in her blue eyes as she met his gaze. His heart contracted. He longed to hold her and comfort her but her greeting was brief and polite and he thought he must have imagined that fleeting look of need. Only when she saw Tania did Rosie show any reaction.

'Save a seat for me at your table,' she whispered. Tania was startled. 'Are you sure?' she asked, casting an uncertain glance towards Catherine. Although he was not greeting everyone Lindsay was hovering nearby and he stepped forward.

'Yes, keep a seat for her, Tania. I will look after Catherine, Rosie has done more than her duty. She needs her own friends from now on.'

'Alex wanted to be here but he has an oral examination as part of his finals today,' Tania said.

'There will be other days.' Lindsay gave a faint smile and stepped back to his former position.

'They're lucky to have your father's help and support,' Tania said to Avril when she reached the table where she and Dean and the twins were already seated.

'Yes. He and Catherine are only half cousins but he is the only relative she has. He has been staying up here at Langton Tower for the past few days,' Avril said. 'He says Rosie has shown tremendous strength but he fears the reaction will set in once today is over. She has bottled up her own feelings. She has handled everything, including hiring the new chef, the staff and the funeral arrangements, but my father says she's as tense as a fiddle string.'

'Poor Rosie,' Tania sympathized. 'She will miss her father. They had grown very close.'

'How could anyone not love Rosie with her beaming smile and pretty face. I suppose he forgot the stiff upper lip and showed his feelings.' Avril said. 'Catherine has always given me the impression she considered it a weakness to show emotion but Rosie must often have longed for a little tenderness. No wonder she spent all her spare time at Bengairney with your family, Tania.'

'She's almost like a sister,' Tania agreed.

'What about your Grandfather Oliphant? I saw him at the funeral but I don't think he's here, is he?'

'No,' it was Megan on her other side who answered. 'This has been another big shock to him. First Mr Turner and now Mr Palmer-Farr. Almost all his working life has been spent between the two of them. He can't accept they're both gone while he's still here. It has upset him. I think I shall try to persuade him to come and live with us at Bengairney soon. Rosie has been wonderful at making sure he is all right each day but we can't expect her to go on looking out for him. She has her own problems and a business to run.'

When the meal was over Lindsay came over to their table.

'I shall stay here again tonight, Rosemary, so if you want to take the opportunity to escape to your own wee house this is as good a time as any.'

'Do you think so?' Rosie's eyes lit with relief, then dulled. 'But what about Mother? She has scarcely let me out of her sight since — since . . . '

'You have to make the break sometime for

both your sakes,' Lindsay said. 'I promise you your mother will be all right. Some of the people who are staying over are old friends. It will do her good to talk with them. I know where you are if she does need you but I'm sure she will be fine. You have your life to live too. We must all move on.' He looked around the table and smiled at Steven and Megan, changing the subject. 'Any news about the offer for Martinwold House yet?'

'Yes, good news,' Steven said. 'The buyer is an American. He is coming to work in Dumfries for an American company establishing some sort of manufacturing process over here.'

'And is the deal signed and sealed?'

'It will be by tomorrow,' Steven said. 'The solicitor asked twenty thousand. I thought he would frighten them away but the man has settled for nineteen thousand and that's without the five-acre paddock. He only expects to be here four or five years but he told the solicitor he wanted a top quality residence so that his wife and two children will be happy to live over here with him.' Steven cast an apologetic look at Rosemary.

'I'm pleased for you all,' she assured him.

'You're a good lassie,' Steven said. 'We haven't seen so much of you since you took over the gardening business. You must be sure and come to Bengairney more often.'

'We'll see,' she said with a wary look at Sam.

'I could stay at your cottage with you tonight, Rosie,' Tania offered when Lindsay left them.

'That would be a good idea,' Megan said. 'It is time we were leaving now. It will not be long to milking time, and the same for you too I suppose, Dean?'

'That's right. No rest for the wicked.'

'If I were you, Rosie, I'd take my father's advice and go down to your own house now,' Avril said.

'Yes, we'll come with you, shall we Sam?' Tania offered. Rosie looked at him.

'That's a good idea,' he said and stood up. 'I feel like a fish out of water amongst all your aristocratic friends.'

'I shall need my car in the morning to get to work. I'll get a lift home with Mum and Dad and bring it back, and a change of clothes,' Tania decided.

'That's OK,' Sam said, taking Rosie's hand. 'We'll walk down to the house. We'll see you later.' He was more than happy to be left alone with Rosie. If he was considering how he would get home himself he didn't mention it.

'How are you feeling, Sam?' Rosie asked

when they were alone. 'I didn't know you were out of hospital.'

'I'm fine. I got home last night. The doctor reckons I'm lucky I didn't lose my arm, or worse, so I'm thankful for that. Things were a bit of a blur for a while. I think they drugged me with painkillers.'

'Everything was a blur?' Rosie asked. Sam wondered why she looked relieved.

'Well I remember Lidia coming. I kept thinking the chainsaw was falling on top of me but I expect I was dreaming.' There were some pictures in his mind he would never forget but he couldn't be sure whether they were real or whether he had been hallucinating. He kept seeing a picture in his head of Rosie bending over him in a pink lace bra. He was fairly certain that bit had been real because he had overheard his mother and Tania discussing buying a new blouse to replace the one she had used to try and stop him bleeding. But had she said she loved him? If she said it, did she mean as a woman loves a man, or only as a childhood friend? One thing for sure, he intended to find out, but he must wait until she'd had time to come to terms with her father's death.

'I suppose shock and drugs can make things hazy,' Rosie said, feeling relieved.

'I'm the one who should be asking how you

are,' Sam said, releasing her hand while she unlocked the door of her cottage. He followed her inside. She went straight to the kitchen and filled the kettle and switched it on. 'So how are you really, Rosie? It must have been a terrible shock. Your father had never complained of being ill, had he?'

'It was a huge shock.' She shuddered. 'Oh Sam, I'm so relieved to get away from them all.' Her voice shook. She turned to the draining board and looked at the two mugs which had been washed and set to drain. She lifted them, then set one down. She cradled the other in her hands. 'This was Daddy's f-favourite. He-he always came for his m-morning coffee.' Her voice broke and she bit back a hard little sob. 'I miss him, Sam — oh so much.' Without warning the tears she had held in check for days now poured down her pale cheeks. Sam moved to her side and drew her into the curve of his one good arm, cradling her head against his chest. He let her weep unrestrainedly, knowing it was a release of pent up emotion. His fingers reached up to stroke the nape of her neck and the soft curls which nestled there. His heart filled with tenderness but he didn't speak. Instinct told him she needed this outpouring of grief and he was glad he was the one to be with her.

The tears subsided and she rubbed her face. 'I'm sorry,' she gulped. 'S-so sorry, Sam. It was just seeing Daddy's mug sitting there waiting for him. He'll never use it again.'

'You loved him, Rosie. It wouldn't be natural if you didn't grieve.'

'I know b-but I've made your best white shirt d-damp. I didn't mean to cry in public.'

'Oh Rosie.' Sam's arm tightened and his voice was gruff. 'I'm not public, my wee love. I'm glad you can share your tears with me. That's what old friends are for, to share the sorrows as well as joys, and we are very old friends, aren't we?' He lifted the arm in its sling and put a finger under her chin so that he could look into her tear-drenched eyes. She nodded, sniffed and strove for a smile.

'I'm better now. Thank you, Sam.' She found her handkerchief and blew her nose and wiped away the remaining tears. 'I must get out of these clothes. Mother insisted we must both wear black but I don't think Daddy would have been bothered.'

'You go and change while I make us some tea. Tania will be back soon. I ought to have asked her to bring me a change of clothes then we could take a walk around your gardens and you can show me what you're doing. Lindsay says you've built another greenhouse.'

'Yes. It's smaller so I can afford to keep it heated in winter. There's nothing to beat the natural sunlight, at least in my opinion, but commercial growers can't depend on the weather.' Rosie knew she was chattering. There was no need to fill the silence with Sam. She grimaced. 'I'll go and change.'

Tania returned from Bengairney with a basket of food, a can of milk and a change of clothes for Sam, as well as her own clothes for work in the morning. Although they all enjoyed the cup of tea which Sam had brewed, Rosie couldn't sit still.

'I'd like to see Paul and find out what's been going on in the gardens,' she said, 'then I wondered whether we should walk down to Papa Oliphant's? We could take him some of this food your mother has sent, Tania.'

'That's a good idea. Maybe we could stay a wee while and make sure he eats something. Mum is really worried. She's thinking of making our sitting room into a bedroom and asking him to live with us.'

'But he loves Honeysuckle Cottage, and he comes here most days in fine weather.'

'I know. Mum appreciates the way you keep an eye on him, Rosie, but she says we can't expect you to keep on doing that now he's getting frail. You already have so much responsibility.'

'There's nothing frail about his mind. He's always alert and he has a fund of stories to tell. I'd miss his company and his advice, you know.'

'Well I don't suppose Mum will get round to doing anything for a while. She'll need to wait until this useless brother of mine is back to work.' She nudged Sam's chest with her elbow and grinned.

'I made the tea. I'm not useless, am I Rosie?'

'Of course not, Sam.' She summoned a smile in response to their familiar banter. 'And it will not be long before Alex is home to help.'

★ ★ ★

It was rare for John Oliphant to get depressed but the death of both his former employers within the year made him consider his own demise. He was surprised and delighted to see the three young folk walking up his garden path. Tania was carrying a basket. He guessed it would be food. He hadn't felt like eating all day but an hour later the smell of Megan's bacon and egg pie wafted from the oven and he found himself eating more of it than his young companions.

'We had a three-course lunch,' Sam told

him. 'It was excellent, especially the roast beef. It was lucky your young chef was able to get his brother here to help, Rosie.'

'Yes, I hope Mother approves of him.' Her mouth firmed. 'He would have liked to prepare a more elaborate menu but I insisted there must be nothing ostentatious. That was not Daddy's style. He would not have wanted it, even though some of the local gentry were there. Chef John can show off his talents some other time.'

'Everyone thought you had done a good job,' Tania assured her, then changed the subject as she saw Rosie's mouth tremble. She looked at her grandfather. 'Mother will be glad to know you have eaten something, Grandpa,' she said with a smile. 'But I think we should go as soon as we have washed the dishes. You look tired out.'

'Aye, I shall sleep better tonight,' John Oliphant agreed with a heavy sigh. 'Ye'll take care o' yourself, lassie?' He looked at Rosemary. 'I'll be back up at the gardens tomorrow. Will ye be there?'

'I intend to be,' Rosie said. 'It's a busy time of year so there's a lot to do. Uncle Lindsay says I must get on with my own life,' she added, 'but I've never seen Mother go to pieces like this before. I can't turn my back if she needs me.'

'Lindsay Gray is a wise man, lassie. You follow his advice.'

'Are you going to give me a lift home, Tania, or can I cadge a sleep on your sofa, Rosie?' Sam asked, as the three of them walked towards Langton Tower and Rosie's cottage.

'You can use my sofa if you think you would get any sleep,' Rosie said.

'Yes, you do that, big brother,' Tania said. 'I'll drop you off at home when I go to work in the morning. It's not as though you're much good for anything if I did take you home anyway,' she said with a grin, and ducked out of the way of Sam's good arm.

Rosie slept soundly for the first time since her father's death and she wakened early, feeling ready to work. She climbed over the low windowsill of her bedroom and ran down the outside stone stairs, which had once provided the access to the hayloft over the stables. She didn't want to disturb Sam in the living room. The world looked newly washed and sparkling in the clear morning light. Rosie breathed in. The sky was wreathed in silvery wisps of cloud like ripples of sand on a clear blue sea, and she marvelled at the vastness and beauty of it. Her gaze moved to the long line of the Galloway hills, still purple along the skyline, in contrast with the bright green of the sheltered pastures lower down. She stretched her arms high above her head with a sense of exhilaration. It was good to be alive with the promise of a beautiful summer's day ahead. Her beloved father would never see such beauty again. Was it wrong to be happy when he could no longer share her joy? Her eyes were drawn again to the morning sky and it was almost as though she felt her father's presence. In her heart she knew he would not have wanted her to go on grieving. She had once heard him say people didn't grieve for the person who had passed on, so much as for their own loss. It was true, and it was selfish in a way. Perhaps he was right. She was here and alive and she was young and healthy. As Uncle Lindsay had said, life does go on. She was blessed with her friends, Tania and Sam, and she was at ease with them again, the way they had always been when they were children — well perhaps not quite as a child with Sam. She lifted her small chin with an air of resolution. She would never forget her father, and she would miss him often, but she would live her life as he would have wished, doing her work and making a success.

She didn't hear Sam come out in his stocking feet until he spoke.

'You're up early, Rosie. How did you get

out here without wakening me?'

'I came down the old stone steps.' She pointed to the corner of the building. 'It could be a lovely house if I built a balcony and extended it to use the whole of the stables but developing the gardens must come first.'

'It would be a family house then, though,' Sam said. 'Do you see yourself living here forever, Rosie?'

'I don't know.' She hesitated. 'Who knows what the future holds?'

'None of us, I suppose,' Sam said. He looked at her. 'You will remember Rosie, I am your . . . your friend. I will always be there for you whenever you need me. You're not alone.'

'Thank you, Sam.'

'You saved my life. If you hadn't been there . . . ' He shuddered.

'Lidia would have helped you. Shock made her panic.'

'I doubt if Lidia ever helped anybody. Mother says she didn't wait, or telephone, to see what had happened to me. Did you hear? But no, how could you with so much happening here,' he added. 'Lidia left her flat straight after. She didn't give notice to her employer. According to Tania's hairdressing friend she's gone back north without leaving a forwarding address.'

'She was in a panic at the sight of so much blood, but isn't that a bit drastic?'

'I think she knew I meant it when I said I would never marry her. I'm not saying she meant to cut my arm off, but she could be both spiteful and neurotic sometimes.'

Rosie was struggling to take in the implications of Sam's news. 'So you — you don't mind that she's gone for good?'

'It's a relief. Whenever I tried to end our relationship she threatened to harm herself. I never knew whether she meant it or not. Dean thought she was being dramatic. He reckoned she hadn't the guts to risk hurting herself. Anyway I've learned my lesson; it takes more than a beautiful face, or a great dancer, to make a genuine and trustworthy person.'

'I'm glad you've no regrets, Sam.'

'I came out to say we're leaving soon. Tania is getting her things together.'

'So early? But you haven't had any breakfast. I'll cook some — ' Sam stepped closer and laid a finger on her lips.

'We haven't any milk left. We left it at Grandpa's.'

'Oh gosh! I forgot about milk. I can get some from the hotel kitchens. You must — '

'No,' Sam said softly. 'Tania will grab something to eat when she drops me off at home. Promise to come down and see us soon?'

'Y-yes, I'll try.'

'Good.' Sam leaned forward and kissed her cheek. He cursed his clumsy arm in its sling but he stretched out his free hand and drew her closer. His green eyes were serious, searching her face before he bent his head and brushed her mouth with gentle delibera-tion. 'Don't forget. Come soon, Rosie,' he whispered.

Tania had been about to call a greeting but she stepped back inside the cottage, sensing this was not the time to interrupt.

★ ★ ★

Lindsay Gray was the only confidant Catherine had so it was natural for her to discuss the future and her situation with him.

'Douglas and I settled our affairs when we put the gardens into Rosemary's name but we never dreamt of anything like this happening,' she added on a strangled sob. 'We are both well provided for financially. It is Douglas himself we shall miss. I never realized how much I depended on him.'

Lindsay told Avril this when he returned home. He knew she was concerned for Rosemary having to cope with Catherine on her own. 'You took care of me and the boys when Mum died,' she said, 'but Rosie and her mother have never been close. She is just getting going with the gardens.'

'Rosemary is intelligent and she's a hard worker. She is doing an excellent job. She loves her work and she seems to have a talent, a sort of instinct. I think she will do well and Douglas has made provision for her. It is her father's love and his company she'll miss.'

A few weeks later Avril and the children were visiting Granny Caraford. It was a Sunday afternoon and Megan and Steven arrived too.

'How is Rosie managing?' Hannah asked. 'She was almost one of your family when she was younger, wasn't she Megan?'

'She still is. She and Tania have become close friends since they've grown up, but we can't help being anxious about her now Douglas is not there to give his support. My father is convinced she will make the gardens into a thriving business. She has extended the cultivated area. He reckons they would be worth a tidy sum already with the greenhouses and her cottage and the orchards, if she ever needs to sell.'

'My father agrees with Mr Oliphant,' Avril said. 'He is impressed by the way Rosemary is planning and improving what she has. She is planning ahead too.'

'Apart from the hotel business I don't suppose there's much else left of the Palmer-Farr estates,' Steven remarked.

'Douglas inherited some investments along with Langton Tower,' Avril said. 'They brought in a moderate income so Rosie will have that. He still owned the buildings and a couple of paddocks from Home Farm so she will have the rent from the three Home Farm cottages and the farmhouse, then there's the little lodge at the back entrance to Langton Tower. It may not make her wealthy but it will be a cushion against a bad season. It's not just about money, though. I worry how Rosie will cope with her mother's overbearing personality and her ambitions to marry her to one of the gentry? My father thinks Rosie is more in need of love than her mother's approval.'

'You're right, money is not everything,' Steven said. 'We all need someone to love us.' He glanced at Megan.

'I'm not worrying about Rosie now I know she will not be dependent on Catherine financially,' Megan said. 'It's the mention of inflation and what the subject does to my own family.' She rolled her eyes at Steven. He smiled across at her.

'We've had a few disagreements about

interest rates,' he agreed. 'It's hard to know which path to take when we don't have a crystal ball, but we had many a struggle when we began farming. So long as we're together, we shall pull through.' He winked at Avril. 'I'd never have managed without Megan but I can't tell her so too often or she might get above herself.'

'Not much fear o' that,' Megan chuckled, 'not with three men in the house.'

'Is Alex home from college now then?' Avril asked, relieved the atmosphere had lightened again.

'He'll be home next week,' Steven said.

Megan related Avril's news about Rosie to Tania and Sam later that evening. Tania was delighted to hear Rosie would have some security, but Sam sat silent, digesting this latest development. Initially he had been more thrilled than anyone at the possibility of his family owning Martinwold but the full implications of having a huge debt to repay had made him realize things were not going to be easy. Would he ever be able to get married? Rosemary not only owned her own home, she was building up a business, and it seemed she would own other property now, as well as having a private income. It might not be a huge fortune in the Palmer-Farr circle but to Sam it represented a huge obstacle between the two of them. As a youngster Samuel had been aware his family were considered low down the social scale as far as Catherine Palmer-Farr was concerned, even though Rosie had been like an extension to his family.

8

Megan made sure Rosie knew she was as welcome at Bengairney as she had always been. Like Lindsay she was afraid Catherine might make too many demands on her only child. She telephoned several times inviting Rosie for Sunday lunch, using the excuse that she would be grateful if she could give her father a lift. Rosie was always happy to help John Oliphant after the years of loving care she had received from him and Chrissie. She enjoyed these Sunday visits, now that Lidia had vanished from the scene but Catherine had always resented the ease with which she fitted into the Caraford family and she began to claim her daughter's company in a way she had never done before. The season was moving on and the hotel was busy but Rosie was concerned about her mother's apparent lack of interest in the business which had once taken up all her time and attention.

'It's as though a light has gone out,' Rosie explained to Megan. 'I can't replace Daddy but Mother seems to need me in a way she has never done before.'

'I understand, dear,' Megan said, but she

was worried that Catherine Palmer-Farr was becoming too possessive. In the past she had put the hotel and her own ambitions before everything, even the loveable child who had so craved a mother's love and approval. Megan wondered whether Catherine had genuine regrets or whether she was being selfish.

Avril was also aware of the situation at Langton Tower and she vowed to do something about it. She made her plans for Christmas well ahead, with Lindsay and Dean's full approval, then she issued her invitation so that Catherine could have no last minute excuses.

'Oh I'm not sure,' Catherine said. 'Sir Henry Braebourne has invited Rosemary Lavender and me to lunch a couple of times since Douglas died. It is so kind of him and his sons, but he is a widower so he understands how I feel.'

'And you think my father doesn't?' Avril asked, knowing how Lindsay still grieved for her mother. 'I'm thinking of Rosie too. She deserves some young company at Christmas and the boys will be home.'

'Oh very well then,' Catherine said ungraciously.

★ ★ ★

221

At Martinwold and Bengairney things were changing. Alex had finished at college and passed all his exams. He was working between the two farms until Sam could move into the old Martinwold farmhouse and take over the dairy when Peter, the dairyman, left for Australia with his family.

Bengairney was a rented farm so they were not allowed to make major changes without the Laird's permission. Alex was frustrated and impatient, knowing that some of his ideas would have been more economical now they were running both farms.

'Cow cubicles are a tremendous saving on bedding,' he insisted, 'even for young stock. At college the figures — '

'I don't need to hear the theory,' Steven said. 'You can make anything fit an argument on paper. College lecturers don't spend their own capital or do the work.'

'I still think the Laird should have agreed to convert the byre to a milking parlour if he insists we must keep on milking cows at Bengairney, or give up the tenancy,' Alex argued.

'I think he is surprised we have bought Martinwold, and that we are keeping both farms. I can see his point of view in some respects,' Steven said. 'Bengairney is leased as a dairy farm. If we stop using the byre and the dairy they would deteriorate. Where would he be if we have to give up the tenancy? He would need to spend money on improvements before he could let to a new tenant.'

'But we're not giving up the tenancy,' Alex objected.

'That's what we hope, but only time will tell. If the Laird sees we are continuing to keep up our standard he may agree to some changes. The new land agent takes over next spring so he may have ideas for improvements.'

'We should count our blessings,' Megan said, joining the discussion. 'We got a better price for the cottage from Archie Pattinson than we expected, and we never thought Martinwold House would make so much.'

'It wouldn't have done if that American hadn't come along at the right time,' Steven said.

'No wonder Natalie and her husband are so furious about her father's will.'

'Pete and his wife and the two children are leaving for Australia next week. I've arranged to move into the farmhouse on Wednesday.'

'We shall have to sort out some furniture for you, Sam,' Megan said.

'I'll take my own bed. I've agreed to buy one or two odds and ends from Pete. I shall only use the kitchen and my bedroom.'

'You'll need a bit of comfort,' Megan protested.

'Dean and I never had much furniture when I lived there as a student,' Sam said.

'I think your father and I should buy you a small freezer and then I shall know you have something to eat. You can come home for your Sunday dinner and bring your washing.'

'Thanks Mum.' Sam grinned at her. 'That would save me buying a washing machine.'

'I'll bet you'll not be there five minutes before you're wanting Mum's settee,' Alex teased.

'He might get it if I can persuade your grandfather to move into the wee sitting room.'

'You'll be lucky.' Sam grinned. 'He was dead against moving the last time you mentioned it. He thinks Rosie couldn't manage the gardens without him.'

'He knows Rosemary is capable enough, but everyone likes to be needed,' Steven chided. 'You'll both be old one day and you'll not want anybody telling you what to do. Come to that, neither of you like being told what to do now, but we shall all need to pull together.'

★ ★ ★

Christmas was drawing near and Avril telephoned Rosie to check they were still coming.

'Mum is trying to back out. I was dreading Christmas without Daddy and I wanted to see Callum and Craig again. I'm afraid we've had a quarrel over it. I refuse to go to the Braebournes, even if they ask us, which they have not done yet. They're not my friends.'

'I suspected this might happen. Don't worry Rosie, I'll speak to her,' Avril promised.

'You had no business making arrangements without consulting me first,' Catherine said when she realized Avril had already spoken to Rosie.

'I invited you both ages ago and Rosie is no longer a child. She has a life, of her own.'

'She is my only child. I need her,' Catherine objected. Avril wanted to say it was a pity Catherine had not realized that when Rosie had needed her mother's love as a child.

'My father will be disappointed if you don't come. He cancelled his visit to Africa when Douglas died. He has been offered another posting and will be leaving in the middle of January. What better time than Christmas to have a gathering of his friends and family. The Carafords will be here to wish him well.'

'The Carafords?' For years Catherine had

barely noticed that Rosemary spent Christmas at Bengairney with the Carafords. Now she was determined to keep her daughter away from them. She had forgotten Avril's mother, Ruth, and Megan Caraford, had been close friends. Hannah Caraford was Avril's step grandmother. They were all connected.

Catherine complained that she had been manipulated but Rosie was grateful for Avril's intervention. Christmas proved a happier time than she had thought possible without her father. Six-year-old Anne and two-year-old William were overwhelmed by so many people but they soon overcame their shyness and were dashing around showing everyone the toys which Santa Claus had brought. Their excitement increased at the sight of the dining room table decked with sparkling crackers and brightly patterned napkins. Their innocent joy was infectious, especially with Tania and Rosie who both loved children.

'It's a shame most of you need to go home in time for the milking,' Avril said. 'I feel more like sleeping after eating so much.'

'I think we all do. It was a lovely meal, Avril,' Megan said. 'Everything was delicious and you're so well organized. Ruth would have been truly proud of you, and of your children.' Dean saw the shadows in his wife's eyes at mention of her mother.

'Shall we have a short walk to see the cows, lads?' he asked looking at Struan, Samuel and Alex. 'It will stretch our legs and shake the dinner down before we need to work.'

'We'll come with you,' chorused Callum and Craig together.

'We knew how to milk when we used to visit Bengairney,' Craig reminded them with a grin.

'Cows! Is that all you people think about?' Catherine demanded.

'Dear Catherine, cows are the chief interest for most dairy farmers,' Lindsay said with amusement. 'They can't shut down the byres like you shut down the hotel, you know. The cows still have to be milked whatever day it is.'

'It's ridiculous, going home at half past three in the afternoon. We should have had an evening dinner.'

'But the children would have missed all the fun,' Avril protested.

'Of course they would,' Rosie said, annoyed by her mother's attitude. 'They have added to the joy. Anyway it would have been very late by the time everyone finished milking and got here.'

'You talk as though you're a farmer too,'

Catherine snapped. 'It's bad enough you choosing to be a gardener when you could have had a good career.'

'Rosie knows the farm routine well enough after the years she spent at Bengairney,' Steven said with a laugh. 'It's a hard life, isn't it lassie?'

'Maybe it is, but it's a good life,' Rosie said, smiling back at him.

'You don't need to leave, Catherine,' Lindsay said. 'You can stay and talk to the boys and me, and Granny Caraford is staying overnight.'

'That's a good idea,' Sam said, turning back from following Dean outside. 'You could come back with us, Rosie. I'll drive you home after milking. You said you had never seen a milking parlour working. Now's your chance.' Catherine opened her mouth to object but Avril said, 'That's a splendid idea. I'll lend you some old clothes, Rosie.' Rosie flashed her a look of gratitude but Catherine's displeasure was obvious. Tania made huge eyes at Avril behind everyone's back and almost caused Avril to burst out laughing.

'Whew,' Rosie breathed as she and Tania followed Avril to the kitchen to help fill the dishwasher and tidy up the remains of the meal before the boys returned. 'Thanks, Avril. I'm sorry Mother has cast a damper on things. I can't decide whether she is missing Daddy or wanting people to feel sorry for her, but it's been a wonderful day. Anne and William are gorgeous children.'

'Mmm, me too,' Tania said. 'Thanks for including Struan.'

'He is almost part of the family,' Avril said. 'Any word of a wedding date yet?'

'No. I don't think Mrs Ritchie wants him to get married at all. He was half serious when he suggested we should go to Gretna Green and tell her afterwards. I'd agree but I couldn't bear the thought of living with her in that huge dark house and there are no cottages vacant at present.'

Outside, Alex and the twins walked together, reminiscing about old times and catching up with events in their lives. Dean and Sam strolled ahead with Struan.

'I wish I'd made the old farmhouse a bit more comfortable,' Sam said. 'Rosie will not be very impressed when she goes back with me this afternoon.'

'Does it still have the cooker in the kitchen?'

'Mr Turner had it changed to a new oil Esse two years ago.'

'The kitchen will be warm then and Rosie will be in the milking parlour most of the time.'

'Mmm, but I can't help thinking about the high and mighty folks who were at the funeral.'

'They weren't Rosie's friends. They are not even her mother's — merely people who knew Rosie's father. Anyway, Sam, don't make the same mistake as I made, thinking you're not good enough. My pride almost ruined things for Avril and me. There's not a trace of snobbery in Avril's father and he's as good as the Palmer-Farrs. He and Avril admire Rosie but they worry about her mother's possessiveness. She needs friends like you for support — or am I right in thinking there's more than friendship?' Dean stopped and turned to look Sam in the eye. Colour mounted in Sam's cheeks but he held Dean's gaze.

'We've been friends since we were children. I admire her determination to lead her own life, rather than do what her mother thinks she should do. She's making a success and I'm proud of her.'

'That's not what I meant, Samuel Caraford, and you know it.'

'All right. I love her. I want to marry her and keep her with me all the time,' Sam admitted. 'But I don't know whether she loves me in that way. Even if she did I can't afford to keep a wife the way things are now and they're not likely to get any better for years.'

'I suppose you'll all need to ca' canny for a bit,' Dean agreed, 'Avril and I are relieved you've got Lidia out of your system. You'll have chance to find out how Rosie feels now.'

'Lidia has been out of my system for a long time, but I couldn't get her out of my life.'

'Forget about women. Come on and see my latest heifer. She's a beauty and she's coming to the calving any day now. She's out of the calf Mr Turner gave us as a wedding present.'

Sam persuaded Alex to take a lift home with his parents so that he could use their little car for himself and Rosie. They were both aware of her mother's disapproval as she climbed in beside him.

'The milking parlour is not like the byre at all, much easier on the back for one thing. The cows' udders are about eye level,' Sam said with an exultant grin. 'The worst bit is if they lift their tails; you can get the sort of shower nobody appreciates.'

'Now you tell me!' Rosie said, laughing. 'I guessed as much from what Avril said.'

'I'll find you a waterproof smock. I'm glad you're coming with me, Rosie.'

'So am I. It was good of Avril to invite us all. Mother is missing my father more than she expected. I miss him too. But it's no reason to make everyone else miserable. I was ashamed of her waspish remarks today. Thank goodness Uncle Lindsay understands her.'

'Don't worry, Rosie.' Sam reached out and patted her hands where they lay clasped in her lap. 'I'm afraid she disapproved of you coming with me, though.'

'Yes, no doubt I shall hear about it tomorrow.' She smiled at him. 'But for now it will be like old times and the milking at Bengairney. I always loved the animals, and especially the cows all lined up in their own stalls in the byre. In the winter it was always warm in there.'

'Mmm, well, the milking parlour is anything but warm in winter,' Sam warned. 'But it takes a lot less time to milk the same number of cows, even on my own, so it has its advantages.'

Rosie saw what he meant when she followed him into the large shed which housed the milking parlour and a collecting area where the cows gathered prior to milking. There were three steps down into a concrete pit. On either side of the pit were zigzag bars and tucked beneath a sort of shelf there was a row of large glass jars with the tubes and teat clusters attached, ready for putting onto the cows' udders. At the other end of the pit three more steps led up to a large concrete area where the cows were beginning to gather.

'Goodness, I see it is different to the byre. No buckets to empty? Are all the cows loose? Do they wander around at will?'

'They sleep in the cubicles in the adjoining shed and they can get up and stretch and walk around when they feel like it. They all feed at the same time through the metal barriers at the far end. We put out the silage twice a day, but some go for an extra feed if there is any left. Most of them go to the same cubicle to sleep just as they used to have their own stall in the byre. We're all creatures of habit, if you ask me,' Sam said with a grin.

'It's amazing. Do the cows come into the parlour of their own accord?' Rosie asked, delighted she had been able to come and that Sam seemed pleased to explain everything.

'Most of them come forward once they've been through a couple of times. Some of the heifers can be difficult at first. They all stand at an angle with their rumps against the zigzag bar next to the pit. That's why this one is called a herringbone parlour. Each one has a feed trough. That encourages them to come in and stand still while they eat their cake. Not all parlours have troughs. This was Mr Turner's choice and I think he was right.'

'Does the milk come down into these jars?' Rosie asked, touching several as she walked along counting eight on either side.

'Yes. We can see how much milk each cow has given, and the milk recorder can take a sample from the jar when she comes to record the yields and quality. When the cow finishes milking we release the milk and it flows to the refrigerated tank in the dairy.'

'No wonder you find it faster and easier than milking in the byre,' Rosie said. 'There's no big buckets of milk to carry to the dairy as your mother used to do. But you don't get to know the cows.'

'You learn to recognize them all as individuals in time. I always walk round them in the cubicles before I go to bed, especially if I suspect one may be on heat or if one seems unwell.'

'So you still need to be an observant stockman, and keep your eyes open for anything unusual, as your father used to keep telling us when we were children.'

'You remember all that, then, Rosie?' Sam asked with amusement. 'My father always said you were the best little farmer of the lot of us.'

'I loved being in the byre with him,' Rosie said. 'He was always patient at explaining things. I knew the names of all the cows at

Bengairney,' she said.

'If you come often you will soon know the names of these cows too,' Sam said.

'I'll come if you want me to,' Rosie said, 'at least when I'm not too busy with the gardens.'

'Of course I want you to come, Rosie. Mr Turner modernized the parlour while Alex was working here as a student. It was a big upheaval, but I'm glad Mr Turner did it then. We could never have afforded to update it ourselves.' He sighed. 'There'll be no spare cash for anything for years.'

'It will be worth it, Sam,' Rosie said. 'Your family will own Martinwold and that's what Mr Turner wanted. You and Alex will be proud of yourselves one day.'

'I hope so,' Sam said, looking her in the eye, 'but we may have to make some sacrifices in the meantime — even in our personal lives.'

'Happiness doesn't depend on money, Sam,' Rosie said, surprising him by stepping up close to the rails to put one of the milk units on the cow next to him. She knew how to put the milking machines on the udders but instead of bending low as they did in the byre she had to struggle to reach high enough now.

'I'd forgotten how small you are,' Sam said

with a smile. 'I'd need to stand you on a duckboard if you were here every day.' He reached round about her to nudge a cow a little closer and make things a bit easier. Rosie was conscious of his breath against her cheek and the hardness of his body against her back, but Sam was concentrating on the cows and she thought he was oblivious to their closeness until he said, 'Your hand is trembling, Rosemary Lavender. You were never nervous with the cows before.'

'I'm not nervous with them now,' she said.

'No?' he gave her a sideways look and cocked one dark brow at her. 'Then why . . . ? You can't possibly be nervous with me. I'd never hurt you, Rosie.' His voice was deep and husky.

'I know.' The air was charged with tension as they stared at each other. Rosie was almost glad when a cow kicked off the milking unit and Sam had to hurry to grab it and put it back on. They both relaxed and Sam teased her about her five foot three inches to his five foot eleven. She was holding the sprayer which they used to wash the cows' teats before putting on the milking units and she raised it and aimed it at Sam's face. He gasped in surprise, then chuckled, remembering how often they had played tricks on each other when they were young. But they were not children now.

'Just you wait until I'm finished and you'll pay for that!' he threatened with a grin. Rosie's heart warmed, knowing he was enjoying their old teasing camaraderie as much as she was, but she saw there was more than childish mischief in Sam's green eyes and her heartbeat quickened.

* * *

Rosie and Paul were meticulous about cleaning and washing out the greenhouses and preparing tools and pots for the spring, turning over compost and digging in manure to enrich the soil for spring planting. They had cultivated another acre and a half of grass paddock and hoped the winter frost would help break down the clods to a finer tilth by the time spring arrived, but shorter days meant Rosie had more time for leisure.

Sam had left her in no doubt that he enjoyed her company since she had gone with him to the milking at Martinwold so she often went down to join him when she was free and every Saturday evening he collected her to go to a dance or a film. His visits soon increased to mid week as well. Sam was honest and sincere. It did not occur to him to visit in secret or to hide his car from view so Catherine noticed his frequent visits and their deepening friendship. She expressed her disapproval to Rosie, and then her anger.

'You've always disapproved of me spending time with the Carafords, Mother,' Rosie reasoned, after a longer harangue than usual. 'I enjoy seeing the farm and the animals at Martinwold, just as I did at Bengairney.'

'Things are different now,' Catherine snapped. 'You're a young woman with independent means.' Rosie choked on a laugh. Is that what owning a few acres of land and her cottage made her?

'Then treat me like a woman,' she said, still smothering a grin.

Catherine was determined to prevent any developments between Rosie and Sam. She invited Sir Henry Braebourne and his sons to lunch with increasing regularity. Rosemary grew exasperated. Catherine issued veiled threats; Rosie ignored them. She didn't want to hurt her mother but when she was with Sam she was happier than she had dreamed possible after the shock of losing her father. They were back into their old easy camaraderie, able to tease and laugh together, as well as discussing the serious world of business which affected them both. They were never bored with each other as Rosie was in the company of her mother's guests. She avoided them whenever possible but Catherine claimed they were old friends of her father and it was her duty to help her entertain them.

The more Rosie endured her mother's dinner parties the more she appreciated Sam's company but she craved more than friendship. She often sensed he was holding back too when he kissed her goodnight. Did he want a more passionate relationship? Rosie trembled at the thought. How should she let him know it was what she wanted too? She could never throw herself at him, as Lidia had done. Rosie had never had a serious relationship so she felt naïve and inexperienced, but she knew her feelings for Sam ran deep and true. Alone in bed at night she wondered whether she would be able to control her own emotions if Sam wanted more. Could she resist if he wanted to make love to her as Struan and Tania had done? It was different for them; they were engaged and Struan could afford to get married. Tania admitted he was becoming impatient to make her his wife; his mother's attitude and hypochondria were driving him to consider desperate measures.

'All we want is a cottage to call our own,' Tania said, 'but it would have to be within reasonable distance of the farm.' Rosie sympathized, but she reasoned with Tania too.

'It sounds as though Struan's mother only considers herself,' she agreed, 'but your parents would be hurt if you present them with a fait accompli. You're their only daughter, Tania. Surely they will want to see you married in church with your friends around?'

'I suppose so,' Tania agreed. 'But Struan and I love each other so much. We want to be together all the time. His father wants to move out of the farm and let Struan take the responsibility. Why can't his mother see that and be happy for us?'

'Maybe she's ill in her mind.'

★　★　★

Rosie attended many of her mother's lunch and dinner parties but she refused to give up her Saturday evenings. Catherine knew she was being unreasonable but she believed Rosie lacked ambition and needed her guidance. Neither appeals nor threats had any effect. Rosie was independent and enjoyed earning her own living.

'I want to prove I can make a success of the gardens,' she told the solicitor when he called her in to discuss changes he had made to her small portfolio of stocks and shares. 'Daddy had faith in me. He knew I could do it.

Meanwhile I want the income to be reinvested. One day I may need the capital.' She had not expected to inherit anything more than the gardens and she would far rather have had her father's company, his quiet humour and his wisdom.

The solicitor respected her wishes and told Catherine she should be proud of her daughter but Catherine was dismayed and angry. Rosie had not even consulted her. She had no influence over her any more, and even less over the company she chose.

Catherine felt she was making sacrifices by forcing herself to entertain some of the local families with eligible sons. She had always felt inferior in the company of some of the county's more exalted families with their long pedigrees and deep roots. Her ambition was that Rosemary Lavender should become one of them. Her daughter must do better than marry a working farmer.

'For goodness' sake, Mother, I'm a working girl myself,' Rosie said in exasperation after one of her mother's lectures. 'I get my hands dirty too. I would never be considered wealthy in comparison to the families you invite to dinner. Their sons and daughters only get dirty when they go hunting in the rain.'

'Well you're far too good for Sam Caraford

and his ilk,' Catherine snapped. 'Some day you will own all of this,' she spread her arms wide, indicating the hotel. 'The antique furniture alone is worth a small fortune.'

'Oh Mother! Don't talk like that. Isn't it bad enough losing Daddy? Anyway I don't want to inherit the hotel.'

'Perhaps you don't but other people will. I have seen the admiration in the eyes of several of the young men who have been to dinner with us. You're very pretty when you make an effort with your appearance.'

'Don't talk rubbish.' Rosie laughed at the idea. She paid scant attention to her appearance, apart from keeping up a six-weekly hair appointment with Tania's friend, Betty. Catherine's irritation increased when John Oliphant became ill. Rosemary insisted on seeing him two or three times a day. He had developed a chesty cough and Rosie made a point of taking him soup and eating her own lunch with him. His condition had grown worse when Rosie arrived at Honeysuckle Cottage on Thursday morning. She didn't want to leave him alone. Catherine had seen her drive off in the van but when she had not returned by late afternoon she walked through the gardens to ask Paul Keir where she was.

'Rosie is worried about Mr Oliphant,' Paul

told her. 'She went down to his cottage. She said he was very short of breath yesterday.'

'It is not her business to care for Mr Oliphant,' Catherine snapped. 'I wish to see her when she returns.'

'Er — yes, but we shall be leaving soon. Perhaps you could telephone her at Honeysuckle Cottage if you need her?' Catherine scowled. She didn't need Rosie; she resented her lavishing so much time on an old man. She had arranged a Friday luncheon party for the Braebournes and she intended to make sure Rosie would be there. Catherine was so used to organizing it didn't occur to her to consult Rosemary beforehand. Twice she had refused to change her schedule to attend, but still Catherine steamed ahead, determined to get her daughter attached to one or other of the local gentry, ignoring her lack of respect for most of them.

Rosemary persuaded John Oliphant to go to bed when he could barely manage a few sips of soup. His breathing was laboured so she had propped him up with a mound of pillows. While he dozed she telephoned Megan at Bengairney. There was no reply. Megan was boiling kettles to help Alex thaw out frozen pipes in one of the sheds so that the young cattle could get water.

'I'm worried,' Rosie said with relief when

Megan answered her third call, still catching her breath after running in from the yard. 'I wanted to phone for the doctor but he forbade me.'

'I'll come and see him,' Megan said at once. 'I do appreciate everything you do for him, Rosie. He can be stubborn and independent but you handle him so well.'

'He has gone to bed without any argument. I'm sure he needs the doctor.'

Megan agreed as soon as she saw her father. She telephoned the surgery without his permission. Doctor Burns was out on a call but said he would visit as soon as he could. Rosie and Megan waited together but it was late afternoon before the doctor came.

'He is adamant he does not want to go to hospital,' he said when he returned to the living room. 'I think he is afraid, but we may have to override his wishes if he gets worse. He ought not to be left alone. I will call in again after evening surgery. Meanwhile could one of you ladies collect this prescription for him?'

'I'll go,' Rosie offered when the doctor had gone. 'Sam said his father was selling bullocks at the market today. Does that mean you are needed at the milking?'

'I said I would start the milking with Alex. We've been thawing out pipes most of the

244

day.' Megan stifled a yawn and Rosie thought how tired she looked. 'My father is more important.'

'I could stay with him after I've been for this prescription?' Rosie offered.

'I'd be truly grateful, Rosie. I'll come back as soon as Steven gets home.'

They persuaded John to take the medicine but he seemed to have difficulty getting enough breath to swallow and there was an alarming rattle in his chest.

'He's getting worse,' Megan said. 'Are you sure you feel able to stay, Rosemary dear?'

'Yes. I'll telephone if — if he deteriorates. Unless the medicine can work magic I think we shall need to get Dr Burns back sooner, though.'

'I agree.' Megan was reluctant to leave but she knew Rosemary was sensible and reliable. Rosie loved John Oliphant as though he had been her own grandfather and she was glad Megan trusted her, but her heart was heavy. Every instinct told her he was getting worse.

When she returned Megan agreed at once. Doctor Burns came before he started his surgery. John was too weak to argue when the doctor phoned for an ambulance.

'Ye'll look after ma cat, lassie?' he gasped, 'and see the pipes dinna freeze?'

'Of course I will,' Rosemary said pressing

his fingers, struggling to hold back her tears. He seemed small and frail, a shadow of the man she had known all her life. Megan went with him in the ambulance.

'Will you explain to Tania, please, Rosie? I'll telephone when I'm ready to leave the hospital.'

It was late by the time Rosie had fed and comforted Papa Oliphant's old grey cat, Jen. I'll come back and feed you in the morning, she promised, stroking the thick fur. She stoked up the living room fire. It controlled the central heating. John and Chrissie Oliphant had enjoyed an open fire but at times like this there was a danger the pipes would freeze if the fire was out for long periods.

It was touch and go for two days and nights but John Oliphant had a strong constitution and he had never been a smoker. He began to improve but the illness had shaken him. He looked all of his seventy-five years when Rosie and Tania visited him in hospital together.

'I'm worried about ma hoose,' he fretted. 'It needs the fire to heat the pipes.'

'Rosie is lighting it every day and looking after things, Grandfather,' Tania said trying to reassure him.

'Thank ye, lassie,' he rasped, dredging up a smile. He closed his eyes, gathering strength.

He seemed to reach a decision. 'It would be less bother for Rosie if ye'd move in for a while, Tania? Keep Jen happy. Ye'd be nearer your work. And Struan,' he added.

'I can do that, Grandpie, if it's what you want?' Tania said.

'It is.' He closed his eyes. 'It'll be yours one day.' Both girls thought he was confusing Tania with her mother. They waited until he was sleeping then crept away together.

'I'm happy to stay at Honeysuckle Cottage,' Tania said, 'but I'm glad Grandfather suggested it himself. Mother is making plans for him to stay at Bengairney when he gets out of hospital.'

'Yes. He looks so ill. Paul and I will miss him if he stays at Bengairney.'

★ ★ ★

Catherine had always liked John Oliphant and she'd had good reason to be grateful to him and Chrissie when she and Douglas first began reclaiming Langton Tower but she was annoyed with Rosie for getting involved, especially when she absented herself from two luncheon parties but still had time for Samuel Caraford. This was the crux of the matter. Catherine had introduced her to young men who were far more eligible. The

Braebourne brothers regarded her with open admiration. Harry Braebourne showed an interest in her work and asked if she would show him round the gardens, telling her they needed her advice to improve the gardens belonging to the family estate. Rosie agreed, but without enthusiasm.

It was the last straw for Catherine when she saw Sam's car parked for the whole of a Saturday evening. It was bad enough when he took Rosemary to the dances but it was worse to imagine them spending hours alone together. She knew Rosie had been helping Tania move into Honeysuckle Cottage most of the day but she refused to believe she was too tired to go dancing. Sam's car was still parked when Catherine peered out before going to bed at midnight. She fumed silently, longing to go to the cottage and tell Sam he was compromising her daughter's reputation, but she knew Rosemary would never forgive such humiliation. She resolved to tackle Sam on his own instead.

Rosemary's future had become an obsession with Catherine since Douglas's death, even though the solicitor respected her as a capable and independent young business woman. Rosemary Lavender was not twenty-one until May. She decided to visit Sam at Martinwold and appeal to his conscience.

Douglas had admired the Carafords for bringing up their children to be kind and considerate but Catherine had always felt Megan Caraford made her feel inadequate as a mother, however unintentionally.

Catherine drove to Martinwold intending to catch Sam at the house when he stopped for lunch. Sam was ravenous and he was looking forward to the dish of shepherd's pie he had taken from the oven. He saw a car turning into the yard through the kitchen window and swore silently, thinking it was one of the men selling cake or fertilizer. His eyes widened at sight of Mrs Palmer-Farr. He shoved his dinner into the bottom oven of the Esse. Rosie? Something must be wrong. Was she hurt? He pulled open the door.

'Has Rosie had an accident?'

'May I come in?' Catherine asked. 'There is a dreadful smell.' She sniffed in disgust.

'Yes, the men are spreading slurry,' Sam muttered. He had never expected Mrs Palmer-Farr to visit, let alone enter his house. He couldn't show her into the sitting room without any furniture.

'Rosie? Is she all right?'

'It is my daughter I wish to discuss with you, Samuel. May I come inside?' she repeated, 'Or do farmers always keep their guests standing on the doorstep?' There was an edge to her voice. Sam's dark brows rose. He was tempted to tell her that guests were invited. He stood aside and allowed her to enter, indicating she should go through to the kitchen. At least it was warm and comfortable, even if things were a bit shabby. His mouth tightened as he saw Catherine surveying everything, including his breakfast dishes, still soaking in the washing up bowl. He seldom left dirty dishes but Ned had come to get him in a hurry that morning.

'I canna start the tractor to feed the silage to the cows. You'll have to come, Sam, they're milling around the feed barrier, pushing and shoving and making a racket.' Sam had grabbed the remains of his breakfast, shoved the dishes into the sink and followed Ned. His heart sank as he saw Catherine's lip curl in disdain. All his possessions were somebody's cast offs, but they were adequate for his needs. He straightened his shoulders. As a little boy he remembered visiting here when Grandfather Oliphant had been dairyman for Mr Turner. It had been warm and comfortable and always welcoming. Rosie had thought it was cosy having the old leather settee in the kitchen. His eye fell on the film of dust on the dresser where he kept his little television and the radio. Mrs Palmer-Farr had seen it too. It was all right for her with maids to do her cleaning. He could smell the shepherd's pie his mother had given him after Sunday lunch at Bengairney. His stomach rumbled.

'You wanted to talk about Rosie?' Sam asked. 'Will you take a seat?' He pulled out one of the pine armchairs from the table. Catherine took her time folding her coat beneath her, but her mind was racing. How best to convince Sam that he must stay away from Rosemary Lavender? It had seemed easy enough until she looked at Sam's set young face, the tilt of his square jaw, the glint in his green eyes and the thick mop of burnished chestnut hair. She could understand why her daughter found him so attractive.

She rushed into speech. Sam gasped and stared at her as her words, or rather her meaning, sank in.

'You're telling me not to see Rosie again? Did she ask you to come?' His thoughts flew back to Saturday evening and a pulse beat in his jaw. They had indulged in some heavy petting. They had grown bored with the television programme and it had seemed natural to turn into each other's arms in the peace and privacy of the cottage. Even now Sam felt his heart throbbing as he remembered the feel of Rosie's firm young breasts and her little gasps of pleasure. She had been shy and diffident about exploring his body in return but her response to his kisses had been wonderful. He longed to make her his but he knew how innocent she was. He was the one who had drawn back. God, it had taken all his self control. He became aware of Mrs Palmer-Farr, watching him with narrowed eyes. Her lips were pursed. Surely she didn't know? Rosie would never confide in her mother over such things? 'Did Rosie ask you to come?' he repeated.

'Not directly,' Catherine said. She had seen the expressions passing over Sam's face. She was all too aware how long he had spent alone in her daughter's company on Saturday night. Please God Rosemary had not let him make love to her! Catherine knew little about the younger generation and their changing standards, but she could guess at the temptations for a girl as naïve as her daughter. In many respects the world had moved on without Catherine realizing it. She would have been shocked to know unmarried girls visited family planning clinics and took their own decisions about birth control. She had been a virgin when she married Douglas and she had been shocked when she learned he was not. She trembled at the memory. He had been a good lover. He had known how to thrill her. She had never slept with another man, or wanted to. She was convinced that's the way it should be for all girls, but could she be sure Rosemary had not already given herself to Samuel Caraford? She had always hero worshipped him and his younger brother. Catherine had seen the fleeting expressions on his handsome young face, and his guilty flush. Anger surged in her.

'I suppose you are looking for a wife with money now that you and your family are burdened with debts to buy this place.' Again she gave a disparaging glance around the kitchen. 'You couldn't afford to keep Martinwold House I understand, but you could never expect my daughter to live in a place like this.' Sam bristled with indignation.

'The Turners lived here when they started out. My mother was brought up here after Mr Turner built the big house.'

'No daughter of mine will live in a hovel like this. I am here to remind you that Rosemary is not yet twenty-one and you are ruining her chance of inheriting — '

'I'm not interested in Rosie's money!' Sam snapped. 'I wouldn't — '

'Then you will not mind proving it by promising that you will not see her again,' Catherine stated and made to rise.

'You must be crazy! I love Rosie. I may not be able to afford to marry yet but if she loves me enough I hope she will wait for me.' Did she love him? She hadn't said she did in spite of her passionate response to his lovemaking. Catherine saw the uncertainty in his eyes and sat down again.

'It is not her inheritance from her father which is at stake. If she marries against my wishes she will get nothing from me. We gave her the gardens to humour her, to occupy her until she marries a man with breeding and education, who can keep her in the style to which she is accustomed.' Catherine saw Sam's chest expand indignantly but she rushed on before he could speak. 'Sir Henry Braebourne and his sons have become frequent visitors. Harry is attracted to Rosemary. Did she tell you that? No, I thought not,' she carried on without waiting for an answer. 'He shares her interest in plants and gardens. He has asked her to visit and advise him about landscaping the gardens at The Manor.'

It had never occurred to Rosemary to mention the Braebournes to Sam. Neither had she considered it necessary to inform her mother she had sent Paul Keir to make sketches and discuss suggestions with Harry Braebourne and Sir Henry. Catherine spoke again, less acerbic now she could detect doubt on Sam's expressive face.

'If you care for Rosemary Lavender you will give her time and space to meet other young men. She is innocent in such matters. She has never had a steady boyfriend. You wouldn't want her to rush into marriage because you were the first man who asked her, would you, Samuel? After a few years of drudgery she would realize what she has missed and regret tying herself down to a working farmer. For your own sake, as well as hers, I'm asking you not to see her again, or make contact with her.'

Sam stared at her. Catherine smiled. She could be charming when she wanted. She sounded so reasonable, Sam thought. Was it possible he had frightened Rosie a little? Had her mother sensed her fears and uncertainties? She had seen how aroused he was. He couldn't hide it. Her blue eyes had been round as saucers as she felt the hardness of him. He had known he must go slowly with Rosie. He loved her. He would never do anything against her wishes.

'I can't promise not to see her again. We've always been friends. We move in the same circles.'

'You could avoid her company for a few months at least, Samuel. Allow her friendship with the Braebournes to develop,' Catherine said. 'If she discovers you're the one she loves what difference does a few months make?'

A few months. That sounded like a lifetime to Sam. He longed to have Rosie in his arms again, to hold her close, to kiss her. Her mouth was soft and yielding. She must love him or she would never have responded as she had.

'A month!' he said, surprising himself, and startling Catherine. 'One month.' Sam's face was set. He went to the door and opened it. 'I promise not to see Rosemary, or get in touch with her, for one month. That's to the end of March. After that I shall consider we are free to meet, or not, as we please.' His tone was firm and decisive and Catherine realized that was the best she could hope for. She would have to work on Rosemary, sow the seeds of doubt his silence would cause.

'Thank you, Samuel, I'm sure you will not regret allowing a young and innocent girl her freedom to find friends of her own class.'

Sam was silent, waiting for her to leave, already regretting his promise. As she stepped outside he said, 'If you love your daughter so much, Mrs Palmer-Farr, may I extract a promise from you in return?'

'Why of course,' Catherine said, smiling now.

'If Rosie and I still love each other six months from now, will you give us your blessing to get engaged?' Catherine looked at him, frowning.

'Six months? Engaged . . . ' she repeated. 'Very well,' she agreed. After all anything could happen in six months, or even in one month. Engagements could be broken if need be. Catherine climbed into her car and drove away.

Sam watched her go with a sinking heart. He no longer had any appetite for food, not even for his mother's shepherd's pie. He had been a fool. A whole month — and not even chance to talk to Rosie, to explain that her mother wanted to break up their friendship. Catherine Palmer-Farr had always disapproved of the time Rosemary spent with his family, even though she had never had time for Rosie herself. Her disapproval would be twenty times greater if she thought Rosie was marrying into the Caraford family. If only he had told Rosie how much he loved her. A month would feel like a lifetime.

9

John Oliphant's illness had taken more out of him than he realized. He settled into Megan's little sitting room with relief. He had a comfortable bed and his armchair in front of a cheery fire, all without any effort on his part. There was a toilet and shower room across the passage. It was good to have company. Steven and Alex drew him into their discussions about the farm and the stock as though he were still a young man. Megan cooked his favourite meals. He began to think he would be foolish to move back to his empty cottage.

'Ye're sure ye dinna mind having me to share your home, Steven?' he asked, one evening when the pair of them were sitting alone together before the fire.

'Mind? Of course we don't mind. In fact it's a relief to know you're here, safe and warm. Megan was worried about you being at the cottage in the cold weather. It troubled us knowing young Rosie was looking out for you every day.'

'She's a grand lassie, young Rosie, always has been, but I was a cussed independent old man.' He smiled and stared into the leaping flames of the fire. 'Now that I'm here I enjoy the company.'

'And we enjoy having you,' Steven assured him, 'so what's on your mind?'

'The cottage. I want to leave it to Tania. Your sons will get their share of the farm stock and machinery, and now there'll be Martinwold to pass on to them some day so I'd like to leave my wee hoose to Tania. I'm thinking I ought to do it soon, while I can still see to things.'

'I've no objections, if you're sure about this,' Steven said. 'Some day I expect Tania and Struan will have to move into the farmhouse but Mrs Ritchie is a peculiar woman so goodness knows when that will happen.'

'Tania could let the cottage when that day comes,' John Oliphant said, 'or sell it if she wants. Either way it wouldna do any harm for her to have a wee bit of money of her own, would it?'

'No, you're right of course,' Steven agreed.

'So will ye arrange for your solicitor to come to see me and put things in hand?'

'Yes, I can do that. Tania is a lucky girl to have you for her grandfather. Don't think we don't appreciate what you're doing for her,' Steven said.

'She's a grand lassie and she's aye been good to Chrissie and me, especially since I've been on my own. Where farms and farmers are concerned the lassies always seem to get less than their brothers so I thought this might help even things up a bit. I wouldna like to cause any trouble in your family though, Steven.'

'I'm sure Sam and Alex have enough to think about since we bought Martinwold. They're full of enthusiasm. Sam is making a good job of managing the men and organizing the work at Martinwold, but he's seemed a bit down in spirits this past ten days.'

'Aye, Megan was a bit concerned about him on Sunday. He'd lost his appetite. He loves her bread and syrup pudding with sultanas and the crunchy top. She says he usually takes some back but he didn't want it this week.'

'It's not like him,' Steven agreed. Megan had confided her concerns about Sam when they were in bed on Sunday night. She wondered if he and Rosie had quarrelled when Rosie didn't come for lunch two Sundays in a row.

'If they have it will only be a lovers' tiff,' he'd said, intending to reassure her.

'I'm not so sure. Tania went up to see Rosie

on Friday evening to ask if she was going to the Saturday dance. She shook her head and would have gone on working if Tania hadn't insisted on stopping to chat. She said Rosie looked pale and tired and she's lost her sparkle, but she insisted there was nothing wrong.'

As usual when Megan was anxious Steven had taken her in his arms and soothed away her worries, reminding her that young people always sorted out their own problems. A tender smile curved Steven's mouth as he remembered. He and Megan had had their own ups and downs when they were young. He remembered being jealous as hell of Lindsay Gray and there had been no need. He was the one Megan loved — and still loved, even though their sons probably thought they were too old to make love anymore.

When Sam didn't call for Rosie on Saturday evening she had expected he would telephone to say he had a cow calving, or some other urgent task with the animals. She'd had to miss Sunday lunch at Bengairney two weeks in a row because her mother had already arranged lunches and expected her to attend. They had never entertained so much when her father was alive but she felt it was her mother's way of dealing with the void he had left and she felt a pang of guilt and sympathy.

She wanted to explain to Sam, but he hadn't phoned or called since the Saturday evening they had spent alone together. Her cheeks burned. Had he thought she was cheap? Too forward? Or too inexperienced?

She telephoned Martinwold but there was no reply two evenings in a row. Was she chasing him, as Lidia had done? Every instinct told her something was wrong but Tania would have told her if he was ill.

She knew Sam could not afford to marry because he had told her there was no spare money for anything major since his family had bought Martinwold. Rosie understood that, but was it only lack of money keeping him away? Passion had flared between them the evening they had spent alone together. Did he feel the need to cool things? Was he drawing back in case she made demands as Lidia had done? Was he afraid of commitment? Surely he knew her well enough to know she would never force him into anything he didn't want? So why hadn't he phoned?

The weekend passed. The days passed. Rosie had never felt so miserable. She was convinced Sam was drawing away from her before it was too late. Her mother had had people to dinner both Saturday and Sunday and Harry Braebourne had even dropped in to see her in the gardens in the middle of the week on the pretext of discussing Paul's ideas for laying out the main garden at The Manor. If Rosie had not been feeling so miserable she might have noticed the gleam of speculation in his brown eyes. When he had gone, Paul joined her in the greenhouse with a grin on his face.

'He didn't want to discuss the plans at all,' he said. 'That fellow is after you, Rosie. Anybody can see that.'

'Don't talk rubbish, Paul. You sound like my mother.'

'Heaven forbid!' Paul said. 'Seriously Rosie, what with Sam, and now Harry Braebourne running after you, it's reasonable to suppose you'll end up married before too long.' His expression sobered. He looked so anxious when Rosie turned to face him that she bit back her sharp retort. She liked Paul and she couldn't manage half so well without him. He had the ideas for both garden planning and marketing their produce while she knew about plants and growing them. They worked well together.

'You'll be the first to know if — repeat if — I ever think of getting married, Paul,' she said.

'Mmm, we-ell I wanted to ask a serious question, but I don't want you to take offence, or think me presumptuous. Mother agrees a pretty girl like you will be snapped up in no time.'

'Your mother said that, Paul? I shall never marry without love.'

'I believe you.' He was convinced she did love Sam but he sensed there was something not quite right. 'But supposing you did marry, what would you do with the gardens?'

'The gardens? I don't know. I mean I've never thought.' Rosie looked at him, then realized Paul might be worried about his job. Her expression softened.

'Can I ask you to consider a suggestion?'

'Of course, but I shall always consider you, Paul,' Rosie said.

'Would you give me first opportunity to buy the gardens if you decide to sell?' Paul asked in a rush. 'Or if you didn't want to sell outright, would you consider taking me on as a partner, selling me a half share?'

'Goodness Paul! I never thought of anything like that.'

'Maybe I'm being a bit — a bit presumptuous, but I enjoy my work here. I've lots of ideas and plans. I could afford to buy a place of my own but this is so convenient. I'd like a house of my own before I'm too much older, but I don't want to move far away when Mother is on her own.'

'I see,' Rosie said. 'You've taken my breath away, Paul.'

'I'm sorry, but I didn't want you telling me you've sold out to someone without giving me an opportunity to buy you out. I know Mother would feel happier if I went into partnership as a first step. She feels you have a better grasp of the business side than I do.'

'You've discussed it with your mother?'

'Of course. She had control of the money my father left me until I was twenty-one. It's up to me what I invest in now but it would be rather inconsiderate not to discuss my plans with my mother after all she's done for me while I was ill, don't you think? Anyway if you were selling it all, including your cottage, and the Gate Lodge, I would need a loan from her.'

'What does she think to that?'

'Oh she's all in favour except that she would prefer to invest the money, as a sort of sleeping partner, rather than give me a loan. Mother's family were well off and we have talked a lot about the future since my medical reports have been so positive. I believe Mother would give every penny she has so long as I'm well and doing something I enjoy. Besides, she shares my love of the gardens.'

'I can understand her point of view,' Rosie said. 'This is all such a surprise, though, Paul. You'll need to give me plenty of time to mull things over. I must confess I have contemplated all sorts of plans of my own but they all need capital. Do you think we could get on well as business partners?'

'I don't see why not, so long as we're open and honest with each other and discuss everything before we make changes.'

'It would have to be done with a solicitor,' Rosie said, 'and we would need to decide how much income we could each take out to live on. We would need an accountant so you knew I was doing things fairly.'

'So you don't mind me mentioning it?' Paul asked with relief.

'Not at all, but I need time to think things through.'

'You can take as much time as you like. I was beginning to be afraid you might tell me you'd sold up one day and were marrying Sam.' A shadow clouded Rosie's blue eyes and she turned her head.

'I can please myself whether I want to take you into partnership or not, Paul, without getting married.'

★ ★ ★

Tania couldn't believe it when she heard her grandfather was giving Honeysuckle Cottage to her. She would own her very own home. Struan had stayed overnight with her a few times while she was looking after the cottage but they both knew the locals would notice his car and speculate. They loved each other and they would have been married by now if it were not for Mrs Ritchie but they knew their families would not appreciate gossip. The more time they spent together the more impatient Struan was to be married. Mr Ritchie had suggested building a bungalow to retire in but Mrs Ritchie had refused to consider the idea. Tania loved Struan dearly but she could not do as his mother wished and live in the same house, unable to change anything or make it her home. Struan's frustration increased each night he had to leave her.

'I wouldn't care if we lived in a caravan, so long as we're together,' Struan had said. 'Father knows how I feel but he doesn't seem able to persuade my mother to do anything once she makes up her mind. My sister thinks Mother needs a psychiatrist, or firmer handling. That's easy to say when you're on the other side of the world. Mother was never as bad as this when we were young and Pam lived at home. One day she will really be ill and we shall take no notice.'

Tania's spirits soared. They would have a home of their own at Honeysuckle Cottage. Struan was elated when he heard her news.

'We could be married in three weeks,' he said with all the eagerness of a schoolboy.

'You'll not mind having to travel four miles to the farm?'

'Not when I can come home to you every night, sweetheart. It will be worth getting up at five o' clock and that will only be when I'm relief milking at weekends and holidays.'

'I don't want pomp and ceremony, Struan, but I can't get married and not tell my parents,' Tania said. 'Papa Oliphant has made everything possible. He would be hurt if we didn't tell him. I wonder if he guessed how frustrated we are.'

'I'll agree to anything you say, my darling girl,' Struan said jubilantly, 'so long as you'll marry me soon. I'll tell my father our plans. It will be up to him to deal with Mother.' His mouth firmed. 'However ill she makes herself, I'll make it clear we shall not postpone our wedding.'

Tania was longing to share her news. She called on Rosie on her way home from work on Friday evening. She was so full of plans it was a while before she realized Rosie was too quiet.

'I do hope Alex and Sam will not be jealous or think Grandfather is favouring me,' Tania said. 'I would hate a family quarrel.'

'You've been kind to Papa Oliphant. It is up to him what he does with his property.'

'I suppose so. He says I can decorate it how I like and I can keep any of the furniture and ask Sam if he can use the rest at Martinwold. His house is almost empty so I think he'll agree. I can't believe it's going to be my very own, Rosie. I'm so excited. There's some ornaments and a very pretty vase which have to go to Mum, and Grandfather would like his own armchair and his own bed. I'll ask Struan if he will move them in his Land Rover and trailer and — ' She stopped, realizing that Rosie seemed distracted.

'Oh Rosie, here am I chattering on about my own good fortune and you look so sad. Is it your father? I know you must miss him. Is that what's wrong?'

'There's nothing wrong.'

'I know you too well to believe that. You've always had such a happy smile. You've lost your sparkle. You're pale too, and strained. It's as though you have all the worries of the world on your shoulders. Is it to do with money? Will you be able to manage?' Tania asked with concern. 'You must tell me if there is anything I can do, whatever it is that's troubling you. Rosie?'

'There's nothing the matter.' Rosie's voice was almost angry.

'I-I see.' Tania swallowed and changed the subject, or so she thought. 'Are you and Sam going to the dance tomorrow night?'

'No.'

'Oh.' Tania frowned. 'Have you two quarrelled?'

'No.'

'Are you sure? Mother says he's going round with a long face and he doesn't look as though he's sleeping properly. He's lost his appetite too. Even injuring his arm didn't have that effect.' Rosie didn't answer. 'Mum says he's been the same for the last two weeks. It seems strange that you're so down in the dumps too and it's ages since you've been to Bengairney.'

'Mother keeps holding dinner parties. She expects me to be there.'

'I know that, but are you sure you and Sam haven't quarrelled?'

'Of course I'm sure. I haven't seen him for three weeks. Everything was fine the last time w-we were to-together. He — he hasn't phoned either.' Rosie's voice faltered. She was near to tears, but it was true they hadn't quarrelled. 'It might be better if we had quarrelled,' she said. 'At least I would know what I'd done wrong. I expect he's got tired of me like he did with Lidia.'

'That's nonsense. There's no comparison between you and Lidia. You and Samuel have always been the best of friends.'

Maybe that's the trouble, Rosie thought. Maybe friendship is all Sam wants from me. Perhaps he got carried away and now he's regretting it.

'He never used to go silent,' she muttered aloud.

'No, that's not Sam's style,' Tania said. 'He gets things off his chest, but he never bears a grudge. Hasn't he said anything — anything at all?'

'He's never been here, or telephoned, or — or anything.'

'Well there's no use moping at home being miserable,' Tania said. 'There's other fish in the sea and maybe my handsome big brother needs a lesson. Anyway Alex is hoping you'll be his partner at the Young Farmers' Dance tomorrow night. It is a competition for aged twenty-one, and under. You two have danced together since Alex's first school dance. Struan and I will be going to watch. We'll give you a lift. Can I tell Alex you'll partner him for the competition?'

'I suppose so,' Rosie agreed, then she added, 'and Tania, I'm pleased for you

— about the cottage I mean, and having a home of your own.'

'Thanks, Rosie,' Tania said and turned back to hug her young friend. As she drew away she was sure she glimpsed the sparkle of tears on Rosie's long lashes but she said no more. She was convinced there was something wrong between her and Sam, or why else would they both be so unhappy at the same time? She would tackle Sam about it when she went to Bengairney on Sunday.

Alex was jubilant at having Rosie for his partner. She was so light he could lift her off her feet, or swing her round at will, and she had more stamina than most of the girls who worked in offices and other sedentary jobs. Unless they were knocked out in the first few rounds he guessed they would both need plenty of energy for the more risky moves they had often done together.

He telephoned at lunchtime on Saturday, eager to make sure Rosie would be there.

'I could collect you,' he offered. 'Sam's not going so I'll have the car.'

'Tania is giving me a lift. I'll see you there,' Rosie said. Her heart was heavy. Both Sam and Alex were good dancers and she had always enjoyed being with them but tonight she had no enthusiasm.

'What are you wearing?' Alex asked, taking her by surprise.

'My jeans with the flared bottoms and a new blue and silver top.'

'Oh.' She could hear the disappointment in Alex's voice. 'I er . . . I hoped you might wear that blue dress with the white bits on it. The one with a short skirt that spins out when you're dancing.'

'It has no sleeves. I'd be frozen,' Rosie protested. 'Besides if it's a competition you'll be trying all sorts of twists and turns and throwing me in the air. I know you, and — '

'Of course I shall,' Alex agreed with a chuckle, 'so you'll never feel the cold once the competition starts. You'd better dress decently underneath.'

'I always dress decently underneath,' Rosie protested. 'Anyway there'll be ordinary dancing first.'

'You could wear something on top, couldn't you? A cardigan or something, until the hall gets warmed up?' he pleaded.

'I'll think about it.'

'Please, Rosie. You know how good we are together on the dance floor — in fact I reckon we're good together all the time. Better than — '

'Alex!' Rosie warned. 'Don't start that again or I'll refuse to come.'

'Well I don't know how you can prefer Sam. He's like a bear with a sore head.'

The following evening when they called to collect Rosie for the disco, Tania and Struan were in high spirits and full of plans for their future.

'We're going to tell Mum and Dad tomorrow while we're both at Bengairney for Sunday dinner. I do hope you'll be there, Rosie. I would love you to be my bridesmaid or witness or whatever, even if it's a quiet wedding,' Tania said. 'Struan's father has promised to fit in with whatever plans we make.'

'He says he'll do his best to persuade Mother to cooperate too,' Struan added, 'but I'll believe that when it happens. He's delighted to be getting Tania for a daughter.' He grinned and gave Tania a quick hug. 'He's going to phone Australia tonight. They'll just be getting up. He wants to tell Pam our news.'

They were almost ready to leave when the telephone rang. Struan was standing beside it in the tiny hall. 'Answer that for me, please, Struan, while I fetch my cardigan,' Rosie said, already half way up the stairs. 'I'm wearing this dress to please Alex but I shall be perished.'

'You look good enough to eat,' Struan said,

grinning. There was still laughter in his voice when he picked up the telephone receiver and gave the number. He recognized the voice of Catherine Palmer-Farr.

'Samuel!' Her voice was sharp. 'You gave me your word! You've broken your promise! I shall — '

'This is Struan Ritchie, Mrs Palmer-Farr.' Struan interrupted, his brows rising in surprise.

'Oh. Oh I beg your pardon. Please tell Rosemary Lavender I wish to speak to her.' He signalled Rosie as she came down the stairs. She was gesticulating to say she was not there.

'Er . . . we're leaving now. We shall be late for the disco . . . '

'Disco? Tell her I must speak with her,' she insisted. Struan shrugged and handed the receiver to Rosie.

'Hello, Mother, we're in a hurry. What? You're having the Braebournes *again*?' She listened in exasperation. Tania stifled her giggles as Rosie pulled faces at the telephone. 'I know there's no Lady Braebourne but they will have a cook. Anyway if they enjoy your chef's cooking so much they should book a dinner and pay for it. No, I'm not being mean. I wish you'd stop trying to arrange every minute of my life! Oh, all right, I'll come tomorrow but that's the finish. Don't count on me for any more luncheon parties if you insist on including the Braebournes every time. Now I must rush. Goodbye.'

'Sounds as though you're booked up for Sunday dinner again,' Tania said, throwing her a sympathetic look.

'Yes, I am.' Rosie had mixed feelings about going to Bengairney and seeing Samuel anyway. 'You'll have to come here one evening and tell me all your plans instead.'

'I will. You seem to be seeing a lot of the Braebournes,' Tania remarked as they settled themselves in Struan's car.

'Too much if you ask me. They want suggestions for landscaping their gardens. I sent Paul to do the preliminary discussion. He's good at that side of things but we think they're expecting I'll do it free, like Mother and her meals. They'll get a bill whether Mother approves or not.'

'Business is business,' Struan agreed, 'and they could afford it if the sons earned their living like the rest of us.'

'Do you think your mother is trying to pair you off with one of them?' Tania asked.

'She'll be disappointed if she is,' Rosie said. 'Harry Braebourne seemed all right in the beginning but he's becoming a pest. He comes wandering round the gardens. He

276

asked if I had any plans for this weekend. When I told him about the disco he made derisory remarks, like 'I'd forgotten you went to the local school. You'll know all the local yokels. We had a proper education.' '

'He sounds an awful snob.'

'I answered him in French but he hadn't a clue what I'd said. He didn't like that.'

'Did he see the funny side?' Tania asked.

'No. He muttered about it being better to mix with ones own cla-ass. He sounded like my mother, but she wouldn't be so pleased if she heard him arranging her life.'

'He sounds self-opinionated to me,' Tania said, but she was delighted to catch a glimpse of Rosie's usual spirits.

Rosie fell silent as they approached the hall. Would Sam be there? Would he speak to her, or would he avoid her? Alex was waiting for them.

'You're late! I wanted to have time for a practice. There's a couple of new lifts I'd like to try.'

'Give Rosie time to get in and get her coat off,' Struan teased. 'The competition doesn't start until ten o'clock. Anyway I'm having first dance with Rosie. I want a word in her ear.'

'Well only the first dance then.'

'You'll be lucky to get a dance at all when

the other fellows see the dress she's wearing underneath that coat.'

'You're wearing the blue dress?' Alex asked eagerly.

'You do want to win tonight, don't you, little brother?' Tania teased.

'We'll give it our best shot, won't we Rosie?'

'If you say so,' Rosie answered. Her eyes were scanning the crowd at the other end of the hall. There was no sign of Sam and she didn't know whether she was disappointed or relieved. She wished she knew what she had done wrong. Her cheeks burned as she recalled their ardent lovemaking. Had he found her too inexperienced compared to Lidia, or had she responded too eagerly? Struan drew her onto the dance floor and Rosie tried to put Sam out of her thoughts. Alex claimed her as soon as the dance was over and proceeded to show her the new moves he had in mind. They had danced together since they were children so she knew he wouldn't let her fall when he tossed her in the air or round his back, and through his legs. He was young and strong and light on his feet and music seemed to give Alex a whole new persona.

'You're light as a feather. I reckon we're even better together than we used to be,

Rosie,' he said with glee.

'I'm the same as I always was but you've developed a man's strength and muscle since you finished at college.'

'At least you've noticed I'm a man then?'

'Oh Alex, please don't start that. I think the world of you as a brother, I always have, but I know I shall never think of you in any other way.'

'So you keep telling me.' He swung her up into the air then caught her close to his chest, holding her there longer than the beat of the music. 'What I don't understand is why you feel differently about Sam. Why isn't he still like a brother?'

'I don't know how I feel about Sam,' she said. 'Let's concentrate on the dancing.'

By the time the competition started some of the couples were exhausted and eliminated after the first couple of dances. The numbers grew less. Alex's vigorous enjoyment was plain to see as he made use of the extra space. The record changed to play the entry for the Eurovision Song Contest — *Save All Your Kisses For Me*. Alex spun Rosie up in the air. Over his shoulder she caught a glimpse of Sam standing in the doorway. Her lips parted, but Alex was lowering her to glide between his legs and catching her again.

'Rosie!' his voice jerked her attention back

to the dance. When she looked again there was no sign of Sam. She knew she had not imagined him. Why couldn't he have waited, to say hello? Her small jaw set and she threw herself into the dancing. Alex sensed a change in her and responded with renewed energy. Then there were only three couples remaining. When one of the judges called their number Rosie thought they had been eliminated. She didn't realize they had won until Alex lifted her high above his head and danced towards the podium.

Sam had been unable to resist looking in at the dance hall. He knew Rosie was partnering Alex. His younger brother was elated because she had agreed. He had talked of little else, unwittingly rubbing salt into Sam's wounds, making him more miserable than ever. Common sense told him his young brother would be no more acceptable to Catherine Palmer-Farr than he was, but it was little consolation. He had assumed Rosie would be as unhappy as he was during this month of separation. He had thought she would refuse to go to the dance without him, even though she and Alex had always made a good pair on the dance floor, and it was for the competition. Obviously she didn't miss him as much as he missed her. He was a fool to have promised her mother not to contact her for a whole month. Tania had told him that Rosie seemed to be in constant demand for her mother's lunch and dinner parties. To make matters worse he had run into Paul Keir in the village shop a few days before. After they had exchanged greetings Paul explained he was on his way back from the Braebourne's place.

'Sir Henry and his sons have asked Rosemary to advise them on landscaping their grounds. That's the sort of thing I enjoy so she sent me to give them a few ideas before they decide whether to go ahead.' Paul grinned. 'I don't think they're interested in ideas for their grounds.' It dawned on Sam that Catherine Palmer-Farr had selected the Braebournes as frequent guests because Sir Henry's sons would provide a suitable match for her daughter. Some time ago he had met them briefly. He considered them a pair of stuffed shirts. They had been following the hunt over Bengairney land because their landlord had given permission to the leader of the hunt. The Braebourne boys and three of their friends had thought they would be clever and take a short cut. They galloped through the middle of a field where their in-lamb ewes were grazing. The frightened flock had scattered in alarm. Sam remembered how furious his father had been. He had not hesitated to confront them. Sam remembered standing beside his father and longing to aim a fist at their arrogant noses as they sat up on their horses and smirked down on his father as a mere tenant. Was that the kind of husband Rosie wanted? He went home without entering the dance hall. He felt sick at heart. He should have known Catherine Palmer-Farr would lose no time in providing other company for Rosie. He couldn't bear the thought of her in the arms of another man — not even his own brother.

Rosie was tired when she wakened on Sunday morning. Apart from the energetic dancing, she had lain awake wondering where she had gone wrong with Sam and considering the future. In the wee small hours she made a decision. Sunday was not ideal for discussing business but she wanted to see Paul and his mother together when they were both at home. If Mrs Keir was in favour of Paul becoming a partner they needed to discuss terms and draw up an agreement. They each had their own ideas but that had proved a benefit so far. If Paul paid her for a half share she would have enough capital to start converting the first of three stone buildings at Home Farm into detached houses. Her father had modernized the farmhouse so she would have four good houses to let, as well as the three farm cottages. It might even be possible to make the Home Farm stable and hayloft into flats if she could get planning permission. The property would give her a reasonable income if she ever decided to sell all of the gardens to Paul. Then there was the Lodge at the back entrance to Langton Tower. Paul had expressed an interest in it.

Rosie showered and dressed in her flared jeans and a new multicoloured top with flattering diagonal stripes. She grimaced at herself in the mirror knowing her mother would disapprove when she turned up for Sunday lunch, but business came first, as her mother had demonstrated. If ever she had children Rosie vowed she would love them before anything else.

Paul and his mother had discussed his future at length and Rosie got the impression Mrs Keir was happy to discuss business, Sunday or not.

'I am thankful Paul is alive and well and he has discovered work which promises him satisfaction,' she told Rosie, 'but he has ideas and ambition.'

'I understand that,' Rosie nodded.

'Paul could afford to buy the gardens but their value is increasing as you improve them. Also I would be happier if he could be in partnership with you for a few years to learn the business side of things. Do you need your mother's permission?'

'No, the gardens are mine but we would need a valuation and a legal agreement. The turnover is growing each year. Between us the business could expand in various directions, so it would be better to become a partner now, Paul, and expand together.'

'That's what I thought,' he said with a grin. 'More importantly I need to know I have a future. What about the Lodge?'

'Could you still afford it?' Rosie asked.

'I think so but I would want a strip of additional land on the two sides away from the road. I'm thinking very long term. I'd be content to make alterations in the future so long as I know it's mine.'

'How long term? What sort of alterations?' Rosie asked.

'If we start selling our plants direct to the public it would be better to have a centre near the entrance. Yes?'

'It would, if we ever get that far.'

'Together we shall, some day.' Paul smiled.

'We would need to mark out the area you have in mind, Paul, and get it valued. We'll discuss the details later now I know both of you agree about this, but I must hurry. I'm going to be late for lunch. Mother will be annoyed,' she said with a rueful grimace.

'That's super, Rosie!' Paul stood up and hugged her. 'You're my lucky star. Life has improved ever since I met you and your father and John Oliphant, hasn't it, Mother?'

'It has indeed. These things take time though, Paul, so you must be patient.' Mrs Keir smiled at Rosie. 'I do appreciate you coming here and talking things through. I confess I have been a little worried. I shall be happy for Paul to enrol in another correspondence course in landscape gardening.'

'Yes. Gosh, I must fly!'

Rosie was half an hour late for lunch. Catherine was furious.

'You could have worn some decent clothes,' she hissed. Rosie sighed in exasperation when she saw the three Braebournes again, along with an elderly couple, and the Wilshaws. They owned the estate which included Bengairney. Rosie had not met their two offspring before but she appreciated the conspiratorial wink from Trevor Wilshaw and the twinkling eyes of his twin sister, Ellen.

'I am sorry to be so late,' she apologized, allowing them a glimpse of her own mischievous smile.

'What kept you so late?' Catherine demanded.

'I had some business to discuss with the Keirs.'

'On a Sunday?' Harry Braebourne drawled.

'Strike while the iron is hot. Better the day, better the deed. Take your pick. The outcome was satisfying. Now I'm ready to eat.' She reached for the basket of bread rolls and urged the Wilshaw twins to follow suit.

* * *

Megan and Tania were enjoying a chat over a cup of coffee when Struan arrived at Bengairney on Sunday morning.

'Alex can't stop grinning after winning the dance competition, and now you're looking pleased about something, Struan?' Megan said with smile.

'Alex and Rosie were terrific. My father phoned Australia last night. He's as excited as a schoolboy and Pam's delighted with our news. Tania, she thinks it's a good excuse to come over and bring the two children if we can arrange an Easter wedding. My parents have never seen them. Father explained about Mother but Pam says she will manage her.' He shrugged. 'She reckons Father and I, and the doctor, are too soft with her.'

'Seeing her grandchildren might help,' Megan said.

'Yes, Pam is hoping my parents will go back with her for a visit.'

'That's wonderful news. Maybe Struan's niece would like to be a flower girl, Tania? She would have Avril's wee girl for company and I'm sure Rosie will keep an eye on them.'

'Mum, we're supposed to be having a quiet wedding. I haven't asked Rosie yet and Struan hasn't asked Sam.'

'Asked me what?' Sam asked appearing at the back door.

'Er . . . we're planning our wedding,' Struan told him. 'I wondered if you'd be my best man?'

'Best man?' Sam frowned.

'Don't sound so enthusiastic,' Tania groaned. 'Say no if you don't want to do it. Struan can ask his pal, Bert. Or Alex would jump at the chance if Rosie agrees to be my bridesmaid.'

'Rosie? Have you fixed a date?' Sam asked.

'No, but Struan's sister is coming over from Australia so we shall try to make it at Easter. Is your social calendar so full?'

'You know damn well it isn't, except with milking cows,' Sam retorted. 'Thanks for asking me, Struan. Easter is late, isn't it? I mean into April. Yes, I'd love to be your best man.'

'Easter Sunday is the 18th,' Tania said, 'but

that's not long. We could try for Easter Monday if the minister is agreeable.'

'We must book a meal at one of the hotels,' Megan said. 'It will be short notice but we may be lucky if it's not a big wedding. You did say you were not having a dance afterwards?'

'But the money, Mum. I thought we were economizing.'

'Don't worry about that, sweetheart,' Struan said. 'Dad wants to pay for the reception. He can afford it and I'm all he has left to launch into the world.' He grinned.

'That's a kind offer, Struan. Please thank your father,' Megan said, 'but we're not so short of money we can't afford a wedding for our only daughter. And Sam, speaking of money your father has decided to pay you a regular wage. It will only be in accordance with the Wages Board regulations for stockmen. Alex will get the same. We don't like to see either of you working so hard and having no enjoyment in life.'

'But Mum . . . I thought with buying Martinwold and everything — '

'Paying the bank will be an ongoing expense for years, like paying a rent. We still have to live normal lives.' She looked at Sam. 'I know we told you and Alex not to squander money, but there's no need to be as miserable as you have been recently.'

'You can say that again,' Tania muttered.

'What's the promise you've been making to Mrs Palmer-Farr, Sam?' Struan asked.

'What?' Sam stared at him. Twin patches of colour mounted his cheekbones. 'Who told you that?' His green eyes flashed.

'Sorry.' Struan's brows rose. 'I didn't mean to offend. I answered Rosie's phone last night. Mrs Palmer-Farr thought it was you and accused you of breaking your promise. She sounded furious until I explained.'

'I see.' Sam pursed his lips. 'I should never have agreed to her bloody demands.'

'What demands, Sam? What promises have you made?' Megan asked.

'Oh nothing,' Sam muttered and sat down at the kitchen table with a dejected thump. Megan eyed him. She knew Sam had not been to see Rosie, or anywhere else. He hadn't brought any of his good shirts for washing for at least three weeks.

'A promise is not 'nothing', Sam. What does Catherine want from you? You haven't done anything — I mean hurt Rosie or . . . ' Megan floundered.

'Of course I haven't done anything!' Sam shouted. Then his shoulders sagged. 'Sorry, Mum.' He put his head in his hands. 'She's never thought we were good enough,' he

289

muttered. 'She always resented Rosie spending time with us, even when she was little.'

'We've always known that,' Megan said, 'but Rosie is like a member of the family. Your grandfather was remarking how much he's missed her company and her cheery smile. So what did you promise? And does Rosie agree?'

'She doesn't know. That's the trouble. Her mother said I was preventing her meeting young men from her own class,' he feigned a posh accent. 'She said I was selfish and if I kept on seeing Rosie she would be in danger of losing her inheritance. I told her I wasn't interested in her money. Then she went on about us being tenant farmers and how we couldn't afford to keep Martinwold House and we have a huge debt hanging over us. Everything she said was true. In the end I agreed to do as she asked.'

'Which was?' Megan asked.

'She didn't want me to see Rosie again, ever. I couldn't promise that so she said I should stay away from her for three months. And not even speak to her, for God's sake! In the end I agreed not to see Rosie, or speak to her, for a month.'

'Not see her, and not tell her why?' Tania asked incredulously. 'No wonder Rosie has been so down in the dumps. She always ran to you with her problems. She'll think you've deserted her.'

'I'd never do that,' Sam exclaimed. 'I love her! I mean — I really love Rosie — not like when we were kids. I want to marry her — if ever I can afford a wife.'

'Oh Sam!' Tania got up and hugged him. 'So that's why Mrs Palmer-Farr has been entertaining half the gentry in the district, especially the Braebournes. She's trying to fix Rosie up with one of the boys. You needn't worry, though. Rosie has always been a shrewd judge of people, even when she was little. She thinks Harry Braebourne is a supercilious snob.'

'Does she? Did she say so?' Sam asked.

'More or less. As for her inheritance, Rosie already has the gardens and some cottages. She's trying to make you feel guilty, big brother.'

'Maybe Catherine was referring to the hotel?' Megan said. 'That will be Catherine's now.'

'Ah that could be right!' Tania said. 'Rosie told me Harry Braebourne was keen to know what the hotel would be worth.'

'I don't think Rosie would care about that anyway.' Sam said.

'Catherine is still a young woman. She will need the income, or the proceeds from the sale, to live on. I suspect she was indulging in a bit of blackmail, Sam. So long as you and Rosie love each other, that's the most important thing of all.'

'I should have discussed it with you before, Mum. You always put things into perspective.' Sam smiled and his face was transformed. 'I've only one more week to go then I've kept my blasted promise. I only hope Mrs Palmer-Farr keeps hers.' His eyes widened. 'What if Rosie doesn't believe me when I tell her why I couldn't see her?

'Oh she will,' Tania said, her mouth firming.

'I'm sure she will.' Struan caught her eye and winked. He knew that determined look. 'You'll be going up to see Rosie this evening? To ask her to be a bridesmaid, of course?' he said, his grey eyes dancing.

'You bet I will.'

10

Rosie was bored with the polite conversation at the dinner table. Her mind was on Paul and the decision they had reached. There would be a lot to discuss but it was a relief to know Mrs Keir was enthusiastic. She wished she had been free to spend the rest of her Sunday with the Carafords and share her news. She respected Steven Caraford's opinion. She would need a valuation. She longed to discuss it all with Sam if only —

'Rosemary Lavender! How rude you are,' Catherine exclaimed. 'Harry asked you a question.'

'Oh?' Rosie jerked her attention back to the guests. 'Er, what did you say?' she asked.

'I was asking why you sent one of your underlings to us. I expected you to come yourself.'

'Underling? Paul Keir can give advice on landscaping better than I can.'

'We Braebournes only deal with the boss.'

'I thought he had some good suggestions,' his younger brother protested.

'You know even less than the labourer she sent,' Harry snapped. His condescending tone and superior smile inflamed Rosie's temper.

'Paul Keir is my partner. I believe his family is as wealthy as yours, or mine. More importantly he is intelligent. He has a strong character too.'

'What nonsense! Paul Keir is not your partner,' Catherine snapped.

'Yes he is, as of this morning. We need a legal agreement but I don't foresee any problems.'

'You should have discussed this with me and — ' Catherine broke off, reluctant to quarrel with her daughter in front of guests. Rosie was not sure what devil possessed her, whether it was the glint in the eyes of the Wilshaw twins, or the supercilious smile on Harry Braebourne's face, or that she was tired of her mother's organizing — or just tired after the dancing.

'I need to make my own decisions, as you have always made decisions concerning the hotel. Harry has some advice for you in that direction.'

'How could Harry ever give me advice? Especially about the hotel?'

'He thinks it is a gold mine and that you ought to sell before you get too old. He's afraid you might let it dwindle away now you're a widow. Isn't that right, Harry?'

Harry Braebourne's face had gone white, then flushed puce. Rosie eyed him. He was a most unattractive colour.

'I didn't say . . . well not exactly . . . ' Catherine was staring from one to the other. 'I er — I er, I don't think you're all that old, Mrs Palmer-Farr . . . ' he stammered. 'Only that — '

'Son, close your mouth right now,' Sir Henry snapped.

'Harry wanted to be sure I'd have a decent inheritance,' Rosie said. 'He doesn't realize I've got my share of the dwindling Palmer-Farr fortunes and I'm happy with it. I am not looking for a title or a rich husband.' She threw her mother a challenging look. Catherine felt herself sag. Rosemary had tried to warn her. Now she was making a public statement. Oh God. She wanted to hide. There was an awkward silence, then everyone started talking at once.

'Would you mind showing me round your gardens, Rosemary?' Ellen Wilshaw asked.

'I'd like to see them too,' her brother said.

'We'll make our escape now, shall we?' She threw them a mischievous smile, 'while the — ahem — older guests take coffee in the lounge.' Harry Braebourne glared but Rosie had made her point. She smiled and escorted the Wilshaw twins outside.

'Did you design and plant the shrubbery on the drive up to Langton Tower?' Trevor asked. 'My parents think it's impressive.'

'The curve of the drive lends itself to an impressive layout but the island in the middle of the forecourt with the fountain and flower beds were Paul's idea. I'm pleased you like it. My father thought it was an improvement.' She sighed.

'I expect you miss him,' Ellen Wilshaw said with genuine sympathy. 'My father says you had grown very close since you came home from boarding school.'

Rosie enjoyed the company of the Wilshaws. They seemed interested in her business.

'Father keeps telling us we must be prepared to earn our own living,' Ellen said. 'Trevor is going to do a course in estate management at a college down south but Mother thinks girls should find a suitable husband and settle down to married life.' She pulled a face.

'Tell me about it!' Rosie sighed. 'But my mother built up the hotel from a near ruin so she shouldn't object to me wanting to be independent. She admits she misses my father's support, though, so she thinks she should choose a 'suitable' husband for me.'

'I reckon you'll do your own choosing when you're ready,' Trevor said with a grin. 'I like a girl with spirit.'

When they had gone Rosie went to her own cottage instead of returning to the luncheon party. She felt dejected and tired after her sleepless night. She was feeling guilty about behaving badly to her mother and Harry Braebourne too.

Restlessly she spent time tidying and dusting. She was making herself a cup of tea when she heard a car coming up the back drive.

'Looks like you've had some good news,' she said, opening the door wide as Tania bounced out of her car. 'I'm in need of cheering up.'

'Like that is it?' Tania smiled in sympathy. 'Well I do have got some good news.' She told Rosie about Pam's proposed visit from Australia. 'So we've no time to lose. Easter Monday is four weeks tomorrow and Struan and I are going to see the Reverend Carmichael tomorrow evening to try and fix the date and time. It may have to be a morning wedding and then a luncheon. Mother thinks I should ask Avril's and Pam's wee girls to be flower girls. You will promise to be my bridesmaid, won't you Rosie?'

'I'm flattered to be asked.' Rosie moved over to the settee and hugged her. 'You and Struan deserve to be happy. I'm pleased things are working out for you, in spite of Mrs Ritchie. It will be wonderful for everyone if Struan's sister can handle her, with a bit of help from the doctor.'

'Oh yes,' Tania agreed. 'Struan makes light of it but I know his mother's imaginary illnesses do affect him. He's afraid she might be ill sometime and nobody will take any notice. She spoils his joy. We're not having a big wedding though. Sam has agreed to be best man and Alex will be one of the ushers.'

'Sam?' Rosie's face paled a little. 'I er . . . I'm not sure I should be bridesmaid, Tania.'

'Oh but you must, Rosie. The wedding will be well into April so Sam can look forward to you being there too by then.'

'What difference does it make?'

'He'll have kept his promise by then.'

'What promise? Did he make a promise to Lidia?' Rosie sniffed. 'Not that I'm interested.'

'Oh Rosie, Sam loves you, and I don't mean the affection we all shared as children. He told us. He loves you as a man loves the woman he wants to marry. He has been so miserable.'

'I-I don't . . . I c-can't . . . He's never said anything to me. We haven't spoken for three weeks.'

'Of course you haven't!' Tania clapped a hand to her forehead. 'I'm so wrapped up in my own plans I haven't told you about the promise he made to your mother.'

'He made a promise to my mother? What sort of promise? Why?'

'It's driving him crazy not being able to explain to you.'

'I don't know what you're talking about, Tania.'

'Didn't your mother tell you she'd been to Martinwold to talk to Sam? She told him he was keeping you from mixing with your own class and meeting young men who could give you a decent lifestyle. She said he was being selfish in keeping you to himself so she appealed to his conscience, or his better nature, or something. She didn't want him to see you again, ever. He couldn't agree to that, but she begged him to stay away from you for three months to give you an opportunity to meet other young men.'

Rosie groaned aloud. 'The Brabournes,' she muttered.

'Sam said three months was like a lifetime but she made him feel guilty enough to compromise. He promised not to see you, or contact you, for a month — that's another week yet.'

'I-I can't believe this!' Rosie's face was pale

now and her blue eyes looked huge, smudged with violet circles from lack of sleep.

'Oh Rosie,' Tania hugged her. 'All parents want the best for their children and we Carafords have always been way out of the Palmer-Farr league. Grandfather Oliphant was your parents' gardener. My father and brothers are working farmers.'

'How can you say that, Tania? You are all like family to me. It was your mother — not mine — who nursed me until I was well after Sam found me half dead in the loft. Daddy said you were true friends and worth more than gold.'

'Mmm, but that was your father, Rosie. Your mother convinced Sam he was denying you the freedom to mix with young men of your own class. She said if you persisted in seeing each other you would risk losing your inheritance. Sam told her he didn't care whether you had an inheritance or not, but she said he would be selfish if he deprived you of a better life than he could give you.'

'I can't believe this!' Rosie stood up, her blue eyes blazing now. 'How dare my mother go to Martinwold. How dare she interfere with my friends? Sam could never make such a promise if he did love me.'

'It's because he loves you,' Tania said. 'Your mother convinced him he was taking

advantage because you're young and innocent. Sam's afraid she may be right and you
will be attracted to someone else. He's like a
bear with a sore head, but it is what your
mother hoped for, isn't it?'

'I should have guessed,' Rosie said, pacing
around the kitchen. 'No wonder she's been
organizing every free moment of my time and
throwing me into the company of Harry
Braebourne and his brother. I'm going to tell
her exactly what I think of her.'

'No! No, don't do that, Rosie.' Tania pulled
her back down onto the settee. 'You're not
supposed to know why Sam hasn't been to
see you. He made a promise. But I didn't. I
think it's so unfair when he can't explain.'

'Mother wants to cause trouble between
us.'

'Yes, but let Sam keep his promise, Rosie,
then she can't accuse him of breaking his
word, or cast it up at him later. Let her think
she's won. It's only one more week. Please?'

'Maybe you're right,' Rosie said, but her
lips were tight and her small jaw jutted
with determination. Tania guessed Catherine
Palmer-Farr might get more than she
bargained for with her devious dealings. 'To
think I was feeling guilty about being rude to
Mother and her guests!' Rosie said and gave
Tania an account of the luncheon.

'Rosie, can I come up to see you?' Sam had seized the earliest opportunity to telephone.

'In the middle of the day? This is April fool's day! Are you . . . ?'

'Yes. No — I can't wait a minute longer. I need to explain why I haven't — '

'Tania told me, Sam. I can't believe you would make such a stupid promise if you love me.'

'Oh God, I do love you, Rosie. More than life itself. If anything this month apart has made me realize that more than ever. Please, Rosie, I have to see you.'

'All right. Come by the back drive. We'll have lunch at my cottage and talk then.'

'I need more than talk, Rosie,' Sam said. Rosie smiled at the phone. She wanted to be cross with him for allowing her mother to manipulate him, for making her so miserable for four whole weeks, but the sky seemed bluer, the grass greener and the birdsong more glorious. She sang as she went to find Paul.

'Sam is coming up to see me, Paul, so I may not be around for a while this afternoon.'

'That's OK by me,' Paul said and grinned. 'You look like a different girl.'

'I feel like I'm walking on air,' Rosie said,

spreading her arms to embrace the world.

It was late afternoon before Sam and Rosie emerged from the cottage and only then because Sam had to get back to do the milking at Martinwold. Rosie's cheeks were flushed, her eyes bright; her mouth tingled from being so well kissed, but that didn't stop Sam snatching another as they walked together to his car.

'You will come to Martinwold, Rosie?'

'Of course I will, as soon as we finish work tomorrow. Oh Sam, I can't tell you how miserable I've been. Don't ever, ever, let anyone come between us again.'

'I won't, my darling. I hope your mother keeps her promise, now that I've kept my side of the bargain.'

'Her promise?' Rosie asked.

'She promised not to object if we were still together and wanted to get engaged in six months' time.'

'Oh Sam, that's wonderful. At least I think it is,' she added. Sam pulled her into his arms again. 'So do I. I may not be rich but I'm earning a proper wage now and saving up. I long for us to be together, Rosie, all the time.'

'Oh Sam, so do I, and I know we shall manage fine.'

Paul glimpsed them through the trees,

locked in each other's arms. He smiled and crept away.

★ ★ ★

The next three weeks passed in a flurry of wedding arrangements; choosing dresses, making arrangements and keeping appointments. Three days before the wedding Struan's sister, Pam, arrived with her two children.

'If the Carafords are such good friends of yours,' Catherine said, 'why didn't they book the wedding reception here, at Langton Tower?'

'I shouldn't think you need to ask that, Mother,' Rosie replied. 'If you ever try to interfere in my life again, or try to sacrifice my happiness for your own snobbish ambitions, I shall never forgive you and you can forget you ever had a daughter.'

'Rosemary Lavender! You can't mean that. I only wanted what was best for you.'

'No, Mother, *you* wanted what *you thought* was best. You don't know me at all if you think I would ever have married a man like Harry Braebourne, even if Sam didn't love me. So do you promise you'll never try to come between us again? Do you?'

'Yes,' Catherine sighed, 'yes I promise.

You're all I have now. I don't want to lose you Rosemary Lav — sorry, Rosemary.'

'That's better!' Rosie said. 'You'll never know how much I hated my name.'

★   ★   ★

Tania and Struan glowed with happiness as they walked down the aisle as man and wife. Later even Mrs Ritchie seemed pleasant and relaxed as she chatted to Steven at the top table. As soon as the formalities were over Sam moved from Struan's side to pull up a chair beside Rosie.

'You look so lovely in your blue dress,' he said in a low voice. 'I wish I could carry you off and be married too.' Mr Ritchie overheard him and chuckled.

'I agree Rosemary looks very pretty,' he said. 'I'm sure you both want to go and chat to your friends now.' Sam needed no urging to get Rosie away from the top table where they were in full view of everyone.

'We'll go for a stroll in the hotel gardens until you need to help Tania change.' Mr Ritchie watched them go then turned to Megan.

'It looks as though you will be having another wedding in the family before long,' he said with a smile.

'I think they're very much in love,' Megan agreed as her gaze followed them. 'Rosie has been like part of my family for years. We all love her. I'm so happy to see her smile and the sparkle in her eyes again. The trouble is,' she said, 'Sam isn't in the same class. He can't afford to give her the lifestyle Mrs Palmer-Farr thinks she ought to have.'

'Class? Bah! There's no such thing since the war. I respect Mrs Palmer-Farr for what she has done with Langton Tower, but love and loyalty are beyond price. I doubt if Rosemary would change Sam for the wealthiest young man in the county — or the country, for that matter.'

'I agree money is not everything,' Megan said with a smile. 'We were young and we didn't have much money when we married but I wouldn't change anything. We've enjoyed building our life together.'

In a secluded part of the hotel grounds Sam drew Rosemary into his arms and kissed her.

'I wish it was us. I wouldn't care about a honeymoon so long as I knew you were my wife, Rosie.'

'I love you so much, Sam.' She snuggled against him, oblivious of her headdress as she lifted her face to be kissed.

'I shall never be able to give you the

lifestyle you deserve. I can't blame your mother for wanting someone better for you, my darling. I want to give you the moon.'

'I don't want the moon, or anything else — only you, Samuel Caraford.' Rosie ran her hands over his chest and then down his thighs. He was surprised. She had been so tentative and shy about caressing him, even though her own responses were everything he could desire. He groaned and seized her hands, holding them close to his chest.

'We have to be sensible, Rosie. If I didn't love you so much I'd take everything you have to offer, even if it did lead to a shotgun wedding . . . ' He smiled against the soft curve of her cheek, then found her mouth. They were quiet for a long time but Sam knew he had to call a halt. 'I want to love and cherish you, Rosie, and give you everything your heart desires.'

'Oh Sam, my heart desires you, to be with you, all the time. I want to cook your favourite meals and wash your clothes and — and love you.'

'It's what I want more than anything else in the world, too, but I have to be able to give you a home and look after you. I want to be able to keep my own wife, not ask for anybody's charity.'

'Especially my mother's?' Rosie teased. 'I

wouldn't want that either, but between us we have all we need. I'm a good gardener remember, and I can cook.'

'I have a big enough garden to feed a multitude,' Sam laughed.

'Seriously, Sam, with everything we can produce I shall be the thriftiest of wives.'

'You'll be the best wife ever, sweetheart, but — '

'I shall be twenty-one at the end of May.' She looked up at him, her blue eyes dancing. 'How about fixing our wedding date for my twenty-first birthday?' she asked.

'What! That's only six weeks away, Rosie. Your mother will have me hung, drawn and quartered.'

'We could be married in a register office.'

'You'd do that? But no . . . ' Samuel's voice was firm. 'So long as I know you love me, as I love you, I want to tell the world, including your mother. We'll tell her together. After all, you're all she has, my darling, and now we know how much we love each other we can afford to be reasonable.'

'How reasonable?' Rosie's hands moved over his body in tantalizing circles.

'You're blackmailing me,' he whispered as her fingers became more insistent. 'So how long, Sam? August? September? We can't wait longer than that — can we?'

'No! I can't anyway.' He clutched her hands in his. 'You're a witch,' he whispered 'and I love you to distraction. We'll tell your mother at the weekend.'

'And you'll stand firm whatever she says?' She sighed. 'I do wish Daddy had been here. He would have made her understand.'

'Yes, I know, sweetheart,' Sam said. 'In the circumstances we have reason for a quiet wedding but I'd like it to be in church, especially after today, seeing Tania and Struan so happy with all their friends around them. You deserve that too, my darling.'

'Yes, I'd like that,' Rosie nodded. 'I could ask your grandfather to give me away. Papa Oliphant is the only grandparent I've ever had, even if he is really yours.'

'He'll belong to both of us once we're married.'

'Mmm, once we're married. I can't wait,' Rosie said, her eyes sparkling.

'I do love you, Rosie,' Sam said. 'I think I always have. We were meant to be together.'

We do hope that you have enjoyed reading this large print book.

Did you know that all of our titles are available for purchase?

We publish a wide range of high quality large print books including:
Romances, Mysteries, Classics
General Fiction
Non Fiction and Westerns

Special interest titles available in large print are:
The Little Oxford Dictionary
Music Book
Song Book
Hymn Book
Service Book

Also available from us courtesy of Oxford University Press:
Young Readers' Dictionary
(large print edition)
Young Readers' Thesaurus
(large print edition)

For further information or a free brochure, please contact us at:
Ulverscroft Large Print Books Ltd.,
The Green, Bradgate Road, Anstey,
Leicester, LE7 7FU, England.
Tel: (00 44) 0116 236 4325
Fax: (00 44) 0116 234 0205

Other titles published by
The House of Ulverscroft:

DRIFTING SHADOWS

Christina Green

Life on a Dartmoor tenant farm is hard and when Becky Yeo meets Joseph, a travelling labourer and folk-singer, her desire is to change her own life. Then, disobeying her family, she refuses to marry Nat, the farm bailiff. She finds work as a kitchen maid at the Manor House, which harbours a dark mystery concerning her family. Meanwhile, Nat, seeking revenge, blackmails her. When Joseph returns, his love for Becky becomes clear and he must challenge Nat for Becky's hand. But after her secret is revealed, can Becky keep her family together and prevent Joseph from leaving once again?

THE STATISTICAL PROBABILITY OF LOVE AT FIRST SIGHT

Jennifer E. Smith

Stuck at New York's JFK airport, seventeen-year-old Hadley Sullivan faces being late for her father's second wedding in London. And she's not even met her new stepmother. Then, in the waiting area she meets the perfect boy. Oliver is British, with his own reasons for not wanting to return home to London. He's booked in seat 18C. Hadley is in 18A. On the long flight from New York to London they get on very well . . . Unfortunately, landing at Heathrow, Hadley and Oliver lose track of each other in the airport chaos — and she doesn't even know his last name . . .

THE WOUNDED HEART

David Wiltshire

There was no doubt in Lt Mike Gibson's mind that he was going to die. As a lieutenant in the Royal Army Medical Corps, death and carnage had been with him every day from the beaches of Normandy to the crossing of the Rhine. One moment eclipsed all others, in a forest clearing in Germany; where he had the experience of hell on earth. He owed his life to one woman, Lily de Howarth, the woman he adored. And now he was planning to kill her in the name of love . . .

OVER HIS DEAD BODY

Laurie Brown

Ever since Caroline Tucker moved back home from Hollywood to the bright lights of Haven, New Mexico, she's been trying (and failing) to avoid her ex-husband, town sheriff Travis Beaumont. However, she's forced to call him when her niece stumbles across the perfectly preserved body of a cowboy at Girl Scout camp. But is this a crime scene? Or is it just a potential tourist attraction? The mystery of the mummy unravels and Travis digs up some sinister evidence. And the more Caroline tries to keep away from trouble — and Travis — the more they come knocking at her door . . .